The Affliction
Provenance

M.J. Petrin

ISBN: 13-978-1-7334-6442-0

CONTENTS

CONTENTS

CONTENTS

CONTENTS

ACKNOWLEDGMENTS

I cannot express enough gratitude for the love and support from my wonderful wife, Misae. Without her amazing attitude, I would have been so lost.

My son Dylan offered his expertise and time to help me create the covers for my books. I could not have done it without his help. I am forever grateful.

Prologue

The Herald Project is now complete. After many attempts and many failures, J9-1-7 has surpassed expectations. It was the 917th attempt, and through all the upgrades and enhancements, success. Discovering the right subject with the combination of biology and physiology to combine with Wen technology was imperative to the Herald Project's success. So many different species were used, and the success rate was higher initially. However, when Wen introduced tech enhancements, one subject after another rejected the tech. One by one, the heralds reacted poorly and eventually died until J9-1-7. He was the first to adapt to biotech enhancements successfully.

At the end of a long hallway within the Island Steel Tower, several Traa'zel High Council members were assembled. They gathered on this day to discuss the successful completion of their Herald Project. Another species may have used this success as a call for celebration, but on Wen'q'rixsh, there are no celebrations. Celebrating is not logical. Logic states that if you follow the protocols and procedures the research prescribes, the probability of success will be higher. There is no need to celebrate an expected outcome.

The Council members proceeded through the meeting room door. The consultation room was an open, colorless area with no decoration. Logic, according to the Wen, needs no embellishment. The only piece of furniture in the room was a long metal table with seven chairs, three on either side, and one at the head.

Suspended above the conference table on a transparent screen, floating in the air, was the J9-1-7 project information. The suspended file was visible from any angle on the table. Participants could touch the table, and the data became visible as if it were directly in front of them on a computer.

The six council members wore hooded blue robes, the fabric hanging over their faces, completely obscuring their facial features from sight. No one spoke or uttered a sound. All six members sat and waited for the head of the table to enter the room to start the meeting. The head chair was reserved for the Traa'zel, who had the most experience and the highest intellect of all Wen'q'rixsh. The other members were not required to obey or follow him. Still, it was logical to be in his presence as much as possible to learn and gain valuable insight. Logic stated that if you did the work, you would improve.

Krix'x walked into the room and approached his seat. The six council members bowed–not in servitude, but out of respect.

Krix'x began to speak. "We have completed our first herald with independent thinking capabilities."

Silent nods of approval were the only response.

Krix'x continued, "I believe we are ready for the next phase to commence."

"We have verified our information concerning the Xanoclax invasion, Krix'x. It is time to proceed," replied the robed figure in the first chair to the right of Krix'x.

Krix'x nodded. "Xanoclax warships are converging on the planet as we speak. We shall proceed immediately."

The seven council members stood, and most walked away from the table. A lone Traa'zel approached the head.

"How does logic dictate that we travel so far to aid another species?"

Krix'x looked down at the blue robe from which the question had emerged. Krix'x was the tallest of the Traa'zels. He knew this Traa'zel, who sought knowledge now as the council's youngest member.

"Artekx, I know it may appear illogical, but if we know of the need, is it not logical to aid their survival?"

Artekx nodded.

Krix'x started toward the door, with the young Traa'zel following.

As they were walking, Krix'x continued to speak. "We are responsible for all species in and around our universe to offer aid in times of crisis. Our higher intellect enables us to make all choices logically and without prejudice. If we stand idly by while the Xanoclax enslave other civilizations, are we not as the Xanoclax?"

Artekx answered in a soft-spoken voice, "I understand, Krix'x. I only question if our resources would better serve those closest to our planet."

"We cannot choose who needs our help. When a crisis arises, we act in the most logical way possible. To judge one species over another is not to use rational thought. We need to treat all species with identical respect. The death of any individual grants no one honor."

"But are we not interfering with their future, and thus changing their fate?"

"There is a difference between natural evolution and accidental circumstance. If we do nothing and allow the Xan to destroy their planet, are we not deciding their fate?"

Artekx stopped walking and stood still as he contemplated Krix'x's explanation. He took only a moment before hurrying to catch back up.

"You are saying that it is logical to preserve life to enable a culture to evolve from within its constructs. Outside intervention is illogical."

Krix'x nodded, but he knew where Artekx was going with his statement. If pleasure were logical, he would have been pleased with the conjecture.

"We are not initiating outside intervention. We are preventing it."

"And you believe that this planet is worth our efforts?"

Krix'x stopped and turned toward Artekx. "It is not for me to decide if our efforts are worth saving a planet. It is up to us to logically evaluate the situation and make our decision. There is no room for judgment when developing an analysis. This primitive planet is no match for a species of higher intellect like the Xanoclax. We can offer assistance, and they can decide to accept our help. Our core belief is to preserve life throughout the universe. Therefore, we must do what we can."

Artekx nodded. "Yes, Krix'x, it is logical to aid this planet. By what name do they call their planet? Our designation, Terra X, is the only one listed in our research documents."

Krix'x began walking again. "They call it 'Earth.'"

1 AND SO, IT BEGINS

Sheriff Bill Jackson stared at his reflection in the hardware store window. Without thinking, he wiped the sweat from his forehead with his right sleeve. The late July heat in Bends Creek, Mississippi, made for a high dry-cleaning bill. He looked at his sleeve and sighed at what he had just done. He could hear Mrs. Grandy from BC Cleaners scolding him when he turned in his weekly laundry. "What am I going to do with you, Bill Jackson?" she would ask him. "Do I need to provide you with hand towels? It would be best if you stopped wiping your sweat on your shirt sleeves. Didn't Betsy teach you better than that?"

"Yes, ma'am," Bill would answer politely.

Bill Jackson was a third-generation sheriff. He'd lived in Bends Creek his whole life and wanted to be a sheriff like his father and grandfather. Bill stood about six-two and weighed a slim-looking 210. Turning sideways, he looked over his midsection, then did a 180 and checked from the other side. He looked from his reflection down at his stomach. This morning, he'd had to loosen his belt a notch when he dressed for work.

He grimaced, "Don't know why I can't lose weight in this heat; I sweat enough," he said under his breath as he critiqued himself in the window.

Turning to his opposite side, Bill noticed a man standing behind him in the window's reflection. He watched as the man mocked his movements, never seeing the window. When Bill turned sideways, the other man followed, and so on. After a few twists from side to side, both men stood there and stared into the window. Neither looked at the other.

Bill broke first, smiling and looking toward the man in the reflection. "Okay, that's very funny, Rufus."

Rufus laughed and put both hands on his belly. It protruded so far from his body that his t-shirt didn't completely cover his stomach. His suspenders kept his dirty, baggy jeans from falling, but exposed the top of his butt. Rufus's fat cheeks were between shaves, scruffy but not quite sporting a beard.

"You got a ways to go before you get this pretty, Sheriff," Rufus laughed, moving his belly up and down with both hands.

Bill grinned. "I ain't in no hurry to look as good as you."

"There will come a day when just lookin' at food will put five pounds on you! There ain't no escapin' it."

Bill turned to face his friend, "Thanks for the pep talk." He chuckled, patted Rufus on the shoulder, then turned and walked away.

"Anytime, Sheriff," Rufus yelled at Bill's back.

Bill tugged on his holster slightly as he walked down the sidewalk; it always seemed more cumbersome in the hot afternoon hours. He hated wearing a gun and was glad he hadn't used it in over ten years as Sheriff. The last time he'd used a gun was in Afghanistan. He loathed guns but knew they were a necessary evil, especially in violent altercations. Also, people tended to listen better when he wore a gun. It was a sad truth that Bill would like to see changed, but until people shifted their mindsets, the firearm would remain on his waist.

Today seemed like any other Saturday afternoon. People were walking in the streets, visiting different shops: nothing unusual. Bends Creek was just far enough away from any of the nearby tourist traps so as not to attract outside visitors. Just another day in Bends Creek, the "same old, same old," as his Dad would always say. But that was about to change.

"Sheriff! Sheriff!" a voice came from behind him. The Sheriff turned around and saw an older, bearded Black man walking toward him, his expression anxious. It was Virgil Porter, one of the town's homeless citizens. Virgil was quickly recognized by his long, grimy coat and old rain boots. His beard and long white hair were dirty, and he reeked of alcohol.

"Virgil, you are going to have a heart attack wearing those heavy clothes in this heat," Bill said, looking Virgil up and down.

"You want I should take it off, Sheriff?" smiled Virgil, exposing the few teeth he had left.

"Hell no, Virgil! I don't know what's under that coat, and I sure don't want to." The Sheriff smiled.

"Sheriff, I gots to talk to ya," Virgil's expression shifted to become serious.

"What is it now, Virgil? Aliens? Ghosts? What?" Bill crossed his arms and shot Virgil a skeptical look. Virgil had a history of sensationalization with made-up stories.

"Sheriff, you gots to prepare for it." Virgil moved closer to the Sheriff. The smell of alcohol was strong. Bill covered his nose and mouth with the hand towel from his back pocket.

"Come on, Virgil, go down to the shelter and shower! And go wash your clothes while you're at it."

"Right away, Sheriff, but you gots to listen to me this time. This is the real deal; you gots to listen." Virgil spoke with a desperate tone. The Sheriff had never seen Virgil like this before. He was always calm and laid back. Now, he was standing before him, anxious and excited about something.

"Okay, what is it? I'll hear you."

"There's a change happenin', Sheriff. People done started losin' their minds."

"Like you?" Bill laughed.

"No!" Virgil raised his voice. "This is diff'nt. This is so diff'nt. This changes everything." Virgil sounded scared now.

"Alright, Virgil, calm down, and let's go to the shelter. I was heading that way anyway to pick up my patrol car."

Virgil stumbled alongside the Sheriff toward the shelter. He kept mumbling and looking up at the sun, all the while, "This is diff'nt. This is diff'nt."

"Okay, Virgil, take it easy. We're here; why don't you do me a favor? Wash up and grab something to eat. I'll come by later, and we'll talk about it some." Bill wasn't just saying this as a sheriff; he liked Virgil. Virgil had served in Vietnam with Bill's father, and like his father, Virgil had come back from that war a different man. The returning soldiers with a support system around them fared better than those without. Unfortunately, Bends Creek never offered much veteran support, and Virgil had no relatives. So Virgil didn't benefit from what help there was.

"Okay, okay, but you gots to come back; it's important," Virgil said as he walked into the shelter.

"I promise, Virgil. You know, I will." Bill looked past Virgil and saw Maggie Carter greeting and welcoming Virgil into the shelter.

"Hey, Virgil," Maggie said with a soft, welcoming voice. "You coming to clean up and grab a bite?"

Virgil looked at Maggie, and his concerned face lightened up and relaxed. He gave her a big smile and said, "Yes, ma'am." He walked by her and left Bill and Maggie alone at the front entrance.

"How's it going, Maggie?"

"I'm doing alright, you?"

Bill didn't realize he was staring past Maggie, watching Virgil walk inside.

"Sheriff? You okay?"

Her voice snapped him out of his daze. He looked at her, standing at the entrance of the shelter. Maggie was Bill's age. She was wearing tight jeans, sneakers, and a white t-shirt. The sun was hitting Maggie's face and making her soft, brown skin glow, and the combination of her smile and the glow of her skin was almost angelic.

"Yeah, Maggie. Seeing you just makes my day a little better, that's all." Bill smiled and turned away.

Maggie's smile grew, and her round brown eyes opened wider. "See you later?" Maggie asked as Bill walked to his car.

"Absolutely." Bill waved to her before he closed the car door.

Maggie smiled and watched the Sheriff drive away. Then she closed the door and went back to work.

Bill still smiled and thought about Maggie when he saw two men yelling at each other in the street. Bill parked his car a block away from them and got out. He drifted slowly toward the argument, observing their behavior. A white man on Bill's left and a Black man on his right were shouting at each other. As Bill approached the two men, he noticed their argument seemed bizarre. The two men were yelling and cussing at each other while using their first names. They knew each other but acted confused and angry as they looked at each other. Each man was physically scrutinizing the other.

The closer Bill got to the argument, the more confusing it seemed.

"You ain't, Bob," the Black man screamed.

"The hell I ain't," the white man yelled back. "You sure as hell ain't, Franklin."

"The hell I ain't," Franklin replied.

Bill squinted his eyes, "What's going on here?"

The two men stopped at the same time and looked at Bill. The white man looked at Bill, confused and scared, and asked, "Sheriff, that you? Sheriff Bill Jackson?"

"Come on, man," Bill said. "You know who I am."

The man squinted and was visibly shaking. "Do you know me, Sheriff?"

Bill looked at the man and said, "Yes, Bob, I know you. You're Bob Stanton. Now, what's this all about?"

The other man, who was Black, looked at Bill and asked, "And me, Sheriff? Do you know me?"

"Yeah, Franklin, I know you. Why wouldn't I? I've known you my whole life."

Franklin was in his mid-sixties, with a muscular build, just a few inches shorter than Bill. He was still doing side work on the old Wilson farm. All the hay baling and working heavy farm equipment had kept Franklin in great physical shape. As a result, he looked ten years younger. Only a few white hairs on his head and beard gave his age away.

The sweat dripped down Franklin's face, shoulders, and arms. Franklin approached Bill slowly. He stopped within an inch of Bill's face, their noses almost touching. As Franklin looked over the Sheriff fretfully, his eyes nearly popped out of his head. He reached up and started touching Bill's face. Bill jumped back, putting some distance between himself and Franklin's hand.

Bill's eyes widened. "Now, hold on a minute, Franklin. Why are you acting all weird and foolish?"

"Bill, I'm losing my mind." Franklin was tearing up as he pulled his shaking hand from Bill's face. Franklin took a few steps back and looked at Bill, then at Bob, and then back to Bill. The frightened look on his face was starting to worry Bill even more.

"Franklin. Talk to me, man. What is going on?"

Franklin's eyes became even more prominent, and he stepped back further, looking Bill over from top to bottom and back up again. He inspected Bill as if he were seeing an alien for the first time.

"Bill, you're Black, man! You're Black!" Franklin shouted, shaking his head.

Bill started laughing nervously. "Franklin, come on, man. The joke's over. What's going on?"

"My God, Bill! You are Black!" Franklin was pointing his finger at Bill and Bob as he spoke.

"And so is Bob over here! Y'all Black as the night. What the hell, man! What the hell!"

Franklin bent over at the waist and placed his hands on his knees as though about to vomit. Then, as quickly as he had bent over, he stood straight up with a terrified look. Bill thought Franklin's eyes would pop out of their sockets. Franklin began rubbing his eyes, stopped stroking, and then started again, trying to rub away what he saw.

Bill was perplexed as he watched Franklin rub his face with both hands several times. Then, finally, Bill realized Franklin wasn't kidding. He needed help.

"Okay, Franklin. Let's get you to the hospital and have them check you out. There has to be a good explanation for this." Bill grasped Franklin's arm and started guiding him toward his police car. Franklin was coaxed along, defeated, to the vehicle. He stared straight ahead without blinking.

Bob gazed at Franklin and Bill from behind as he stood frozen. He had the same terrified look as Franklin, and he didn't say a word the whole time Franklin and Bill spoke to each other.

Bill looked over his shoulder and yelled, "Bob! Don't just stand there; give me a hand."

Bob Stanton was approximately the same age and height as Franklin. But that's where the similarities stopped. Bob was so thin that his protruding bones made him look almost sickly. He had a dirty white T-shirt and jeans on. He wore an old straw cowboy hat and black work boots. Bob looked up at Bill and started tearing up. He looked like a child whose ice cream cone had just fallen to the ground. He stared at Franklin and pointed in his direction.

"He's white, Bill. He's white." Bob's voice was almost a whisper. It sounded eerie, and for the first time, Bill felt fear. Not the fear he felt when he served in the Rangers; this was a different type of anxiety. The stress of watching someone close to him suffering and feeling helpless was a lot different than pulling an injured soldier to safety.

Okay, get a hold of yourself. These guys need your help, Bill reasoned with himself.

Bob's arm appeared locked in place as he extended his finger toward Franklin. He just left his arm in the air, frozen, pointing.

"What? What's wrong, Bob? What are you saying?"

"My God, Sheriff, that man is white! I known him all my life, and he ain't Black no more. He's white now. And it's scary!" Bob was starting to panic, getting more anxious. He was shaking all over as he stood, still pointing.

Get a grip, Bill told himself.

"Okay! Okay! Both of you get in the back seat. We're going to the hospital. Let's go!"

After Bill helped Franklin into the car, he walked back to Bob. Bob was still pointing in Franklin's direction. Bill lowered Bob's arm slowly. "It's okay. Let's get you to the doctor and fix this, alright?"

Bob didn't respond to Bill. Instead, he slowly moved toward the car.

Bill drove the two men to the hospital. He looked in his rearview mirror repeatedly; his passengers stared out the window, refusing to look at each other. Neither man said a word. Just stared out their windows, expressions of shock frozen on their faces.

"Guys, it's all going to be okay. We'll get it all sorted out at the hospital," Bill said softly, looking into the rearview mirror. Bill noticed his palms were damp on the steering wheel.

Get a grip. Man. That's easier said than done, he thought.

He wasn't sure what would happen, but he couldn't let the two scared men in his car know that. Bob and Franklin reminded Bill of two teenagers who had gotten into trouble and whom he had to bring home to their parents in his patrol car. They sat in silence, scared, waiting, not knowing how their parents would react when they got home. Only home, in this case, was the hospital. And they had no idea how the doctors would respond.

Bill was confused as he tried to understand what they were going through. One person acting insane was one thing, but the two men seemed to be stricken with the same problem. He hoped the hospital had an answer because he didn't.

He pulled into the hospital's parking lot and opened the back doors to let the two men out. He let them walk in first and followed behind them. Both were taking short, deliberate steps as if they were scared to discover what was wrong with them. Bill came up behind them and put one hand on Bob's back and the other on Franklin's. He gave them each a gentle push. "You guys go sit, and I'll get the doctor."

The two men turned in unison and walked to the seats in the waiting room, keeping their heads down and refusing to look at each other. They sat opposite each other in the patient waiting room, and neither man was taking their eyes off the floor directly in front of them. Instead, they stared blankly and occasionally reached up to wipe the tears running down their cheeks.

Bill approached the receptionist. "Hey, Judy, how ya doing?"

"Just fine, Sheriff. What's going on?"

"I have a small problem with these two; they need to see a doctor ASAP."

"They look okay to me, sheriff. What's the problem?" Judy said as she looked over at Bob and Franklin.

"I don't know exactly; it may be in their heads, but whatever it is, they both got it."

"Got what? I got to tell the doctor something to get him out here."

"Come on, Judy; this is serious. Tell him they're having a nervous breakdown or something."

"At the same time?"

"Yes, that's why I brought them here. What Bob and Franklin are going through is the same for both of them. So please get the doc out here."

"Okay, give me a minute, Sheriff. I'll be right back." Judy exited her desk and walked toward the door directly behind her. She paused as she opened it, looking back at Bob and Franklin. Then, she sighed, shook her head, shrugged like she didn't understand the problem, and walked through the door.

Bill walked over to the two men sitting in the waiting area. They looked as though they were about to explode any minute. He wanted to fix this problem for them, but he knew it was out of his wheelhouse. Not being able to fix this situation made him feel weak and useless.

He started talking in a calm voice. "Guys, it's all going to be okay. The doctor will be right out. He'll probably get you something to calm your nerves."

Neither man looked up; they both kept staring at the floor. Franklin talked first. "This ain't about my nerves, Bill. It's more than that."

Bob talked over his shoulder to Bill, not looking at either man. "Franklin's right. This ain't no nerves."

"Okay, alright, maybe so, but we've got to calm you guys down so we can work through this."

Bill gazed at Bob and Franklin sympathetically, knowing that was all he could do. Both men nodded their heads in agreement.

"We'll figure this out. Let's take it one step at a time." Bill gently patted Bob on his shoulder. Bob just nodded slowly in agreement.

The men appeared calmer, but Bill noticed they were still shaking in their seats.

"What's going on, Sheriff?" It was Doctor Darryl Brown, an older Black man, just a little shorter than Bill and sporting a short white beard. He wore a white clinician's coat and had a stethoscope hanging from his neck.

"Hey, Doc," Bill greeted him with a handshake. "We got a peculiar one here."

The doctor came up to Franklin first. "What's going on?" he asked Franklin.

Franklin looked up at Doctor Brown with tears in his eyes. "I see Black people, Doc. I see them everywhere."

The doctor looked at Franklin incredulously. "And that's a bad thing?"

"Hell no," Franklin raised his voice a little. "It ain't a bad thing! It's just terrifying!"

"Seeing Black people is terrifying?"

"No," Franklin shouted, "what's so scary is everyone I see is Black! People I know is white; they look Black now!" Franklin was getting hysterical.

"Okay, let's calm down and go into a patient room and see what we can do." The doctor turned to address Bob. "You seeing Black people too?"

Bob slowly turned to the doctor, and when he was face to face with him, he said, "No, sir, I'm seeing only white people."

"You see me as a white man?" the doctor asked, confused.

"I do," Bob said, tears running from his eyes. Bob's sad, helpless look started to concern the doctor.

"Alright, let's get both of you into a patient room and run some tests."

Doctor Brown turned to Bill. "I'll run some tests and see what's going on."

"Thanks, Doc," Bill said. "Could you please call me and let me know what you find? Just in case, God forbid, I run into this again?"

"Absolutely."

Bill stood there, watching the three men walk through the door to the emergency room, and stood there for a minute after the door closed behind them. He had never experienced anything like this before. It was confusing and scary at the same time.

"You okay, Sheriff?" Judy asked from her desk.

"As okay as I can be right now, Judy," he smiled and left the hospital.

Driving back through town, Bill noticed a lot of street activity. There were crowds of people gathered in the middle of the road. People were yelling, crying, and laughing.

"It's here! It's finally here! Judgement Day is upon us!"

"Praise Jesus!"

"I died and gone to heaven!"

"Now what?" Bill said emphatically.

Everyone acted like they were on drugs or drunk, just wandering around the streets and yelling loudly. Bill stopped his car and stared at all the commotion. It was all around him. He began to feel claustrophobic, like the crowd was sucking the air from his lungs. His palms were sweating on the steering wheel again.

"Come on, really?" Bill screamed out loud, hoping to snap himself out of his panic.

Bill knew he couldn't handle this chaos alone, so he radioed for help. He asked dispatch for a few deputies to come to the downtown area and help with crowd control. Bill sat in his car, watching everyone. He was confused and shocked by how his quiet town had suddenly erupted into mass confusion. Bill wondered if this had to do with what Franklin and Bob were going through.

Bill zeroed in on the individual behavior while he waited for backup to arrive. The one plus was the absence of any physical violence. Everyone in the crowd was walking around the center of the road and yelling. One man walked up to another man and hugged him. That's about as physical as it got.

When the other deputies arrived, they all looked as shocked as Bill. Finally, one deputy shouted at him, "What are we supposed to do with all these people?"

As the other deputy got out of his car, Bill addressed the two of them.

"Okay, try to calm them down!" Bill shouted. "We can't take everyone to the hospital. We need to get everyone to calm down and stop yelling. We ain't sure what this is yet and where it's heading."

The crowds started gathering together, and it was getting harder for Bill to maintain control of the situation. Cars crashed into parked cars to avoid hitting people running in the streets. Some people were acting scared, while others were laughing. But it seemed to

Bill that everyone was confused and in shock. Everyone acted like Bob and Franklin, which was frightening to watch.

Bill kept thinking to himself, *Okay, think. Calm your butt down and figure this out.*

Then, as if a light bulb went off in his head, Bill realized something critical. There were people in the crowd who were acting differently from the others. These people were not hysterical. So, he decided to focus on them first. Off the side of the street, several people stood around and watched the chaos.

Bill walked over to the sidewalk and spoke to a man staring into the crowd. "Sir, what is it? What do you see?" Bill asked.

"Just a crowd of people acting confused, Sheriff. I don't understand the fuss," the man answered.

Bill asked the same of the woman who was standing next to the man.

"I'm with him, Sheriff. I have no idea what is going on," she said.

Bill focused on the relaxed people and separated them from the others. He ordered the two deputies to gather all the calm people, bring them to the sidewalks, and keep them all together away from the chaos. Once the deputies had separated them, the chaotic group was a little more manageable, as Bill had hoped.

Bill went through the crowd to his car and got an air horn from the trunk. Bill then returned to the middle of the group, held up the air horn over his head, and discharged it. The air horn was loud and got everyone's attention. Those closest to Bill covered their ears and yelled, cursing. Finally, the crowd quieted, and everyone looked at the man holding the air horn. Then, after a few "What the hells," and worse, Bill started yelling.

"Okay, I need everyone to get off the streets now! Go home or go shopping or whatever, I don't care. Just get off the streets. I will arrest anyone still on these streets for disorderly conduct, causing a public commotion. My jail isn't that big, so y'all will get to know each other really well if I lock you up. So get on now."

As the crowd was dispersing, they were still acting confused and scared. Finally, the Mayor, Rayburn Samuels, came running over to Bill. "My God, Bill, what is going on?"

Bill was directing people off the street. "Mayor, I don't know. I don't have a clue. People are acting scared and irrational, saying they see everyone as their own race."

"Well, we need to figure this out quickly, Sheriff, before the whole town destroys itself," the mayor shouted as he walked away.

"Yeah, we do," Bill said as the crowd dispersed.

2 REALITY SUCKS

Word travels fast in a small town. So people started calling people they knew, and they called people they knew, and so on. Others talked at their favorite watering holes.

People flooded the mayor's office, seeking answers to the downtown crisis.

"Mayor, what the heck is going on?"

"Why is this happening?"

"Is this a government experiment?"

Others screamed, "It's the apocalypse, time to be judged!"

"Amen!"

"Come on, Samuels, what's going on?" a voice shouted from the crowd.

The mayor's office was one of the largest in the city hall building. It was built before the Civil War and later used as a Confederate recruitment office. The fire department rated it a 40-person capacity room, but it was large enough to hold over 50 people. It was maxed out right now.

The mayor stood on his desk and addressed the crowd in his office. "Okay, everybody, let's quiet down for a moment. Let's see what we got here," he fumbled through a few papers and began reading. "There have been reports all over town that people are having issues with their sight."

"We know that. Tell us something we don't know," someone shouted.

"Let him speak," another retorted. Then, others started yelling, and the room quickly filled with sounds of confusion and chaos.

"Calm down now," the mayor spoke in a firm voice. "Let me tell you what we have on this so far, and then we will try to resolve this civilly."

The crowd suppressed their outbursts, and the mayor started to read the report.

"Here's a report from County Hospital," the mayor held up a file for all to see.

"We have observed and run tests on over 25 patients suffering from these mysterious sight issues. At this time, we have not come to a definitive conclusion as to what is causing these hallucinations. There appear to be no physical or chemical issues with any of the patients that would cause these particular hallucinations. Due to the increasing number of people complaining about this issue, and because we cannot determine a cause, we recommend calling the Center for Disease Control to help with this investigation."

The crowd was getting restless, shouting and yelling out questions.

"The hospital thinks it's a disease?"

"We got a virus or something they don't know about yet?"

"What do we do in the meantime?"

"Did you call the government? They did something to us, didn't they?"

The mayor raised his arms, trying to calm the crowd, "Look, we don't know what this is yet. We need to get some professionals here to check it all out and get us some answers. I already called the Centet for Disease Control in Atlanta. They will be sending a team out here tomorrow. I suggest we all go home and call it a night."

Someone shouted, "How do we deal with this in the meantime? This mess is downright freaky scary! I'm afraid to look at anyone!"

The mayor responded, "Listen up, we're all freaked out. But we're all in this together. We need to keep calm now and let the professionals figure this out. When they get here and find out something, we can take the next steps to try to fix this. But for now, we need to keep our heads together."

"Easy for you to say, mayor. It ain't affecting you, is it?"

"No, I can't say it has, at least not yet. But panicking and freaking out over whatever this is will not make our situation better. If you act paranoid and start screaming at each other, guess what? Your eyes are still going to see what they're seeing. It doesn't change anything. So let's keep cool and take it one step at a time."

The majority of the crowd seemed to agree.

Mayor Samuels looked over the crowd and noticed they were acquiescent. "Good. I always said this town had a lot of good people with common sense. Please go home, try to relax, and spend time with your families. Those of you having these issues with your sight, stay home until we get an answer. The less time outside, the fewer people you see, the better. I promise I will get you answers from the CDC once I get some."

The crowd started to disperse. Rayburn got down from his desk and immediately got on the phone to verify when the CDC would arrive.

Bill was just outside the office, monitoring the situation. When the office emptied, he walked in and sat at the mayor's desk. Rayburn hung up the phone and fell back into his seat, loudly sighing.

As Bill quietly sat, he observed the frustration on Rayburn's face. He seemed oblivious to Bill's presence, staring at the phone. Rayburn Samuels was a simple man. The whole town liked him. He was always willing to help anyone with anything that they needed. He was known to pay out of his pocket for groceries to help people who were laid off or going through hard times. Rayburn didn't have military experience and never received crisis prevention training. He was just a good man now stuck in a complicated situation.

"You keep stressing like that. You're going to add a few wrinkles," Bill started the conversation.

Rayburn replied, not looking up, still staring at the phone, "That's the least of my problems."

Bill nodded, "The hardest thing to do is follow your own advice. It's always easier said than done."

"Yeah, it is."

"We got the Feds coming in tomorrow. Hopefully, they'll have some answers. So why don't you go home and try to relax? You can't do any more here."

Rayburn nodded slightly. Bill got up and walked out of his office. He looked over his shoulder at Rayburn, who was still staring at the phone.

***

Bill walked out of the building and looked around. He kept thinking that nothing like this happens in Bends Creek. And why did it happen now? His mind was racing with questions that had no answers. Then, looking around, he noticed Maggie standing on the sidewalk, leaning against a parking meter.

"Waiting for someone?" Bill asked.

"I was hoping the Sheriff might walk with me for a bit. It seems like the town's going a little whacky, and I shouldn't be walking alone." Maggie said in a soft, sweet voice.

"Well, it would be an honor to walk with you, ma'am," Bill smiled. "But I am on duty, and I have to ensure all the other women walking alone are okay as well."

"Oh, really," Maggie smiled. "I'm pretty sure you won't pay attention to anyone else once you start walking with me."

"Wow, you sure sound confident."

"Oh, I am. I am." Maggie took the Sheriff's hand and started heading down Main Street. "Want to stop for a cup of coffee?"

"I don't know. Things are a little insane right now," Bill answered hesitantly.

"Is there something you can do to fix it right now?" Maggie asked.

"No, not really," Bill answered.

"Are the deputies making sure everyone is staying off the streets?"

Bill smiled. He knew she was right. "Yes, ma'am."

"So let's start over. Would you like to stop for a cup of joe?"

"Sure."

Bill was in his happy place. The relationship with Maggie was going well. They had been seeing each other for over six months now. He was walking hand in hand with the woman he was falling in love with, not thinking about all the madness in the town. All the chaos seemed to drift away for the moment, making Bill feel lighter than usual.

As they walked down Main Street to the coffee shop, an elderly Black woman approached the Sheriff. Grabbing his arm, she seemed frantic. "Sheriff, what's going on? Why is this happening to us?"

"Ma'am, I don't know. But I'm sure we'll have some answers pretty soon. Why don't you go home and try to relax, and we'll see what the CDC folks have to say tomorrow."

"Yes, I suppose you're right," she said quietly. She walked on. Bill turned back with a concerned glance as she walked away.

"It's sweet," Maggie said.

"What?"

"It's sweet how you care about people, Bill. It's one of the things about you I find attractive."

Bill smiled at Maggie, "But not the only thing, right?"

Just as they reached the front of the coffee shop, a truck drove by. The driver blew the horn several times at Bill and Maggie.

"Looks like our white boy sheriff is getting some brown sugar tonight, boys," yelled the truck driver. Three white men in the pickup laughed loudly at what was just said.

"Rednecks!" Bill was upset as they drove off.

"That's just that ignorant racist Elias and his clan. You know better than to let that crap get to you," Maggie said.

"Yeah, well, it bothers me more when they're shouting at you."

"I know, and it's sweet. Don't let those racist idiots ruin our coffee, okay?"

"Yeah, you're right, as usual," Bill turned away from the street and looked at Maggie.

"You are getting smarter all the time."

They both laughed and walked into the coffee shop.

They sat down, ordered their drinks, and stared at each other. Maggie was looking at Bill's face. Usually, she had his undivided attention, but tonight, he was somewhere else.

"So, what's on your mind, Sheriff?" Maggie asked. "You don't seem to be here with me right now."

Bill didn't answer.

"Bill, you okay?"

"Yeah, sure, I'm alright. I can't wrap my head around this, that's all."

"What do you think is happening? Any ideas?" Maggie was curious as well.

"It's bizarre, Maggie. I thought it was just a fluke when it happened with Franklin and Bob this morning. Maybe something they were smoking or drinking. But now, the whole damn town is flipping out. I don't understand what's going on here at all."

"So, how would you normally handle a case under investigation?"

Bill smiled, "Your common sense, that's one of the things I find attractive about you."

Maggie laughed, "But not the only thing, right?"

They both laughed and touched their cups in a toast.

"Okay, Maggie, let's look at the evidence and the clues then."

"Good idea," she said.

"Franklin said everyone he looks at is Black. Bob said everyone he looks at is white. Other people in town are experiencing the same thing. If you're Black, you see everyone as a Black person, and if you're white, you see everyone as a white person. Is that what you have seen too?"

Maggie nodded, "Yes, I've seen it today with a bunch of people."

"So that leaves us with what? What could affect people like this? I have never heard of anything technical or biological that can do something like this. Have you?"

Maggie shook her head as she held her coffee cup with both hands.

"So, what then? Are we talking about something spiritual? Something supernatural? What could cause this?"

Maggie just shrugged her shoulders, gesturing that she didn't know.

Bill looked at Maggie. "You're not much help here."

She smiled. "It's your investigation, sheriff, and I don't want to interfere."

They both laughed again. Bill thought it was good that they could laugh during this crisis. It helped ease the stress. Maggie helped Bill feel like everything was going to work out somehow.

Maggie stopped laughing and said, "Look, Bill, this will make sense eventually. I don't know how, but it has to. There's always an explanation for why things happen the way they do. We may not like the answer, but it will be there; it has to show itself eventually."

"True," Bill said, "but can we survive while waiting for the answer?"

Maggie reached across the table and grabbed Bill's hand. "That, Sheriff, is for you to control."

Bill squeezed her hand and smiled; she was right. His job was about controlling the chaos right now. They held hands as they lifted their cups with their opposite hands to take a drink. Bill looked into Maggie's eyes as they sipped their drinks, and he thought, *This is one of the best cups of coffee I've had in a long time.*

***

As Bill walked Maggie home, he held her hand a little tighter, and she squeezed his hand back. They walked silently to Maggie's house, and before Maggie opened the gate to her yard, Bill looked at her and asked, "Maggie, do you still see me as I am, or do I look Black to you?"

She laughed. "I was thinking the same thing, Bill. I was going to ask you the same question."

"Well, how do I look to you?" he asked again.

"Well," she said, getting closer to him. She started running her index finger up his shirt toward his chin. "I must admit, you would look pretty good as a Black man…But I still see the man I fell for."

She smiled, tapped his chin with her finger, and turned away. She walked through her gate to her house, never looking back. Bill watched her stroll across her yard to her porch. He loved watching her walk, especially while she was wearing jeans.

"Seriously? You left me hanging just like that?" he shouted from the gate.

She turned around. She was on her porch at the front door. "Why, sheriff, I'm not that kind of girl?"

Bill looked at her and smiled. "Yes, ma'am, I respect that. I'll be seeing you tomorrow, then." Bill started to walk away.

Maggie shouted at Bill. "Bill Jackson, you better get your butt up here on this porch!"

Bill hurried around the corner through the gate and walked up to the porch. "Thought you'd never ask," he said.

"You don't lie very well. You knew damn well you were coming in tonight."

They embraced, sharing a long, passionate kiss, Bill holding her tightly in his arms. Maggie had her hands on Bill's face while Bill appreciated her tight backside. Once the kiss ended, they pulled away from each other slowly. Maggie opened the door, took Bill by the hand, and led him inside.

3 THE NEXT DAY

Bill was going to the mayor's office to meet with the CDC officials. The ride through town was quiet and gloomy. With the streets abandoned, it felt like a ghost town. It was difficult not to notice all the empty stores. Bill was glad that everyone listened and stayed home.

Bill walked into the waiting room of the mayor's office. His office door was wide open, and he waved for Bill to enter. Bill walked through the open door.

"Close the door behind you, Bill," Rayburn said.

Bill closed the door and turned around to face the mayor. Sitting off to the right were two people from the CDC. One was a woman with dark black hair, tan skin, and a black business suit. The other was a man in a suit, taller than the woman but slightly shorter than Bill. He had short hair, almost a buzz cut, and looked much younger than the female agent.

"Bill, this is Officer Morales and Officer James from the CDC," the mayor said.

Bill stuck his hand out and shook Officer James's hand first.

Officer James' handshake wasn't as firm as Bill had predicted. Not limp, just not the handshake he was expecting from a Fed.

"Nice to meet you, sir," Bill said.

He pulled his hand away and shook Officer Morales's hand. Now, this was the handshake he was expecting. Morales' handshake was firm. Bill could tell that she was confident and experienced. Bill smiled as he shook her hand.

"Something funny, Sheriff?" Morales asked.

"No, ma'am. Pleased to meet you," Bill said.

"Bill, these officers have questions concerning your trip to the hospital with Bob and Franklin."

"Sure, absolutely," Bill said.

Morales started the conversation. "Sheriff," she began.

"Bill, ma'am. You can call me Bill. We're all friends here," Bill smiled at her.

Bill saw her roll her eyes at him as if to say, "We'll keep this official, and we don't treat each other any other way just because I'm a woman."

"Sheriff," she said, "please explain what happened with as much detail as you can remember."

"Okay, Officer Morales," Bill revised, emphasizing the word officer, "shortly after lunch, I was patrolling Main Street when I saw two men arguing. So I approached them and noticed they weren't angry with each other."

"You said they were arguing," Morales cut in.

"It appeared that they were arguing because both men seemed upset," Bill continued. "I recognized the two men. I determined that they wouldn't get physical with each other."

"Why was that?"

Bill looked at the mayor with a "Can you believe this crap?" look, then answered Morales. "Because I've known these two my whole life. They've never hurt anyone or shown any animosity toward each other in the past."

"Okay, I get it. Continue, please."

"Well, as I approached the two men, they were more scared and confused than angry. They kept pointing at each other and saying crazy things."

"What crazy things, Sheriff? I need you to be very specific."

"The two men, Bob Stanton and Franklin Porter, were looking at each other as if they were seeing aliens or some crap."

"What were they saying?" Morales seemed annoyed that she had to repeat herself.

"Well, Bob Stanton, who is white, was saying Franklin Porter, who is Black, looked white. And Franklin Porter was freaking out and saying Bob Stanton looked Black."

"According to the hospital report, they couldn't find a cause for these hallucinations. We spoke directly with the doctor in charge, and he also mentioned others?"

"Yeah, I was driving down Main Street after leaving the hospital, and there was mass confusion in the downtown area."

"What did you observe?"

"It was the same thing that Franklin and Bob were going through, only it was happening to many more people."

"What did you do?"

"Well, after I called for backup, I noticed that not everyone saw the same crazy stuff as Bob and Franklin."

"What do you mean?"

"Well, some people we observed were not freaking out like everyone else. So, I separated them from the people who were hallucinating. So then we were able to manage the situation."

"Do you have any ideas about what could have caused these hallucinations? Any relatable drug cases?"

"No, not anything I can think of."

Morales took a deep breath and looked at the two men standing there, waiting for an answer.

"Okay, we need to start looking at the commonalities among all those infected."

"You think it's a virus or something like that?" Bill asked.

"I don't know what to think right now, Sheriff. But we are the Center for Disease Control, and that's what we do, no?"

Bill felt a little humiliated, "Yeah, sorry."

"I'll have to get a team down here so we can run tests and conduct interviews," Morales said.

Bill broke in, "How long will all this take?"

"We don't have a cheat sheet for these things, Sheriff. I can't just look up, 'Man sees only white people,' and an answer magically pops up. These things take time. We need to interview people, run tests for infections, find commonalities between them, and find some answers."

"So, what do we tell everyone in the meantime?"

"The best thing to do is to keep this as quiet as possible. It will be hard to do with the social media attention, but we can't raise any panic. We should try to accomplish as much as possible before the rest of the world comes in on this. Our situation here is going to turn into a circus quickly. So before it gets too out of hand, we need to set up stations across town and barriers to keep everyone who has nothing to do with this investigation out of town."

Rayburn finally spoke. "Bill, we need to set up a perimeter around town and keep people out."

Bill nodded at the mayor and looked at Morales. "So, I suppose this means the mayor needs to set up a curfew and restrict anyone from leaving town?" Bill sighed.

"Sheriff, this may be overwhelming for you now, but once word gets out about what is going on here, the governor or even the president may declare martial law and eventually take over."

"Great."

"Yeah, great." Morales went on. "Once that happens, you, the mayor, and everyone in this town will lose all control over this situation. So I advise getting ahead of this and looking like we can handle it before all the chaos hits us hard."

Bill knew she was right; once the Feds got involved and took over the situation, all the citizens' rights would dissolve. "Okay, I'm on it."

4 SETTING UP

Bill had deputies set up roadblocks at the four main entrances to town. There was a lot of open space around town, and Bill knew there was no way to handle that without additional help. So, he concentrated on what they could control. Only commercial vehicles delivering food and other goods were allowed in. The mayor spoke on the local radio station and announced the curfew would take effect immediately. No one was to leave town during the CDC investigation. While at the radio station, the mayor received calls from people and was overwhelmed by all the questions.

He eventually had to end the conversation, "We all need to work together and give the CDC our full cooperation so we can get to an answer a lot quicker."

Morales explained the situation to her superiors on a video call with her headquarters. Her directors shook their heads and said this wasn't a CDC issue. One scientist even offered that it was more of a psychological problem than a matter for a CDC investigation. Morales wasn't pleading her case: she followed the book and reported it as she saw it. No emotional input whatsoever.

"Okay, give me the word, and I'll pull out," she answered. "Just tell me what you want me to tell these people before I go. Are we recommending another agency to help them? Are we saying it's their issue and to work it out themselves?"

"No one is saying pull out yet," the head of the CDC commented. "We just need more facts."

"Sir," Morales went on, "we don't have much time before this breaks out all over the news. Once it does, we will fight much more than this issue."

"Yes, we need to get a jump on this."

Another doctor on the panel disagreed, "If we investigate this matter, then we'll spread even more panic."

The CDC director raised his voice in rebuke, "If we do nothing and we later realize we could have helped by acting quickly, then where does that leave us? Morales, you take point on this. We'll be sending a team down there immediately. Please report your discoveries as you make them. And be as discreet with your findings as possible."

"Yes, sir," Morales ended the call.

Morales was neither happy nor upset that she received the go-ahead. She just wanted to get started before all hell broke loose. She knew it was inevitable that this would be pandemonium once it hit the internet. All kinds of weird theories were going to start popping up. Everyone and their mothers would be choosing a side to follow. Racism would take center stage, and all the crazies would be basking in the light of this discovery. The trolls would be out in full force.

Yeah, she thought, *this is not going to be fun at all.*

***

The mayor assigned Morales a large meeting room in the courthouse to serve as a working office. She had the mayor's staff assemble several tables and set up various computers and laptops. Morales installed dedicated secure Wi-Fi with top-level security protocols to protect against hackers or leaks. She assigned individual work areas as the CDC doctors and scientists slowly reported in. Morales asked the Sheriff about specific strategic places around town to set up for interviews and testing. She wanted to set up areas of the city that allowed higher numbers of citizens to quickly and easily access the interview sites. Bill showed her some vacant office spaces around the town. During interview hours, a deputy was to be stationed at each location to keep the peace.

There were three CDC field teams. They set up in the empty office spaces just outside the downtown area. People who were affected lined up outside the office door to wait for their interviews. When the next person in line entered the office, they were directed into a room and filled out some paperwork. Once they completed their paperwork, they received a numbered paper nametag with an adhesive backing. Morales had several CDC employees enter completed paperwork into their database.

Each citizen then walked into a separate room to have their blood taken. Local nurses volunteered to conduct the procedure, label the samples, and store them. Each of the rooms had equipment brought in from the local hospital to aid the nurses.

The final step in the process was the one-on-one interview. Several rooms on the second floor of the building were set up for CDC officials to conduct individual interviews. Each interviewer had a laptop on their desk, which granted them access to the interviewee's previously provided information.

The interview was the most time-consuming part of the procedure. First, Morales and her team assembled a group of questions for each citizen. Each citizen answered the same questions, so all the analytics had equal weight for internal validity.

"So, Mr. Jones, tell me what's going on exactly." The CDC interviewer in room one was Janet Klausen. Morales assigned Janet, a young white woman, as the interview team leader.

"I don't know exactly," Mr. Jones answered. "I was walking down the street a few days ago, and suddenly, everyone I looked at was the same color."

"What color is that?"

"They were and are all white now," Mr. Jones said, scratching his bald head.

"Can you remember what you did just before this happened? What did you drink or eat, for example?"

"I got up and had breakfast like always—just some cereal. Then, I made a cup of coffee and drank it while dressed. That's about it."

Janet asked Mr. Jones several more questions, which did not lead to anything more interesting. Eventually, she sighed in defeat, thanked Mr. Jones, and asked for the next interviewee.

The next in line was an elderly Black woman.

"Hello. Mrs. Parker, right?" Janet looked over the chart on the screen in front of her.

"Yes, that's me." She smiled.

"You seem to be handling this pretty well."

"Yes, I am," Mrs. Parker kept smiling.

Janet smiled back, "Are you okay with this new condition everyone seems to be having?"

"I believe it's God's work. He is letting me know that this is what I have to look forward to in heaven. Praise Him."

"That's an interesting way of looking at this. So I take it you see everyone as a Black person?"

"I do."

"How do I look to you?"

"You are a beautiful Black woman, and you are making me smile."

Janet just grinned. "Yes, ma'am. Can you tell me what you were doing just before this happened to you?"

"I was kneeling, praying to my Lord like I do daily. Then I went outside, and this miracle began."

"Did you eat or drink before your morning prayer?"

"Yes, I did."

"Can you remember what you ate or drank that morning?"

"Yes, I can. I had some biscuits and gravy and a cup of coffee."

"Did you take any medications after your meal?"

"No. I take a few aspirins a day. I am not on any prescription medications."

"That's good," Janet smiled. "Can you remember doing anything differently that first morning? Or maybe the night before? You know, something out of your normal daily routine."

Mrs. Parker was silent for a moment. Janet could tell by her facial expression that Mrs. Parker was thinking about her question. Then, Mrs. Parker began to move her head slowly.

"No, I can't say that I did anything unusual. My day is pretty much set up the same way every day. Too old to exercise or do anything spontaneous," Mrs.Parker laughed.

Janet smiled, " Yes, ma'am. Thank you for your time. We will let you know if we find anything, okay?"

"Thank you."

All the interviews seemed to go the same way.

"Sir, Mr. Harris?"

"Yes?"

"Can you tell me what's going on?"

"Goin' on?"

"Yes, what are you experiencing right now?"

"Not sure what this is," Harris answered.

"Well, what do you see then?"

"Everyone is white. Every damn person I run into is white. Even though I know they're Black. They're white now."

"Did you experience anything unusual before this occurred?"

"Unusual?"

"Yes, anything different than what you are used to daily."

"No. Nothing happened before I noticed all this. Everything was the same as it always is."

"Are you handling this, okay? Is this causing you any stress?"

"Hell no," he said. "I don't see a problem with this at all." He smiled and walked out of the room.

After two days of tests and interviews, the results were compiled and brought into the meeting room, now the temporary CDC base of operations. Morales was standing against a wall with a big whiteboard behind her. All the team leaders were sitting at the table with their files in front of them. Bill and the mayor were sitting off to one side, quietly observing. Bill struggled to keep his right leg still while Morales managed her meeting.

Morales began. "Okay, we do not have any results from the full toxicity scans yet, so let's see what we have so far."

Janet Klausen spoke up. "I am finding this to be a very unusual case."

"What did you find?" Morales asked.

"From all my interviews, we have one commonality: it's racially driven."

"What do you mean?"

"Well, apparently, it's based on the color of your own skin. The brain is perceiving all others as the same color."

The other team leaders spoke up, "Same with my findings."

"Also, with my results, the same."

Morales looked at the team leaders. "So, what type of pathogen could cause this brain activity?"

All the team leaders just shook their heads.

"So, no ideas?"

Janet spoke up, "Well, we may be looking at an event that is the first of its kind. We may not have any data to support any theories on this."

"Okay," Morales said, "let's go over what we do know and build from there." She went to the big whiteboard behind her and started writing.

Victims see the same skin color.

Facial features and skin color seem to change.

No other external physical reactions other than skin color.

No common exposure to infectious gas.

No common exposure to infectious food or water.

No signs of a common traumatic event.

The event started at approximately the same time for everyone, the same time and day.

Not everyone is affected.

Blood tests not completed.

Morales turned around and asked if this was what everyone else had. They all agreed.

"So, we need the toxicity scan results. Hopefully, we will have some answers there. In the meantime, continue with your investigations. The answer could be right in front of us."

Everyone got up and left. The mayor and Bill walked up to Morales. "So," the mayor said, "what do you think?"

"I don't know," Morales answered. "This is very different from anything we have ever come across."

Bill said, "Well, hopefully, you can figure it out soon. We don't have much time; it's already on the internet. People are going nuts, as you said."

Morales smiled slightly sarcastically, "Yeah, hate being right about that one."

5 WORLD REACTION

Bill was home at his desk, drinking a beer. He had just gotten out of the shower and wrapped his towel around his wet body. Bill turned on his PC and started searching the internet to see how bad things were getting. As he expected, Bends Creek was out there, and it appeared to be getting worse. Videos were popping up all over the web. Some videos were actual news, but the others, the ones that were getting the most hits, were terrifying. Suddenly, Bends Creek, Mississippi, was the center of the world, and not in a respectable way.

Bill knew the freaks would come out, but this was scarier than he thought. The racist groups were making the loudest noise. White nationalist groups were claiming that Bends Creek was the new white heaven. The white nationalists' videos were preaching that Bends Creek was rewarding all-white believers with what they always wanted: a country free of color.

New videos were popping up by the minute. Black groups accused the government of a conspiracy to avoid reparations to the descendants of enslaved people. Videos from different ethnic and religious groups and various individuals sprouted.

Bill was shaking his head. Never in his wildest dreams could he have imagined the world caring about Bends Creek. Bends Creek was a small, insignificant town that no one other than the people who lived here knew existed. In the little southern town where he grew up, the neighbors he came to know throughout the years had been minding their own business. And now, all this.

Some videos warned of the apocalypse and judgment day. The religious videos all seemed to serve up the same message. The message was too crazy for Bill to watch: God is now punishing Bends Creek as an example to the rest of the world. Judgement Day had come to Bends Creek.

Then, there were the videos proclaiming the opposite. Bends Creek was now considered the Promised Land. God had chosen Bends Creek, where all humanity could cleanse its soul.

Bill couldn't handle it anymore and turned it off. He kept thinking that trouble was on its way. People outside of Bends Creek would want to see this for themselves. Bends Creek was the center of all the news; nothing good would come of this. The only thing to worry about now was how he would handle this chaos. Bill knew the uproar that would hit Bends Creek would be too much for his small Sheriff's Department to handle independently. They were going to need outside help.

***

When Bill walked into the mayor's office the following day, he saw Morales standing at the mayor's desk while Rayburn was on the phone. Rayburn looked a little disturbed as he hung up the receiver.

"What's up, Rayburn?" Bill asked.

"I just got off the phone with the governor. He's declaring a state of emergency in Bends Creek. The National Guard will be rolling in shortly."

"Man, this is going to be a cluster!" Bill retorted.

"Now, Bill, I have been guaranteed by the governor that we will still be in charge."

"Yeah, right. We both know how long that's going to last. We are so screwed here." Bill knew that if the government sent troops in, things could go sideways quickly. The military presence around town would cause people to become more scared and stressed.

Morales said, "Gentlemen, the bigger issue is finding out what's happening here. Let them keep everyone out of this town while we figure this out. Let them handle the loonies so we can try to fix this."

Bill nodded his head. "Yeah, we should focus on what's happening in town and let them handle everything else. Agreed."

"Okay, let's get back to work then," Morales said. "We are still waiting on the test results from Atlanta. Hopefully, we can get some answers when they come in."

"Well, I will try to keep everyone as calm as possible. But Rayburn, we will need more deputies to do that."

"Add more bodies as needed; I'll approve any budget changes to support it."

"Thanks, I'll get started." Bill began to walk out of the room.

Just as Bill reached the door, Morales called to him. "Sheriff, can I speak to you for a minute?"

Bill turned around, "Sure, what's up?"

"When you get those new deputies, you should ask them if they are affected by what's happening before you enlist their help."

"Why's that? You think this thing will cause a problem or something?"

"Well, it's more of a hunch than anything else. I mean, if you have deputies that are affected by this, it may cause them some mental issues and stress."

"Yeah, okay. I'll work with that. Thanks."

Morales tilted her head, "Sheriff, a big concern that is coming up in our findings is how only some of the town's people are affected, and others are not. For instance, you aren't, and neither is the mayor."

Bill raised his eyebrows, "Is that an issue?"

"No, not an issue, just an interesting variable. We may have to test the ones that aren't affected as well to see if any differences may help us."

"Okay, sure, whatever you need. Just let me know." Bill walked out.

Morales watched Bill walk out the door. She looked over at the mayor, who was now at the desk on the phone with someone else. Morales usually went with her hunches, and she had always seemed to have a sixth sense of seeing what no one else could. These hunches rewarded her with a quick move up the CDC ladder. Fortunately, she could always back her suspicions with facts throughout her investigations. But this was a different type of case altogether—too many variables, and it was hard to isolate a cause. Moreover, her hunches were going to be tested rigorously in this case. Morales was worried for the first time in all her years at the CDC.

6 THE CALVARY ARRIVES

Colonel Strathern was the typical colonel you would see in the movies: sporting a crew cut over a broad forehead and a square jaw, dressed in military camo. He walked straight and confidently. He reached his hand out to Rayburn and introduced himself.

"Mayor, I'm Colonel Strathern, assigned to cover the perimeter of Bends Creek. Pleased to meet you, sir."

"Pleased to meet you, Colonel," Rayburn said as he shook the colonel's hand. Rayburn noticed how firm the colonel's grip was.

"We'll be setting up roadblocks at all the entrances to town and patrolling the open fields and wooded areas as well. In addition, I'll set up a temporary HQ on the main road outside of town. My communications expert will get you all the communications details so we can keep each other abreast of all activity as needed. Do you have questions or concerns for me?"

"No, sir, I–" Rayburn was interrupted.

"Good. I'll get started. Talk soon, sir." Strathern shook Rayburn's hand again and tilted his head forward while looking at Morales, "Ma'am."

"Colonel," Morales said.

Morales and Rayburn watched the colonel march out of the office. Morales had dealt with the Guard on several occasions before and knew the colonel's type: strictly by the book. Given an order, Strathern would carry it out without batting an eye.

Roadblocks were set up at the four entrances leading into town, as Strathern promised. Three roads ran into the countryside and did not connect to major highways. He set up a command post on the side of the main road leading into town. Strathern knew that since the main road was linked to a few major state highways, it would be the road of choice for visitors. National Guard vehicles were parked just a few hundred yards from the command post's HQ tent. He also set up other tents with tables and cots. One tent was for communications only, where all issues and questions raised by the press were handled.

A map of Bends Creek and the surrounding area was on one table in the main HQ tent. Security around the surrounding areas was a concern. Colonel Strathern set up foot patrols through those areas that were unreachable by vehicles. Three-person patrol groups spread out across the entire region. Soldiers were to patrol 24/7 until further notice. Two dozen tents were set up 20 yards from the HQ tent. These tents had cots for the soldiers to rest while waiting their turn for patrol duty and other orders.

Colonel Strathern was a keep-it-simple type of commander. Strathern was old school: he liked to bark and wanted his men to jump. Of course, it helped when his team leaders were all on the same page with him so that he didn't have to dumb down explanations of his orders. For that reason, he relished the moments when he had a few veterans of distant campaigns under his command. Granted, no one would be in his league after serving over 30 years on many overseas missions. He knew that in today's Guard, he was a dinosaur.

How he ended up with this command ticked him off immensely. It seemed the army was going through a new awakening period with the available technology. Old dinosaurs had to make way for the younger, tech-savvy leaders. Being replaced by someone with zero in-field and command experience was bad enough, but throwing in the fact that he wasn't on Facebook was an issue that took him over the top. The army needs more socially conscious leaders, a general had told him.

He made the mistake of losing his cool and shouting back at the general, "I got their social media right here!" while grabbing his crotch. The general didn't find it amusing and assigned him to the National Guard Command.

Strathern's orders were clear: keep everyone out of Bends Creek who was not a resident, and do not allow any residents to leave the area. General Bronson sent a communications PR officer to deal with the media so that Strathern could concentrate on his duties without outside interruption. Strathern kept communications hot between his post and the Pentagon. He reported daily or as events occurred.

And that's all they're going to get, Strathern thought. *Always by the book.*

Enormous "No Visitors Allowed" and "Area off Limits" signs were posted a few hundred yards before each main entrance into town. Strathern had his men patrol just outside the city limits, creating a ring of signs and manpower circling Bends Creek. With these signs posted, any action his troops needed to take to prevent people from entering was justified.

Bill decided to visit Strathern. He wanted to see if Strathern needed anything from him in the way of support. A soldier walked Bill to the command post tent and announced his visit to the colonel.

"Come on in, Sheriff," Strathern said with a smile.

Bill smiled and held out his hand. "Pleased to meet you, sir."

"Sir?" Strathern seemed surprised. "You serve, Sheriff?"

"Yes, sir," Bill stood a little taller, almost coming to attention. "Did a few tours in the Middle East. Rangers, sir."

"Finally!" Strathern shouted. "Someone I can communicate with on an intellectual level."

Both men laughed.

Bill began, "I just came by to introduce myself and ask if you needed anything from us, sir. We appreciate your help."

"Naw," Strathern declined. "We're just settling in right now. Once we get everything set, we'll get together and give you all a report of what we're doing and how we will enforce our orders."

"Fair enough," Bill smiled. "Here's my card; it has my cell on it. Please give me a holler if there is anything I can do to help."

"Thanks, Sheriff. Will do." Strathern took Bill's card and shook his hand again. Strathern watched Bill leave the tent. He looked down at Bill's card and tossed it onto the table next to the map.

***

As the news spread worldwide about Bends Creek, the people in town were growing more anxious for answers. The mayor was on the local radio station several times daily, keeping everyone updated. Unfortunately, the news wasn't changing after the first few broadcasts, so the listenership fell dramatically. The citizens of Bends Creek were not only upset about not having answers; they were getting cabin fever. They weren't allowed to leave town because the colonel denied passage to every citizen. They felt like prisoners.

As the anxiety level increased, answers became more challenging to come by. Morales finally received the results of the tests from Atlanta and called the mayor and sheriff into her office to share the findings.

When Bill arrived in her office, Rayburn was already there. He was at a desk with his head in his hands, staring down at the top of his desk.

Bill looked at Rayburn and Morales, "Alright then," he said, "what did I miss?"

Morales answered. "Well, we have the test results." She raised some papers with her right hand and pointed them at Bill. "And it's all bad news," Morales said, dropping the papers on her desk.

"What do the results say?"

"Nothing," Morales said, raising her voice. "Absolutely nada. Nothing!"

"I don't understand. There has to be something." Bill scanned through the paperwork as if he knew how to read the results.

"Nope, nada!" Morales exclaimed, walking toward the window. "The CDC found no abnormalities that were a cause for concern. Nothing out of the ordinary. It doesn't make sense." She raised her hands and dropped them straight down. "The only commonality in the tests was that everything was as normal as possible."

"Okay, so now what?" Bill asked. "What are we going to tell these people? Hey, there's nothing wrong with you. All you have to do is wake up from this bad dream you're having?"

"Yo no se," Morales said, drifting off while looking out the window.

"Well, you'd better figure this out quick, or we're going to have that cocky Colonel moving into town. They'll be patrolling our streets before too long, and all hell will break loose!" Bill was starting to raise his voice now.

"Bill," Rayburn looked up from his desk. "We have to remain calm. These folks are counting on us to get them out of this mess. If they see us panicking, then they will follow suit. And yes, then all hell will break loose."

Bill knew Rayburn was right. If they showed any distress, it would just worsen things. He looked over at Morales. "Sorry about that. What happens now?"

Morales couldn't take her eyes from the window. She was drifting far away. "Sheriff, that's the million-dollar question right now. What's next?"

As Bill predicted, Colonel Strathern received new orders, including patrolling the city from the inside. Strathern set up his new HQ tent in the middle of town at Mudwater Park. A few army Humvees patrolled the main streets. The situation was starting to look like a military occupation, and the colonel was all in.

Bill walked up to the colonel's tent at his new HQ and was escorted inside by a sentry. "Bill," Strathern said with a smile, "come on in. I was expecting you."

"Colonel," Bill answered, "good to see you again."

"What can I do for you, Bill?" the colonel asked, not looking up from his war table.

"Sir, are the Humvees necessary? It looks like Beirut out there. These people are scared already, and this isn't helping."

"I understand your concern, Bill, but you know, as a military man, this is just protocol."

"Yes, sir, I do. But these are different circumstances. These people aren't a threat or a danger to your men."

"Not yet, they aren't. But we can't be too careless with these matters. You never know what will set them off. We have to stay sharp."

"So I take that as a no to parking the Humvees for now?"

"That's a 10-4, Sheriff. We'll try to keep the patrols to a minimum. How about that?"

"I'd appreciate anything you can do, sir." Bill shook the colonel's hand and walked out.

The colonel watched Bill leave and went back to looking over his map.

***

About 45 minutes later, the first external intruders were apprehended. As the sun set, two men with cameras hanging around their necks were escorted into Strathern's outer perimeter tent by two armed soldiers.

"Now, what do we have here?" The colonel grinned at the two men. "Gentlemen, trespassing on a military operation is a serious offense."

The two men stood in front of the armed soldiers who were blocking their exit from the tent.

One spoke up, "General, we–"

Strathern interrupted, "Colonel."

The man continued, "Sorry, Colonel. We're just reporters looking for some answers."

"Well, the correct way of getting answers is talking to our PR officer, sir. You, of course, are aware of this?"

"Yes, we are. But PR isn't telling anyone anything."

"Well, I am just an instrument of service to my country. I follow orders. My orders are to keep everyone who doesn't live in this town out of town. You understand that, right?"

"Yes," the reporter said. The other reporter just nodded.

"So, legally, you are trespassing on the grounds of an ongoing military operation. I could have you both arrested. Fortunately, my men did not shoot either of you. Because if they had, no one would've given a crap."

"Sir, there's no need for any of that. We'll leave and never come back. How's that?" The other reporter was still nodding.

Strathern scratched his chin with his thumb as if he were thinking about the reporter's proposition.

"Now, I believe you, I really do," he said sarcastically. He walked around the reporters. "But what kind of message would I be sending to all the other people outside this town who decide to break the law and try what you did if I just pat you on the butt and send you on your way?" Strathern looked up, his thumb still on his chin.

"I think it's a perfect message, sir," the reporter answered nervously.

"Yeah, well, you would think that, wouldn't you? I'll tell you what I'm going to do. Instead of having you arrested, I'll detain you overnight and see how I feel in the morning. How does that sound?"

The reporter's eyes widened, "Do you have to keep us overnight? Colonel, please reconsider."

"It's either that or we take you to a civilian jail and charge you with trespassing."

The two men didn't say anything. They both watched Strathern take the SD cards out of their cameras.

"I'll hold onto these until we get the all-clear from my superiors." Strathern returned the two reporters' cameras and ordered his soldiers to escort them to the holding facility.

"Gentlemen, sleep well."

Strathern watched them leave. He knew charging the reporters would be more hassle, and he didn't want to waste his time testifying in court.

7 TOWNSFOLK

Bends Creek was becoming increasingly divided. Some citizens were scared about what was happening, while others embraced the event affecting their town. Some people were thankful to God for answering their prayers. Others were just thankful.

At one end of town, in the Bends Creek AME Church, the Reverend William Sanders was preparing to greet his parishioners. This Sunday felt more special than any in the past. Today, he felt lighter. A heavy burden was lifted off his shoulders today. Reverend Sanders didn't have to preach about hatred and racism today. He didn't have to focus on how badly the police treated African Americans, and he didn't have to reference a racist crime that was in the news. Today was about hope and the possibility of a new beginning: that was a reason to feel joyous. He stepped up to the podium and looked out across all the Black faces in the pews.

Yes, he thought, *A new beginning.*

No one was more thankful for the present crisis than Elias Stout. He was well known as the town's most vocal white supremacist. Along with six or seven other white men, he formed a local white nationalist group headquartered outside the city on Elias' farm. As Elias put it, they stowed away weapons and explosives in preparation for the war to end all wars.

Elias was always accompanied by two or more guys from his social group when he came into town. Bill was one of the few people in town who could handle Elias. Elias knew of Bill's military record and respected him for serving his country, mostly because he was Special Forces. Whenever Elias started trouble in town, Bill would always be there to ensure it never got worse than name-calling. For example, if an altercation occurred between Elias and a Black citizen, Bill would step in, and Elias would look at Bill, salute him, laugh, and walk away.

But this beautiful sunny Sunday, Elias Stout came into town alone today. He was riding in from his farm in his rusty red pickup. As Elias drove into town, all Elias saw were white people. Elias had the biggest grin as he passed people, waving and yelling out his window. Elias Stout was in his racist heaven. Elias was so happy that he put money in the meter when he parked his truck. Something he had never done before. The unpaid tickets in his glove compartment could attest to that.

He decided to walk down Main Street and take it all in, saying hello to everyone he passed. He started whistling Dixie as he walked down the sidewalk.

"You in hog heaven, ain't you, boy?" a voice called out to him.

"Yes, I am," Elias smiled at the man sitting in a parked truck who had just spoken. The man was JT Crawford, a Black man who had grown up with Elias. They went to the same high school. Suspensions for fighting were a part of their high school experience together. The only thing they had in common was that neither had graduated.

The man spoke from behind the wheel of his truck. "You can't see me, can you? You racist pig."

"Racist pig?" Elias shouted. "JT, is that you, boy?" Elias started laughing.

"Yeah, it's me. I guess you be enjoying this, huh?"

"Ain't you? I know you are; tell me what you see." Elias stood at the front of JT's truck with his arms stretched to the sides.

"You're as Black as the piece of crap you are," JT answered. "What're you seeing?"

"Whiteness, baby. All whiteness," Elias laughed. "How the hell did you know it was me, JT?"

"Ain't no Black man going to be walking down the street whistling that racist song, would they, bitch?"

"Well, JT, get used to it. The times they are a-changin'." Elias laughed and walked off, waving the back of his hand toward JT. Usually, Elias would have confronted JT, as he had done many times before. But not today. Today was for celebrating, and Elias was doing just that.

Elias grew up on a small farm just past the Bends Creek town line. His father, Tobias, always had a bottle of moonshine in his hand. That transparent bottle containing that clear, home-brewed alcohol was a part of his body, as was the hand holding it. Elias remembered how hard the bottle was because it never broke when his father hit him on the head with it.

Elias hated his father. It wasn't so much because his father used his belt buckle when he beat him. No, Elias hated his father for what he did to his mother. His mother, Louisa, was always working around the house, cleaning and cooking. Tobias would come home drunk, going on with his racist rants and getting so riled up that he would start hitting Louisa. If Elias was in the same room when Tobias attacked his mother, his father turned on him next. Elias' mother would always find the strength to stand back up from her beating and try to get between Elias and his father to protect her son.

Elias always remembered the day he stood up to his father. He was

20 years old when his father came home after a night out drinking with his buddies. He came in, ranting with those racial slurs, and yelled to his mother for his supper. His father sat at the table and took another long swig from his bottle. When Elias' mother put his plate on the table, he grabbed her backside and smiled at her. She walked away, and he took a bite.

"What the hell is this crap?" he yelled as he threw the fork down on the table.

"What's wrong?" Louisa asked in her soft southern drawl.

"I ain't eating this crap; come get this pig slop away from me," Tobias slurred.

Louisa leaned down to pick up his plate when Tobias hit her with the back of his hand. Louisa fell backward onto the floor, hitting her head, and her nose started bleeding. Elias heard the noise and ran into the room. He went over to help his mother up. Tobias got up and walked over to the two of them.

"Ain't nobody deserves to be fed this kind of slop, woman!" Tobias yelled as spit and drool left his mouth. Tobias looked at Elias as he was helping his mother up. "You a momma's boy?"

Elias didn't answer.

"I'm talking to you, boy! Are you still sucking your momma's tittie?" He laughed and took another drink from his bottle.

Again, Elias ignored his father. He held his mother and walked her to a nearby chair to help her sit down.

"You ignoring me, boy? I oughta kick your ass, you ungrateful little bastard!"

Elias turned away from his mother and faced his father. As he turned, his father's hand and that damned bottle came down toward Elias' head. Elias caught his father's wrist just before the bottle reached his head. His father looked at Elias' hand as it held his wrist, eyes bulging.

Elias finally spoke. "You are done hitting anyone in this house, hear me?"

His father laughed. "What are you going to do, boy?"

Without saying a word, Elias hit his father square in the jaw. The blow sent him backward, and he fell onto his back, unconscious. Elias never knew if his punch or the floor knocked Tobias out. He never really cared; he was just glad he was out cold. The bottle of moonshine rolled out of Tobias's hand and across the floor. That would be the only time Elias remembered his father was separated from the bottle.

***

Bill was driving down Main Street when he noticed something peculiar. He couldn't help but note how surprisingly calm everyone was. People talked to each other and carried on as if it were just another day in Bends Creek. So many people, Black and white, were mingling with each other. They seemed to enjoy each other's company, acting like old friends.

Unfortunately, Bends Creek had its share of racists, and those who chose to would only associate with people of their own race. As a result, people in Bends Creek always kept to themselves. There was mutual respect by staying out of each other's business.

No one ever talks about racism, but everyone knows it's here, Bill thought.

There was an unspoken agreement between the Black and white people of Bends Creek. Each group had its part of the city. The Black citizens stayed on their side of town, and the white ones stayed on theirs. Only those who are comfortable being with any group would mingle with others. Bends Creek was like many other towns in the deep South with a dark and bloody past, and these racial territorial divisions were the scars left behind from the horrible history preceding them. Bill was not proud of this history. At one point in his life, he considered moving as far away as possible because of it.

Bill always tried to notice little things to make him feel hopeful that change for the better was coming: a white man helping a Black man change a tire, a Black lady and a white lady walking through town, shopping together. He wasn't naïve, though. He knew Bends Creek was a long way from solving all their problems. But it was gratifying that some people on both sides were at least trying.

Most of the town was now afflicted. Bill looked around and noticed that the affliction was succeeding in knocking down racial barriers. Without racial obstacles, people talked freely and understood each other on a level they never could before. There was no fear of speaking your mind or offending someone. They were all merely living in the moment and doing their daily business as usual. With the racial tension eliminated, everyone appeared happier. It was a sight to behold. Everyone was laughing and carrying on together.

He had to stop the car and escape because this atmosphere was an incredible Bends Creek first. People he thought were so set in their southern racial traditions were carrying on with each other as if race had never existed. Right now, given the affliction, it didn't. Bill wished his father were alive to see this. Bill couldn't help thinking that maybe this event was not such a bad thing after all.

But he knew there was a problem with thinking this was a good thing because people were living a lie. Bill shook his head. He realized these people couldn't see it the way he did. They behaved based on a falsehood generated from the affliction. Although it was nice to see, this fellowship was happening for the wrong reason. It was a temporary fix to a centuries-old problem.

Still, Bill thought, *we should all enjoy this while it lasts.*

Sheriff Bill Jackson had grown up with the people of Bends Creek. He knew most of the troublemakers by name. Most of his calls as sheriff involved breaking up fights between loud-mouthed individuals. Everyone knew where they were safest in town, and each side marked its territory. There was a mutual understanding of where trouble would start.

Knowing they could masquerade as the same color, the troublemakers would begin to visit the other side. Problems were coming, and it would take all the men he had to deal with them and try his patience. So, as a precaution, he doubled the patrols around the hotspots, mostly the bars in town. With the patrols being so visible, Bill hoped to avoid any trouble before it started. Bill knew the crazies that saw the patrol vehicles and stayed away weren't his problem. It would be the idiots who ignored the patrol cars and wanted to start trouble anyway.

Unsurprisingly, Bill got his first call since the affliction had started from Connie's Bar. Connie's Bar was at the end of town and was publicly known to cater to African Americans. When Bill arrived, he pulled up alongside his two deputies' vehicles. Bill walked through the front door and pushed a few men aside to make his way to the center of the bar. He passed the band, which was quietly watching the fight. A few pool tables were in the back, and the two men in the center of the room had each grabbed a pool stick. They were screaming at each other, threatening to hit each other with their makeshift weapons.

One man screamed, "Get your racist white ass out of here, or I'm going to shove this stick through your heart!"

The other hollered back, "Come on and bring it!"

The two deputies were holding the men back from striking each other. One deputy was white, the other Black, and they both looked confused.

Bill walked up to his Black deputy. "What's going on, Randy? Why do you need my help with this?"

Randy looked at Bill wide-eyed.

Bill frowned, "Oh shit, Randy, you afflicted?"

Randy just nodded his head. "Bill, they both look Black to me."

Bill looked over at his other deputy. "Freddie, what about you?"

"They're both white, man."

Bill just shrugged his shoulders and lowered his head for a moment. Then he raised it and walked over to the two men. Bill addressed the white male first.

"Okay, Ned, give me the pool stick." He held out his hand.

Ned looked up and laughed. "Come on, Bill, we jus' tryin' to see how the other side lives. They got ridiculous drinks here, and the music is so good." He handed Bill his stick.

Bill looked over and asked the other man to do the same. "Come on, Darnell. Stop this right now and hand me the stick."

"It ain't right, this white racist coming in here, Sheriff! You know it ain't right."

"I gotcha, Darnell. I agree no one should be coming in here to start trouble. So how about we calm down and let me get him out of here for you?"

"That would be good, Sheriff. That would be real good." Darnell handed over the cue to Bill.

"Okay, here's what's going to happen," Bill announced, looking around the bar. "I'm going to give everyone who came here to start trouble ten seconds to clear out peacefully. Before you decide, know I am not afflicted and can see who you are. If you insist on staying, I will arrest you. I will arrest you if you insist on making derogatory remarks as you leave or if you decide to get physical with anyone as you pass them as you are leaving. For those who stay, I expect the same. Right, do we all understand the rules? Okay then. The clock starts now."

Bill watched as five white men walked out of the bar. Some of the Black patrons looked surprised, and others just nodded. Bill grabbed Ned by the arm. "Hold on a minute, Ned, we need to talk. You're coming with me. Randy. Freddie. Escort Ned here to my car and watch him for me. I'll be right there."

"Okay, Sheriff," both men answered in unison.

Bill walked over to Darnell. "How did you know that Ned was white?"

"I said something," said an elderly man sitting at the corner table by the window.

"You aren't afflicted then, sir?" Bill asked.

"Guess not," the man said. "Just like you, I saw all of them. I just commented to the bartender that I thought it was pretty cool we were hosting culture night." The older man started laughing.

Bill couldn't help but laugh with him. "Yes, sir, a first for Bends Creek. Culture night at Connie's." Bill, still smiling, shook the man's hand and told him to enjoy the rest of his evening.

"Thanks, Sheriff," the man nodded.

Bill turned around and addressed the patrons one last time. "I wish there were something I could do to stop idiots from starting trouble," he roared. "But I can't. All I can say is, please don't let them get you so riled up that you end up in a cell right next to them. You call me, and I promise I will come and remove any jerk who starts trouble. That's my job. Goodnight," Bill finished and walked out the door.

Ned was in the back of Bill's car, still laughing, the stench of alcohol reeking in the vehicle. Bill opened the door and pulled Ned out. He got in his face. "Look, you racist scumbag, I have enough crap in this town to deal with right now. I don't need this empty-headed racist nonsense going on, making everything worse than it already is. I catch you over here again, or see you where I don't feel you should be; I will lock you up until this affliction is over. You understand me?"

"Sure, Sheriff," Ned said quietly. "We were just having a little fun, that's all."

"It ain't fun if you piss people off! It's only fun for scum like you because you get off when you upset other people. So I'll make it real fun for you if you upset me again. Are we clear?"

"Yes, sir, we are. Can I go now?"

"Ned, don't forget what I said. And tell everyone you know, too. I am not afflicted, so I can see you, idiots, a mile away!"

"Gotcha, Sheriff. I'll pass it on."

"Good. Now get out of my sight."

Bill looked over his car as he shut the door behind Ned. The two deputies were standing there, looking more confused than before. He walked over to them.

"Look, guys, you have to take it slow now. Agent Morales from the CDC calls this condition an affliction. With her agency's help, we'll figure it out. Please do me a favor and call a meeting tomorrow afternoon after lunch, say 2 p.m. Let's get all the deputies and the whole department together in the station meeting room to discuss this mess, okay?"

"Sure," said Randy, getting into his car. "I'll get everyone there."

"Okay, thanks," Bill said and walked to his car. Opening the car door, he looked back at Connie's Bar. Bill noticed the non-afflicted older man in the window, sitting at his table and smiling. The man raised his glass to Bill. Bill nodded back, got in his car, and drove off.

Bill went directly home. It was late. He had to decide how his department would handle conflicts moving forward. He would have to make some tough choices: the type of options you lose sleep over the night before.

***

"Okay, let's get this meeting started." Bill was at the front of the room, looking over his team. "By now, everyone knows what's going on. What we don't know is how long it's going to last."

"The CDC any closer, Bill?" Randy asked.

"No, they aren't. Everyone tested so far seems to be normal. There's nothing out of the ordinary. No biological explanation for this affliction at all, yet. That doesn't mean the CDC won't find something to solve this. But in the meantime, we have to hold down the fort."

Bill looked around at all the faces of the concerned people in the meeting. They were all whispering to each other. "Okay, listen up. We have some major areas I want to deal with as quickly as possible. First, for those afflicted, I need you to go to the CDC tents or offices and get checked. Second, I need to know who is afflicted to manage this appropriately."

"What do you mean appropriately?" one deputy called out.

Bill looked at the deputy. "If you are afflicted, we need to discuss it. We both need to decide if it will distract you when making any decisions."

"And if it is?" the deputy asked.

"Then we need to figure out the next best step," Bill replied. "So please, if you are afflicted, put your name down on the sheet that's going around. We will discuss this more personally, and all talks will be confidential," Bill went on. "We are moments away from the governor giving the order to impose martial law on this town. If that happens, we will not be able to help our citizens. Their fates will be in the hands of the U.S. government. Ours will be, too. We must do everything we can to show them we can handle this without their interference."

Everyone clapped in agreement.

8 A NEW FACE

"You gonna sleep all day, man?" Virgil asked his new business partner, sitting against the alley wall with his head on his knees. "Lunchtime is a good time to be working, you know: people out walking to eat and all."

The man raised his head; he looked tired. "You are right, sir. We need to get to work."

Virgil stood up and looked down at the man. "Where you say you was from?"

The man used the wall behind him to push himself up. "Honestly? I don't remember."

Virgil laughed. "What the hell you been drinking, man? If that stuff helps you forget, man, you need to be sharing."

"I would if I remembered what I was drinking!"

Virgil stared at his partner and then began laughing. "That's funny, man!"

Virgil couldn't tell how old the stranger was because of his long, messy beard. He looked him over once, then again. Virgil kept thinking the man was out of place. He didn't belong on the street, even though he looked the part. But Virgil knew none of that mattered right now. Now was the time they needed to get to work.

The stranger wore a long, ragged coat almost identical to Virgil's. "Where did you get this coat?" Virgil asked.

"At the shelter. Where'd you get yours?"

"Same." Virgil shook his head and laughed. "You ready to work?"

"Sure, let's do this."

"By the way, what's your name? Or did you forget that, too?" Virgil asked

"Pete. My name is Pete."

"Alright then, Pete, let's go."

The two men walked together, holding their tin cups and asking anyone they passed for spare change. It didn't take long before Pete made an observation.

"Virgil, we need what you would call a gimmick."

"What you mean? It's your first day, and you're already trying to take over?"

"No. Maybe some kind of street performance or something."

"What kinda performance? What you know about performing?"

"I think I can play the guitar. Can you play anything?"

"Harmonica, baby. Ain't no one better than me at that, that's for sure." Virgil lit up.

"Maybe we should try it."

"Where we gonna get the instruments, man? I ain't got no harmonica, and you sure don't look like you got no guitar."

"The shelter. I saw an electric guitar and a small amp in the corner when I was there last time. Maybe we could use that?"

"Maggie runs the shelter. She'd let us use it for sure."

"Won't hurt to ask?"

"Naw, it won't. Let's give it a try."

Both men started walking down the street toward the shelter. As they walked, Pete could see Virgil's face becoming more animated. As they chatted, Virgil got more excited the closer they got to the shelter. "Blues," he said. "We got to make sure we play some blues."

"Absolutely," Pete agreed.

"We can add a few songs, you know that I don't, just to attract diffn't folks, though."

"Makes sense."

They didn't see the two white men walking by as Virgil planned their playlist. Virgil accidentally bumped into one of them, knocking him back a little.

"Watch where you're going, old man!" one man said.

The other chimed in and got closer to Virgil. "What is your problem, gramps? You too drunk to see straight?" Both men laughed.

Virgil looked up at the two men and noted they were three or four inches taller than he was. They were muscular, tough-looking brutes.

"Sorry, fellas, my bad."

The first man Virgil had accidentally bumped into raised his voice, "Your bad? That's all you got to say? How about I push you and just say my bad." The man pushed Virgil with both hands, knocking him into some trash cans and onto the ground.

Pete chimed in. "He apologized. It was a mistake."

Now, both men were facing Pete. "It looks like you're both mistakes. "Maybe we should just take you both out like the trash you are"?

"Trash, you are?" Pete asked.

"Yeah, that's what I said. Like trash, you are."

"I get it," Pete exclaimed, acting like he had an epiphany. "By getting rid of the trash you are, we are all better off."

"Wait a minute, man. You're twisting my words around." The bully was getting annoyed.

Pete went on, "You said to get rid of trash like you. So we need to get rid of you to be happy, right?"

"Who are you, man, some homeless street idiot? I oughta just waste you right here," the bully's face turned red. He raised his shirt to expose a gun handle.

Virgil scrambled up and lurched between Pete and the bully. "Okay, we got it. We'll just be moving on now."

The man lowered his shirt, staring at Pete. "Get out of here. If I see you again, I'll take you out."

The two men walked away. Pete looked back at the men and said, "If I see you again, it will be too soon."

The two men didn't hear Pete, and Virgil jumped in. "Pete, you trying to get us killed or something?"

"No, I just don't think what they were doing was okay."

Virgil looked at Pete and shook his head. "I guess I gotta learn you a few things about these streets here in the south. You ain't got time to be a rookie on these streets, and you have to understand your situation. You just got to roll with the cards you're dealt, man. The sooner you see that, the better off you gonna be."

"Thanks, Virgil."

"No problem, partner; let's get this show on the road."

When they arrived at the shelter, Maggie was the only one there. She sat by herself at a table in the corner of the room, sipping a cup of coffee. She was looking at her phone and shaking her head.

"Hey, Miss Maggie," Virgil smiled as he greeted her.

Maggie looked up. "Hey, good looking, what's up?"

"Well, me and my new partner here want to ask you a favor."

Maggie looked at Pete. "New partner? What do you mean, partner? You don't mean," she stopped, waving her index finger from Pete to Virgil and back again.

"Oh no! Maggie, what the–? You crazy? Pete is my new business partner!" Virgil yelled.

Maggie started laughing, "Okay, Virgil, calm down. I didn't know."

Maggie looked at Pete and smiled, "How are you? I'm Maggie, and you are?" Maggie stretched her hand out to Pete.

Pete shook Maggie's hand. "I'm Pete."

"What's on your mind, Virgil?"

"Pete here said he saw a guitar sitting in the corner over yonder, and we want to know if we can borrow it."

Maggie looked at the guitar and then at Pete. "You want to sell my guitar, Virgil?"

"No, we want to borrow it. Pete had this idea that if we could do a little street jam, we might be able to make some money."

"This is Pete's idea?"

"Yes," Pete answered.

Maggie went on, "I don't know you, Pete. This is the first time I've seen you here. How do I know I can trust you to get me my guitar back?"

"I'm not a thief. If I give you my word, you can trust me."

"Trust you?" Maggie asked. "Do you know how many people have said that to me and still do? Trust me, they say, and the next thing you know, you get screwed over."

Pete smiled at Maggie. "I understand. I assure you we will return your guitar and amp every night before dark."

Maggie looked at Pete. He had a certain innocence about him. He looked like he had gotten a raw deal at some point. Maybe he was taken advantage of for being so pleasant.

"Okay, Pete. I'm going to trust you, but I want you to know that I have friends who will find you if you screw me over."

"Sheriff Bill, I know."

Maggie looked confused. "How'd you know that?"

Pete answered, "I think everyone knows." Maggie and Virgil started to laugh. Maggie thought there was something different about Pete, but she couldn't quite put her finger on it.

Virgil raised his chin, "Oh, by the way, you still got that old harmonica around here?"

Maggie grew excited. "You're going to play too, Virgil? I would love to hear that. I'll tell you what: you play me something, and I'll let you borrow these instruments. Deal?"

Virgil lit up. "An audition? Always wanted to have one of those!"

Pete grabbed the guitar and amp and sat at the table. Pete plugged the guitar into the amp and started tuning it by ear. Maggie and Virgil looked at each other and smiled. Maggie went to the back and came out with a harmonica in a gold case.

"I've always kept my eye on this for you, Virgil."

Virgil's eyes watered a little. "Thanks, Maggie." He took the harmonica from her.

"Well, what's it going to be, guys?" Maggie asked as she sat at a different table, waiting for the entertainment to start.

Pete asked Virgil what the harmonica's key was. Then Pete ran a few riffs to loosen up his fingers. Maggie and Virgil looked at Pete, then at each other, then back at Pete. They were both staring at Pete, their eyes wide open.

Pete looked up from the guitar. "Everything okay?"

Maggie just nodded, still looking at Pete. He was running his fingers up and down the strings, and it sounded like a rock solo.

Pete's playing seemed surreal to her. This homeless man was ripping away at the guitar right before her.

She finally had to say something. "Are you a famous musician who lost his way or something?" she asked.

Pete kept playing, never looking away from the guitar. "No, not likely."

Virgil was warmed up on the harmonica and ready to try it. He was a little more excited now that he knew Pete could play.

"Okay, Pete," Virgil said, tapping his foot. "Let's get this party started. Blues in G."

"G it is." Pete started with a blues progression.

Both men were tapping their feet in time. Pete's blues playing was getting Maggie to tap her feet as well. Virgil came in with his harmonica and played a solo throughout the progression. Maggie smiled, and all seemed right with the world at that moment. All the chaos outside the shelter didn't seem to matter to anyone. Now was the time to enjoy the music.

9 A DIFFERENT TAKE

Morales was getting nowhere fast. Every test they decided to run or try came back with no clues. She seriously considered giving up the investigation, something she had never done in her career with the CDC. Her frustration was mounting, and she had nothing to report to Atlanta. She had nothing to add for the mayor and sheriff. But what frustrated her more than not having answers was that she was considering giving up. Morales never gave up, but this was beating her down. She called her team together.

"Okay, what are we not seeing?" she asked her team. "There has to be something that is staring right at us, and we do not see it. Does anyone have any theories?"

One team member spoke. "I don't think we will find anything biological."

"What makes you say that?" asked Morales.

"Well, it's been over seven days. We haven't seen any new cases, and there are zero reactionary symptoms to what's happened."

Morales looked at everyone at the table. "So…where does that leave us?" she asked.

Another team member spoke. "We must look outside science or consider that the answer is outside our expertise."

The other team members started getting restless, whispering and talking among themselves. Morales noticed that everyone in the room was as frustrated as she was.

"Okay, okay, settle down," Morales said. "What we need are suggestions on how to move forward. We have done this by the book and come up empty-handed. So, let's think outside the book and try something different. I am open to suggestions. Nothing is too far-fetched at this point."

"Maybe we should look at the people who are not victims of this affliction," Klausen called out.

"Why?" Morales asked.

"Maybe the answer lies within the people who are not afflicted. I don't know."

Morales didn't want to leave any stones unturned. "Let's try that then," she agreed. "Let's interview the people who are not afflicted and see what they have in common. Let's not just focus on the biological commonalities. Let's see what comes up through conversation. Personal behaviors, beliefs, and so on..."

The team seemed to be energized by the possibilities. Morales was surprised that most of her team, all scientists, were willing to look beyond science for an answer. Of course, she wasn't sure what they would find, but she was still hopeful.

Bill came into the office as her team was leaving. "Looks like you had a good meeting," he smiled.

Morales looked up at him from her chair. "Any meeting that provides hope at this point is good," she said.

"Really? Hope is good."

"It's just another guess at this point. We will interview the non-afflicted people to see if they have any commonalities."

"Anything I can do to help?"

"No, thanks. We're plugging away, but it doesn't look too good."

"I met with my department and told them we must buckle down and get ready for the government to come in."

"Yeah, it's inevitable," Morales said. "The big problem is we can't identify what this is or isn't. Once they give up on our efforts, then they will come in and quarantine this whole town. Quarantine isn't going to be pretty for anyone here."

"Yeah, I know." Bill shook his head, "The internet is on fire, and the colonel has his hands full already. It won't be long before they order more troops here to help him."

Morales sighed. "He's the scary part of the government. That old-school, by-the-book mentality always seems to mess things up somehow. On top of that, there's no telling which agencies will be coming in to investigate this. Marshal law is going to be a major cluster."

Bill smiled. "I couldn't have said it better."

Morales smiled and sighed again. She wasn't used to feeling this way. Helpless, with no answers or solutions to offer. She wasn't the type to sit around and wait to see what happened next. But the sad thing was, this time, she had no choice.

Bill tried to pick her spirits up. "I'm sure you guys will get this before it hits the fan."

Morales smiled. "I hope you're right, Sheriff. I hope you are right." She couldn't shake the feeling that nothing good would come from this.

"You religious, Sheriff?"

Bill shrugged his shoulders. "I go to church sometimes. But I'm one of those new-wave types. I consider myself spiritual but not actually religious."

"Oh?" Morales' eyebrows rose in surprise. "How well does that go over in the Bible Belt?"

"It goes over great as long as you keep it to yourself," he laughed.

"Yeah, I suppose everything is better when you keep quiet about it." She smiled.

"Why are you asking?"

"I don't know." Morales looked out the window. "Maybe the answer is beyond science. I don't know."

"Well, if it is, I hope we find it. It would be easier to deal with that way."

"True. True." Morales seemed to be drifting off.

Bill spoke softly, "Hey, you got this. It will come to you when you least expect it. So don't be too hard on yourself, if that's even possible."

Morales smiled. "Thanks, Sheriff."

Bill walked out and left Morales, staring out the window.

Morales's team interviewed over 50 citizens who were not afflicted. Then, they returned to the office for the nightly recap and presented their observations. As far as the standard test questions went, all the results were the same as those from the afflicted interviewees.

"I think there is a difference that we need to discuss," Klausen stated.

Morales looked at her and said, "Please go on."

"Well, these interviewees are not happy about the affliction."

"I'm not sure what that means," Morales said.

"Some of the afflicted were okay with this condition. Some were even happy about it. But none of the non-afflicted are okay with this."

"Are you saying the happy people want to be afflicted?"

"No."

"Why are the non-afflicted unhappy?" Morales asked. "Do you think it's because they were left out?"

"No." Klausen shrugged, "They were unhappy that people don't get to see the world as it is any longer."

Morales looked confused. "What does this mean?"

Klausen leaned forward, "Well, we decided to look outside biology, right? All our tests are inconclusive. At this point, we do not have any historical or scientific data to support this event. We have found no evidence of chemical poisoning or geological anomalies reported in the area. We have eliminated the possibility of cultist behavior. We have crossed all logical assumptions off our list with research and evidence gathering. It is also safe to conclude that outside factors, like race and religion, play a significant role in how they feel about being afflicted. So if we conclude that these behaviors can not be supported with scientific evidence, then maybe we are looking at something…." Klausen paused.

Morales said, "Finish, go on."

"It appears to be something supernatural."

The team broke out into chaos. Every team member was talking loudly. Some agreed, while some said the proposition was absurd. It was apparent that this assumption wasn't the consensus of the team.

"Alright, everyone, let's calm down." Morales tried to get control of the meeting.

"Please explain this theory."

"A logical conclusion would be psychological causes, but no events connect these occurrences. Not every afflicted person feels the same way about being afflicted. Race is the only similarity and constant between the afflicted. From our research and lack of scientific evidence, we can logically assume that someone or something is intentionally afflicting these people. "

Morales was still listening, even though others were mumbling and whispering to each other. "Please, everyone, pipe down and let her finish. Go on."

"We can safely conclude from these results and our other findings that people who want to be afflicted have a higher chance of being afflicted than people who do not want to be."

"And?"

"People who don't want to be afflicted aren't, and people who are happy with it are. That implies that there's a connection based on their original mentality. Something has actively allowed these people to ignore race without possible psychological or biological causes. Therefore, we should consider the interference of an external force. Perhaps the supernatural.

"You can't possibly agree with this!" one team member shouted.

"Why not?" another responded.

Morales spoke up, "Please, everyone, please calm down. We haven't determined anything yet. We are taking suggestions and opinions. We need to consider all theories and either prove or disprove them. That's our job."

Morales continued after the room quieted. Morales sighed, "Look, I am not saying I believe in the supernatural or the intervention of a higher being. I am just saying we are at a point where we need to present all the facts and theories we have and test, test, and test some more. We must accept what we don't understand as possibilities because our knowledge database does not answer this dilemma."

One team member got up from his seat. "I have to leave this team," he claimed. "I am a scientist, not a witch doctor or occultist. I want no part of this."

Morales looked at him. "It's okay, I understand. If you are uncomfortable, you can leave without repercussions to your employment status."

"Thank you," he said. Then, he shook Morales' hand and walked out of the room.

Morales offered, "Anyone else uncomfortable with these conversations? Don't be afraid to leave. Leaving right now will not be held against you or written on your record. I cannot punish someone for doing what they believe is right."

Two other scientists got up, nervously shook their heads, and walked out.

Morales waited a few minutes to give everyone at the table time to digest what had happened.

Morales furrowed her brows, "You all were hired to analyze evidence. I mean, that's what we do, no? But we have exhausted all avenues of evidential reasoning. I realize seeking answers outside our wheelhouse of knowledge is a bit unorthodox. But we are running out of time to help this town. Martial law will impose strict rules and limit their freedom. Once the federal government gets involved, these people will be treated like guinea pigs."

The remaining team members were nodding their understanding and approval.

Morales continued, "Okay, look. Let's not call it supernatural or religious or spiritual just yet. Let's look at this with open minds and continue to talk to these people. Maybe we can figure out what is going on that way. So please, let's take tomorrow and see if we get the same results from another non-afflicted group, and we'll take it from there."

Everyone got up and left the room. All the team members talked to each other as they walked out. Morales didn't know where this would lead, but she had to accept all ideas at this point, no matter how absurd they sounded.

10 REINFORCEMENTS

"We've given your team almost two weeks to figure this out. We have no choice now." The governor was on speakerphone in Rayburn's office. Bill, Morales, and the colonel were all listening in with Rayburn.

"But everything in town is business as usual," Rayburn responded. "We don't need any extra police help; there are no issues with violence or—"

The governor stopped Rayburn. "It's not just a question of controlling your people, mayor. We have thousands of people wanting to get into your town. There are expeditions from all over the world that are on their way. The colonel doesn't have the numbers to support the onslaught of people heading your way. So we need to send more support down there."

Colonel Strathern smiled. He knew that meant his command would become more substantial.

Bill frowned, "Sir, this is the sheriff. Could we have just a few more days, at least?"

The governor raised his voice slightly. "Can you tell me what good a few days will do? Are we close to solving this mystery? Is there something I am not aware of?"

Morales spoke. "No, sir, we are no closer to solving this." There was no way Morales would bring up the new theory they were testing.

"Then I will dispatch more troops to Bends Creek, and if necessary, I will declare martial law. Colonel, you will be receiving your orders shortly from your commander."

The colonel smiled and said, "Sir, yes, sir."

"And colonel?" the governor said.

"Sir."

"Remember who you work for. Don't make any stupid decisions without consulting everyone, please."

"Yes, sir." The colonel's smile went away.

"Mayor, please alert your citizens to what's coming. We'll start tonight. Ensure you reinforce your curfew and have everyone off the streets by 11 p.m. every evening. That includes Friday and Saturday night."

"Will do," said the mayor.

"Look, I know this isn't easy for any of you, but if we wait too long, this may get way out of hand. Your town will be overwhelmed with lunatics from all over the world. If they get inside, it will be too late, and I guarantee things will get uglier than they are right now. Good luck." And with that, the governor hung up.

The colonel turned away and headed out of the office. After he was gone, the mayor was the first to speak.

"I'll go on the radio this afternoon and make the announcement. Then, I'll have the station play it every 30 minutes," Rayburn said reluctantly. "This is not going to be received well."

"We'll get through this, Rayburn," Bill spoke up. "We'll work through it somehow."

"Thanks, Bill," Rayburn said. "I'm glad we're on the same side. You know your department will have to help enforce the curfew, right? At least until GI Joe takes over. What a mess that's going to be."

"Yeah, I know. Believe me, I know," Bill answered. "I'll talk to my guys, and we'll start getting the word out."

Morales looked at Rayburn and Bill. "Sorry, I let you guys down. I thought…we… could get this solved a lot sooner."

Bill said, "Look, you did the best you could. We all know there's nothing normal about what's going on. But, frankly, I'm surprised you tried as long as you did. I would have given up a lot earlier than this, but you kept hammering away at it. We can't thank you enough."

Rayburn agreed. "We are fortunate to have you here. Thank you for all your hard work."

Morales shook each of their hands. She felt how grateful they were. That just made it harder to accept that she had failed them.

"We have to go back to Atlanta to prepare to discuss our findings with the new agency assigned to this task."

Bill was confused. "New agency?"

"Yeah, with martial law about to be imposed, the government will want a new team here."

"Great. We're talking quarantine, aren't we?"

"Unfortunately, yes. That's the next step."

Bill nodded, "I don't blame you. I'd hurry and get out of here, too."

"It was a pleasure working with you both," she said softly. "I hope everything gets resolved quickly so you can have your town back."

She smiled and walked out. All that was left was to gather her things and her team and head back to Atlanta. The walk to her office seemed to take forever.

Rayburn went to the radio station. The radio station released an emergency broadcast signal to get everyone's attention.

"Ladies and gentlemen," Rayburn began. "This is your mayor speaking. The governor of the great state of Mississippi has informed me that he is declaring an emergency for our town. Due to the events of the last two weeks, Bends Creek has become the focal point of the world. As I speak, we are attracting groups from all around the globe. The governor is sending more troops to help us keep non-citizens out of our town.

The governor has not declared martial law at the time of this broadcast. So, we still have the responsibility to police ourselves. Let me explain how important it is to work together here. Martial law will allow the military to enforce laws in Bends Creek. We will not have any say in the enforcement of our rules. So, I implore you to listen and to spread the word quickly. We will continue our curfew at eleven p.m. and every night until we resolve our current situation. Once again, please abide by the curfew starting at eleven p.m. If you are walking or driving on the streets after the curfew siren sounds, you will be arrested and spend the rest of the night in jail.

If we cannot enforce the curfew and handle any circumstances that arise, the governor will impose martial law. Our streets will flood with soldiers and tanks. So please, let's all work together to get through this. More to come as we get updates. Be safe, and God bless."

***

The following day, more troops showed up outside of town. Each platoon leader reported to Colonel Strathern. Strathern called for a meeting at 9 am to review the strategy for protecting Bends Creek from outsiders. He doubled up the guard at each of the 4 entrances to the town. Their orders were to bar anyone from passing the barrier into town. He also received confirmation that no one was to leave for any reason. As of 1pm today, anyone in town will remain until this situation improves.

Unfortunately for Morales, she would be the first victim of the colonel's new orders. She was at the gate, trying to leave town, when the colonel was alerted.

"Colonel, what's going on?" Morales asked.

"Our orders are that no one is to leave Bends Creek, ma'am," the colonel smiled.

"You know who I am. Why are you doing this? I am not a citizen of Bends Creek. I work for the Federal Government."

"I have my orders, ma'am. You must turn your vehicle around, or we will impound it and have you arrested."

"Are you serious?"

"Yes, ma'am. Now, please back your vehicle up and proceed back into town," The colonel said, waving a hand at Morales.

Morales jumped into her car, slammed the door, backed it up, and squealed her tires as she sped back toward town.

The colonel just smiled and waved goodbye to her as she sped off.

Morales wasn't happy about being confined to town. She felt she failed Bends Creek. And now she was stuck in a city that had asked her for help and answers that she never gave them.

This is just great, she thought as she headed to the local hotel.

While the colonel was organizing his troops outside the town perimeter, everyone inside the town seemed to be adjusting just fine. Other than a few incidents of mistaken identity, everyone was getting along. However, Bill was suspicious that everyone was getting along too well.

"Maggie, you notice how the town is changing?" Bill asked.

Maggie picked up her cup of coffee, but before she sipped it, she asked, "In what way?"

"I don't know. It's a weird feeling. It seems like everyone is easier to get along with now. I'm not so sure this new affliction is a bad thing."

Maggie looked at Bill. "You think people are getting along because they see what they want to see?"

"I guess so. I don't know, but the only people who aren't that happy are those who aren't afflicted. Shouldn't it be the other way around?"

"I don't know, Bill. I suppose."

Bill looked at Maggie. "What is it? What's on your mind?"

"I don't know if you've noticed…but that new guy, Pete?"

"Yeah."

"He's been preaching on the street and getting a big following. At first, I thought he was just another homeless person down on his luck like Virgil, but there's something different about him."

"Like what? What's different?"

Maggie frowned, "I can't put my finger on it. Pete is just different, somehow."

"Do I need to talk to him?" Bill asked.

"No, he hasn't done anything wrong. Maybe check in on him and see if you read him like I do."

"I can do that."

Maggie smiled. "I know, sheriff; that's why I asked." She winked at Bill.

11 A LOOK DEEPER

Pete played the guitar, and Virgil played the harmonica when Bill approached them on the street corner. He noticed people walking by and dropping money into a hat they had on the sidewalk in front of them. Bill smiled, watching Virgil play the harmonica. Hearing the music brought back good memories of when he was a boy sitting on the porch, watching and listening to Virgil play. When he heard those opening notes coming from Virgil's porch, Bill would run over to Virgil's house and sit on his steps while he played.

Bill smiled and thought, *Those were good times*. He waited for the song to end.

"Wow, you guys are pretty good, huh?" he asked Virgil.

"Sheriff, life is as good as it gets right now." Virgil smiled, showing a mouth missing most of its teeth. "Me and Pete, we be doing alright."

Bill smiled at Virgil. "I'm glad it's going well, Virgil. Hi, Pete. I don't think we've met."

Pete held the guitar up in his left hand. He extended his right to shake Bill's, "No, sir, don't believe we have. Pleased to meet you."

"Same," Bill smiled. "You ain't from around here, are you?"

Pete shook his head, "No, sir, I believe I am not."

Bill laughed, "Well, where do you believe you are from?"

Pete shrugged, "I really can't remember, sir. I ended up here in the great company of this good man, and that's all I know."

"Why don't you come to the station sometime when you guys aren't so busy, and you and I can chat?"

"Sure. I would love to, Sheriff."

Virgil looked at Pete and then at Bill. "There ain't no problem, is there, Sheriff?" Virgil asked, concerned.

"No, sir, there isn't a problem. Just like to get to know who's in my town, that's all."

"Well, Pete is good people; you can know that right now."

"I believe you, Virgil. You know I have a lot of respect for you. And if you say Pete here is a good person, then I believe he is. Just want to get to know him a little, that's all." He turned back to Pete. "See you then," Bill said as he walked off.

"Okay, Sheriff," Pete said.

"Bill is good people too, Pete. You guys will like each other. I know that for a fact." Virgil stated.

Pete smiled and nodded. The two men went back to playing.

***

Three hours went by before Pete walked into the sheriff's department. He sat and waited a few minutes for the sheriff to come out and greet him. Pete looked curiously around the lobby. It was as if he were seeing the inside of a police department for the first time. It felt strange, cold, and unfriendly to him. Pete wondered if he should be nervous about meeting the sheriff. But he was calm and relaxed when Bill finally walked in.

"Hey, Pete," Bill came toward Pete with his hand outstretched.

Pete got up and shook Bill's hand. "Hey, sheriff."

Bill asked Pete to come into the office. Pete felt more comfortable sitting in the chair before Bill's desk than in the lobby.

"Nice digs, Sheriff," Pete said, sitting down.

"Sort of my home away from home, you know," Bill looked around the office as he answered Pete.

Bill sat down and looked at Pete, and Pete smiled back. Bill poured Pete a glass of water from the pitcher sitting on his desk and looked Pete over. Through Pete's long hair and scraggly beard, Bill estimated him to be in his late twenties or early thirties.

"So, what's up, Sheriff?" Pete asked, sipping the water. The glass felt cold in his hands. Pete relieved some of his thirst as he drank.

"Nothing, in particular. I just wanted to chat and get to know you a little, that's all. Mind if I ask a few questions?" Bill asked. "It'll help me get my bearings straight."

"No, sir, ask away."

Bill felt something warm about Pete. He sensed a calmness and peace he hadn't felt in a long time.

Bill smiled, "Okay, Pete. How long have you been in Bends Creek?"

Pete tilted his head, "Not sure. About a few days, I think."

"Do you have any idea why you can't remember where you're from or why you came here?"

Pete could sense Bill was concerned, but it wasn't in an invasive way. "You're worried about Virgil, aren't you?"

"Yeah, Pete. I've known Virgil for a long time, and he's pretty close to family for me."

Pete nodded, "That's cool, Sheriff. Virgil's pretty lucky to have that."

"Well, I think we're both pretty lucky. Virgil has meant a lot to me throughout my life, ever since I was a boy. He's always looked out for me. Now it's my turn. The Deep South has a terrible history of racial injustice, and Bends Creek was no exception to that when I was growing up. I was lucky to have a father who didn't allow racists around his family. My father and Virgil were close friends. There were times each took a beating for associating with the other."

"Sounds terrible."

"Yeah, it was a tough time. My father and Virgil were as close as brothers and stuck together; they even went to war together. They always had each other's backs. After the war, my father returned, and everything was messed up. Agent Orange ate right through him. Virgil claimed my father kept him away from the Orange, so he wasn't affected by it. After my father passed, Virgil came by and took care of my mother and me until she passed away a few years later."

"How did Virgil end up homeless?"

"He wouldn't let me help him, prideful son of a gun." Bill was staring at a picture of his father, Virgil, and himself on the wall. "When I was old enough to care for myself, Virgil disappeared for a while. He showed up a few years later in that alley you're both in."

Pete raised his eyebrows. "What happened to his house?"

"He had sold it years earlier. I believe he spent most of the money taking care of me. I could never verify that, though."

Pete looked at Bill. He was still staring at the picture on the wall. He could see the concern in Bill's eyes. Virgil meant a lot to Bill.

"Seriously, Sheriff, I will look after Virgil as long as I am here."

Bill felt at ease and strangely comfortable with Pete. He had never felt this type of energy from anyone he had questioned. The strangest part was that Bill felt guilty for asking Pete these questions and didn't know why. As the conversation continued, Bill noticed no emotion in Pete's speech. As pleasant as his voice was, he spoke without emotional inflections. That could be a reason he felt relaxed around Pete. Bill continued to stare at the picture on the wall.

"I just don't know, Sheriff."

"What?" Bill felt like he had just dozed off for a minute and was awakened by Pete's voice.

"The question you asked me? I don't know why I don't remember anything. I hope I can figure it out sooner rather than later."

"I hear you are preaching and entertaining on the corner now?"

"I don't know if you can call it preaching, Sheriff. I open my mouth, and people seem to want to listen to me, that's all."

Bill couldn't help smiling. He was starting to feel awkward, smiling through this interview. He had to force himself to stop grinning and try to look a little more serious.

"So, do you have a message for people, or are you just saying whatever comes out of your mouth at the time?"

"That's it exactly. I say whatever comes out of my mouth. People listen to it as a message."

Bill leaned forward, "So, what is the message, Pete?"

"Unconditional love, Sheriff. We're all connected in this universe, and we must stop judging each other and love the moment we're in, you know?" Pete smiled.

Bill looked at Pete and noticed a glow around his face. Bill looked a little closer, and it was gone.

"Sheriff, you okay?" Pete asked, concerned.

"Yeah, thanks. I'm fine. Pete, I don't know. Maybe you were sent here because we need someone like you now. People are scared, anxious, and desperate for answers right now. You aren't afflicted, are you?"

Pete looked down at the glass of water he held with two hands. Finally, he looked up at Bill. "No, and neither are you."

"Yeah, that's pretty well known in town. Thank God I'm not. If I were, there's no telling how I could take this on. Anyways, Pete, if you need any help trying to figure it out, let me know. We have some good people in this town who would love to help."

"Thanks, Sheriff. I appreciate that."

"Well, I appreciate you stopping by as you did. That tells me a lot."

The two men stood up and shook hands. Pete started walking out of the room. He turned around and looked at Bill. "Don't worry, Sheriff. I'll watch out for Virgil."

"Thanks," Bill said. And he watched Pete walk away.

Bill was left sitting at his desk, wondering what had just happened. He had never experienced anything like this before. He wanted information, yet he didn't care about the answers, which was strange. Usually, one explanation would lead to another question, and so on. But all that didn't seem to be relevant to Pete's interview.

Bill just shook his head. "I don't get it. But at least my detective instincts didn't fail me."

He smiled and picked up Pete's glass with a pencil, allowing it to hang upside down.

***

Pete opened the outside door of the sheriff's building and turned right. He walked only a few feet when a female voice inside his head started talking.

You did that on purpose, didn't you?

Pete answered the voice telepathically. *You know it.*

Pete walked down the sidewalk and back to Virgil's corner with a smile on his face.

12 TIME SLIPS BY

Another week went by with nothing changing. The citizens of Bends Creek were getting restless with all the military action and noise outside of town. It seemed to be getting louder and louder. John Daly started charging admission for people to go up onto the roof of his hardware store to check it all out. The rooftop had a perfect view of all the action beyond the barricade on Main Street. People in groups of five were allowed on his roof for 10 minutes for 5 dollars. The line outside the hardware store proved that John Daly's idea was lucrative.

Bill was allowed onto the roof at no charge; Daly knew Bill wouldn't pay anyway. Bill went up with binoculars to understand how crazy it was outside the town limits. He didn't see anything that promoted optimism for a happy ending. Bill saw hundreds of tents filling the open field where people camped outside the military barrier. People were dancing, drinking, and smoking. The landscape looked like an image from an old rock album. And that was just what he saw straight ahead. He could see campfires in the woods just outside those military fences to the left and right of the town. Bill had a scary thought. What if these people decided to group up and rush the barriers? There was no way they could stop the mad rush of people. The question was, how long would it take for them to figure that out? The outside world closed quickly, and

Bill knew what was coming next. The governor must declare martial law and put forces inside the city to protect the town.

Bill went over to Maggie's that night after curfew.

"For the first time in my life, I feel lost, Maggie. I don't know how to help the town. The military will soon be here in full force, and we will lose all our freedoms."

"Bill, you've got to keep trying. If you don't try, then who will? A lot of people look to you for answers. So maybe you should start reorienting your position within what is happening to get some."

"Pretty smart for a shelter lady, you know that?" Bill laughed.

"Shelter lady, my butt…you best be apologizing for that ignorance, Bill Jackson, or you won't be sharing my bed tonight."

"Yes, ma'am, I apologize from the bottom of my heart."

Bill knew Maggie was very bright. She earned her Master's in Business from Mississippi State and decided to return to Bends Creek and help people. She was admired by so many for her selflessness. Maggie could have moved to a bigger city and made better money, but her heart was in Bends Creek.

"And I am not just apologizing because I don't want to sleep alone tonight." He pulled her close to him, looking her in the eyes. "You are one of the most intelligent people I know." Then, starting to hold back a laugh, he said, "And…" he hesitated, "…you complete me." Bill couldn't hold back his laughter, and Maggie pushed him away, laughing too.

"Screw you, Bill Jackson, with your 'you complete me' crap," Maggie smirked. They ended the conversation, amused, lying in each other's arms.

Bill knew Maggie was right. Bill made tea, and they went to her living room to turn on the TV. As usual, Bends Creek was all over the news. Every local channel and news channel was discussing what they called the "Bends Creek Phenomenon," or BCP. Talk show hosts spent their whole hour discussing the BCP with guest speakers. Some were from religious groups, and others called themselves spiritual. The shows that appealed to Bill were those that had several groups with differing points of view. When the yelling died down, which wasn't very often, an interesting perspective would come up. Bill found all the options intriguing because no one knew what this was.

The most prominent viewpoints gathering the most support were all about Judgment Day. All the other opinions seemed even more sensational than the Judgement Day theory. The list of arguments seemed to be endless. Some ideas suggested that Bends Creek must have been the spot of an unrecorded massacre of so many Black people that their spirits returned for revenge on those who had persecuted them. Another popular view was that the government was conducting a secret experiment that leaked out. The opinions went on and on—none of any real substance, so far as Bill could follow. The BCP was just that: an unexplained phenomenon. Not knowing made people anxious for answers.

While watching one talk show, Bill heard a renowned Japanese scientist with a theory that was so outrageous it almost made sense. He had recorded an unknown energy source in space when the BCP started. This unknown energy source made the scientist believe the phenomenon was a message from an intelligent alien life form. He thought an alien race was now trying to communicate with humanity by showing humans how to communicate.

When asked for an explanation, the scientist said, "These aliens are teaching us to look at everyone as we see ourselves. Once we accomplish this, we will be able to see these alien life forms like humans, and we will be able to communicate with them. Because our intellect is not as advanced as theirs, they must dumb themselves down for us. Seeing them in their pure form would cause panic and chaos. The human race would focus on the chaos, not the gift the aliens would bring us."

When asked what he meant by gift, the scientist smiled, looked into the camera as though he was looking right at Bill, and said, "The gift of hope."

Bill loved science fiction as much as the next person, but this was difficult to swallow. He began to compose a long, thoughtful dissertation in his mind. *Could the scientist somehow be right? Maybe there was intelligent life outside of their own. But why Bends Creek? Why now? There were so many questions that seemed impossible to answer. There wasn't any evidence that supported any theories, logical or nonsensical.*

Maybe everyone needs to start accepting some of these non-logical theories and move on with those. If the whole thing doesn't make sense, to begin with, why try to make sense of it? Why not accept it and see where it takes them? Man, I know I'm going crazy now. I'm thinking just like the loonies out there.

Bill looked at Maggie and asked her what she thought of the scientist's claim.

"Well," she started, "it's usually the least expected answer that is correct."

Bill nodded, "True."

"Maybe we should start looking at this whole mess for what it is and not what we want it to be?"

"Makes sense."

Maggie nodded, "Yeah, you know, the whole looking outside the box thing?"

"But do we start accepting whacked-out theories?"

"Well, maybe we should start trying to disprove these theories until all that is left are theories that need our attention?"

Bill leaned forward, "As usual, you're right. Maybe you should get together with Morales and try this new approach."

"Morales? I thought she went back to Atlanta."

"Oh yeah, I never told you. The colonel's new orders have everyone staying put who's already inside."

"Really? Why?"

"Control the leaks, and so on. The government doesn't want any information shared until we get to the bottom of this."

"Kinda dumb, isn't it? We still have the internet."

"Yeah, about that–" Bill sighed.

"No way!" Maggie jumped up, surprised. "They are not going to cut us all off from the outside, are they?"

"Yeah, all cell service and internet will be cut off this week when the governor declares martial law. We may allow a few stations to transmit and receive for emergencies. Still, the general public will have no access."

Maggie gasped, "Oh, this is bad, really bad. You know how reliant everyone is on the internet, right? People are going to go ballistic."

"I know, Maggie. I know."

"How will we do any research without the internet, Bill?"

"That's the reason I mentioned teaming up with Morales. She will have one of the access points that allows her to use the internet. Being with the government and having clearance and all that."

Maggie nodded, "Okay then. When can we start?"

"We can meet with Morales tomorrow. Hopefully, she'll be willing to try something different."

"Well, it's better than just waiting for something to happen, right?"

"Yes. Absolutely. At least we're still trying to figure this out. As long as we do that, there's always hope."

Bill hesitated a moment and looked away from Maggie toward the TV. He stared at the Japanese scientist and shook his head. "No, no way," he said, unconvincingly, to himself.

13 UNIVERSAL CONNECTION

The crowds that continued to assemble around Pete and Virgil's corner seemed to get busier every day. Pete and Virgil played some blues, and people passed the hat around for donations. After the money was collected, Pete would stand up on a crate above the crowd so the people in the back could hear him. Pete looked over the crowd and smiled.

"We have an opportunity to change for the better," Pete started speaking. People in the crowd started saying "Yes, sir" and "Amen" while nodding.

"This affliction is a test for us all. A test to resolve our differences and journey back to where we all came from."

"What place is that?" a voice called out.

"A place of love. We all come from a place of love." Pete gazed across the crowd and opened his arms to welcome everyone. "We all come from a place of love, but somehow, some of us lost ourselves. We started looking at each other with disdain, anger, and hate instead of love. We have turned ourselves into selfish, self-loathing human beings. We are all guilty of the 'what's in it for me?'

attitude. Instead, we should ask ourselves, 'How can I help others?'"

The crowd cheered and applauded.

"We are all connected. We are all the same. As soon as we realize this, we will be able to get on with our mission in life, a mission each of us shares: to take care of each other, be kind to each other, and love each other."

As the crowd applauded and cheered, Pete stepped down. He picked up his guitar, and Virgil began playing along. As they played, the crowd dispersed, with some people dropping more money into the hat. Pete saw that Virgil was having the time of his life. Virgil had a new light about him. He was happy, and he even looked different now. Virgil was bathing daily and bought himself some new clothes. He'd changed for the better. He decided to give some of their proceeds to the shelter to help others, and Pete agreed.

After the crowd left, the two bullies who had harassed Virgil and Pete the day before walked up to them. The one that pushed Virgil down the first time they met kicked their hat and sent their earnings all over the sidewalk while the other bully laughed. They didn't try to hide the fact that they had come by to harass Virgil and Pete purposely.

"So you freaks are the Bends Creek Messiahs now?" Both bullies laughed. With the crowd disbanding, the four were alone at the alley's entrance.

Pete put his guitar down against the nearby building wall and got on his knees to pick up the money. As he picked it up, he never looked at the two brutes or said a word. The men were both the same size, about six feet three, and were bulky. It was clear they liked using their size to intimidate others.

"I didn't tell you to pick that up, did I?" one bully shouted at Pete.

Pete ignored him and kept picking up the money.

103

"Get up, now!" he shouted down at Pete.

Pete ignored him and continued to pick up the money. The bruiser looked at his partner, smiled, and kicked Pete in the ribs, knocking him over onto his back.

"I told you to stop!" he shouted. His buddy just laughed louder, and they fist-bumped each other.

Virgil ran over to Pete, got down on one knee, put his hand on Pete, and looked up at the two men. "That ain't called for," he said to them.

"What, you feel left out, old man, huh?" It was the second bully's turn; he kicked Virgil in his side, knocking him over Pete. Virgil was lying on the ground next to Pete, moaning and grabbing at his rib cage. Pete looked up at the two thugs and stared.

"What you gonna do, Messiah?" one bully shouted at Pete.

The female voice in Pete's head spoke. *Now is not the time.*

Pete looked at the two men who were still laughing. *Yes, it is*, he answered her telepathically.

The two men looked at Pete as he stood up, still laughing at him. Pete looked around and noted that the four of them were alone. He raised his arm and held his palm toward the first man. This action made the bullies laugh.

"What?" the bully asked, "You gonna heal us?" They both started laughing louder.

Pete's outstretched hand began to glow and slowly increased in intensity.

The voice in Pete's head began warning Pete, *"You're energizing the weapon construct. You must calm down before blowing this town into the cosmos."*

"I've had enough of these two, Pete replied.

Before the voice could reply, a ball of light emerged from his palm until it completely surrounded his hand. The two men stood wide-eyed, shocked, staring at Pete's hand. Pete's head was tilted, but his eyes flicked to meet their stunned gaze. The energy glow surrounding Pete's hand slowly started to consume Pete's arm. As the bright light engulfed Pete's arm, the two men froze in their stances. They could only make out the outline of Pete's arm now. The energy collecting around his arm looked like yellow fire. Still, unlike fire, this energy was concentrated only in one place around Pete and did not spread unpredictably. As a result, they could no longer see Pete's arm.

The two men looked at Pete's face, still staring at them. His head remained tilted. That stare would be embedded in their minds forever.

The female voice in Pete's head repeated itself, louder this time. *Pete! This is not the time!*

Pete ignored the voice.

Pete flicked his glowing wrist to the right ever so slightly, and the two men were airborne, heading for the nearby brick wall. They crashed with an awful thud and bounced off the wall, landing next to Virgil.

The voice in his head yelled, *How did you do that? There's no way you should be able to do that!*

Pete stared down at his hand and answered the voice. *I don't know. I just thought about it, and it happened.*

When the glow around his arm disappeared, Pete hurried to see if Virgil was okay.

Virgil rolled over, still grabbing his side. "You okay, Pete?" Virgil asked.

Pete's arm was under Virgil's head, holding him up, "Yeah, I'm good. How about you?"

Virgil looked over at the two men bleeding on the ground next to him. "I'm a lot better than those guys right now." Virgil started to laugh. "Ow. Man, can't laugh."

Pete helped Virgil up, grabbing their money and their instruments. "Let's get you to the hospital."

"Yeah, that would be good. These old bones can't take too much of this anymore. What about them?" Virgil jerked his head back toward the two bullies lying unconscious on the ground.

"We'll call them an ambulance and tell them a wall hit them."

Virgil grimaced, "Oh, ow, man. Pete, don't make me laugh."

The two men hobbled down the street toward the hospital.

"Pete, thanks, man," Virgil said.

"We got to take care of each other, right?" Pete replied. Pete lowered his voice a little, "Virgil?"

"Yeah, Pete?"

Pete kept eye contact with Virgil, "We good?"

Virgil coughed, "Why the heck wouldn't we be?"

On the way to the hospital, Virgil never mentioned what he saw. Pete never talked about it, and Virgil never brought it up again.

***

About 45 minutes later, Bill arrived in the alley, where the two men were lying on the ground, out cold but still alive. The ambulance arrived before he did, and the medics attended to the two victims. Bill stood next to one kneeling paramedic and observed the scene. Bill couldn't help shaking his head at what he was seeing.

"Okay, do you have any ideas about what happened here?" he asked the paramedic.

"Not a clue. There's blood on the wall, but...."

"But what?" Bill asked.

"The blood on the wall is a lot higher than the height of these men. Not sure how to explain that," the medic answered.

"Yeah, I noticed," Bill said. "That's why I asked you for any ideas."

Bill couldn't take his eyes off the blood on the wall as he examined the alley and the height of the blood several times. Finally, Bill deduced that to smash two bodies into the wall at that height, the victims had to be on a flatbed trailer. But a flatbed couldn't fit into this small alley.

"Man, I do not need this right now," Bill sighed. He looked at the medics. "You need anything from me?"

"No, sir, I believe we're good right now. Just not sure what to say on our report."

"Well, good luck with that," Bill said as he got into his car. He turned on his siren and lights and headed to the hospital.

Bill pulled up to the emergency room and walked into the lobby. "Hey, Judy, how are you doing?"

"Pretty good, sheriff. What's up?"

"Did Virgil come in here?"

"Yeah, he's in there with the doctors now. You want to go check on him?"

"Yeah, I need to ask him a few questions."

"He's in room three. Go on back."

Bill walked back into the emergency area. He came up to room three and slid the curtain aside. Pete was sitting there.

"Pete, where's Virgil?"

"He's getting some X-rays done right now."

Bill shook his head, "Can you tell me what happened out there?"

"Not sure, Sheriff. These two guys were kicking us. Virgil and I were both on the ground; the next thing we knew, they were lying on the ground next to us."

Bill frowned, "That's it? So you didn't see anything else? Was anyone else there?"

"Not that I recall, Sheriff."

Bill scratched his head. "I don't get this, man. You get roughed up by a couple of big dudes. And there can't be three hundred fifty pounds between you and Virgil. But somehow, these guys, who are bigger than me, get slammed against a wall ten feet off the ground? How do you explain that?"

Pete looked at Bill with a calm expression. "I don't know, Sheriff."

Bill wasn't buying Pete's answers at all. He sensed Pete knew what had happened, but for some reason, Pete was holding back.

"Listen, Pete. I've only known you briefly, but from what I gather, you're a pretty smart guy."

"Thank you, Sheriff."

Bill pursed his lips, "I'm not trying to compliment you. I'm trying to get some answers that I know you have. I can't figure out why you aren't telling me what happened."

"I am. I really don't know."

"Bull, Pete. Were you knocked unconscious? Or are you too scared to talk to me about something you saw? What is it?"

Pete looked at the floor, "Sheriff, this has been pretty traumatic for me. I'm worried about Virgil right now. Can we talk about this later, please?"

"Man," Bill raised his voice. "You come down to the station after Virgil is released, you hear me? I want to talk to both of you when you finish here."

"Okay, Sheriff, we'll be there."

Bill looked down at Pete. His head was in his hands, staring at the floor. "Okay, see you guys in a few." Bill turned away and walked out of the emergency room.

Bill couldn't get the brick wall picture out of his head. There was no way Pete or Virgil could pick those guys up and toss them that high, especially with enough force to cause those two to hit the wall and bleed like that.

When the doctors said it was okay, Bill wanted to talk to the two bullies.

Maybe they'll remember what the hell happened.

14 POSSIBILITIES

Morales and her team were sitting in the conference room, but no one was saying anything. The atmosphere in the room was one of despair. Like Morales, every team member sitting at the table was forced by the new lockdown to stay in Bends Creek.

Eventually, Morales spoke up. "Well, we're stuck here now. Maybe we can try to work on this from a different angle? What do you think?"

"What do you have in mind?" Donna Grimes, a scientist, asked.

"Well, I have invited Ms. Maggie Carter to join us today. Maggie has some fascinating ideas that I thought might interest some of you. Maggie?"

"Thanks," Maggie said as she stood up. "As you know, some pretty nutty theories about why this is happening in Bends Creek are bouncing around the internet. So I thought checking and disproving each one might be interesting."

"Why would you do that?" a team member asked.

"Well, by disproving those theories, we can accomplish two things.

One would be to calm the chaos by eliminating the number of potential crazies trying to invade our town. And after eliminating as many theories as possible, what's left may be a theory we can work with."

"But why us?"

"Well, we have a collective of scientists in this room who could get answers quickly. And…" Maggie paused. "This is the only place with internet access in town." Maggie smiled at the team.

The room broke out in laughter. "Why not?" said Donna Grimes. "What else do we have to do?"

"Great!" Maggie was excited.

Morales spoke up. "So let's look at these so-called theories and try to group similar ones if possible. This project can keep us busy until we get out of here."

The team broke off into small groups and started discussing the project. Maggie walked over to Morales. "I appreciate you and your team doing this. I think it's going to be a big help. Maybe if we can keep the people outside of town busy fighting among each other about their theories, they won't storm the town."

Morales smiled. "I hope so. And then maybe we'll get to go home."

As Bill entered the room, the two women approached the team table. He headed straight for Maggie.

"Hey, you," Bill said to Maggie. They kissed, and Bill turned to Morales. "Sorry, you're unable to go home."

"Me too," Morales shrugged her shoulders.

Bill looked at Maggie. "Listen. I have a strange feeling about Pete Maggie. It's like you said, something doesn't feel right."

Morales looked at Bill. "Is there anything I can do to help?"

"That would be great, Morales," Bill said.

"Jessica," Morales replied.

"Jessica?" Bill answered, confused.

"My name. It's Jessica." Morales smiled at Bill.

"Cool. Pleased to meet you, Jessica. I'm Bill." They shook hands.

"So," Jessica asked, "what's going on?"

Bill filled Jessica in. "This homeless guy, Pete, showed up a few days after the affliction started. He's not from here, and he doesn't know where he's from or who he is."

Jessica looked at Maggie, then at Bill. "You know, it's not unusual for a person who has suffered trauma in their life to get amnesia. It helps them to cope."

Bill looked at Jessica. "No, I get that, and I know what you're saying because I've seen that first hand. This guy is different; he makes me feel like he's pulling one over on all of us. He's hanging out on a street corner with another local homeless man, Virgil. Each day, around the same time, people gather around them, and Pete gives a little speech about being kind to each other. The crowd eats it up, and they throw in more money. The groups are also getting bigger each day. He's developing quite a following. He's more intelligent than he's putting out there. But today, the incident with Virgil took my curiosity about him over the top."

"What happened with Virgil? Is he okay?" Maggie's eyes widened.

"Yeah, he'll be okay. Unfortunately, two big thugs attacked Virgil and Pete, and they're all in the hospital right now as we speak."

Jessica wrinkled her forehead, "What do you mean all of them are in the hospital?"

"That's what brought me down here. The two attackers were knocked unconscious at the site of the incident."

Maggie's jaw dropped, "Bill, Virgil is too old and brittle. He couldn't be physical with a pet, let alone two thugs."

"I know, Maggie. It wasn't Virgil. It had to be Pete. But Pete says he was on the ground with Virgil and didn't see what happened to them."

Jessica was more than interested now. "What did happen to them?"

"This is where it gets bizarre. The two thugs were on the ground, unconscious and bleeding, when the paramedics arrived. They were slammed against the nearby brick wall and bounced off it."

"So you think this Pete guy pushed them against the wall?" Jessica asked.

"Maybe. Well, not exactly. It's not adding up."

"What's not adding up?" Maggie asked

"They were slammed against the brick wall so hard their blood was on it."

"Maybe Pete is stronger than you think?"

"The blood on the wall was over eight feet from the ground. I've seen adrenaline rushes make men do extraordinary things, but throwing two large men over eight feet high? Come on!"

Jessica and Maggie looked at each other with surprise on their faces. They didn't know what to say or think. Neither spoke.

Bill said, "I need your help figuring out how this could happen.

Can you add this to your to-do list, please?"

Both women nodded, still looking surprised. Bill kissed Maggie, thanked her, turned, and walked out.

Jessica raised her eyebrows, "Looks like we've got crazy to figure out inside our walls as well."

"Yeah," Maggie said softly.

As Bill was driving around town, he couldn't get the incident in the alley out of his head. He hoped he would get some answers once he sat Virgil and Pete down and confronted them.

***

Bill went into his office at the station, sat down, and turned on the television. He was able to pick up the local stations with his antenna. Bill grabbed a cup of coffee and scanned the tube for any stories on Bends Creek. He stopped on one talk show where philosophers and spiritual leaders discussed the cause and effect of the affliction. Bill turned up the TV.

"No, I am not saying that," a spiritual leader from India said. "I am saying that we should all strive to reach the point of love within ourselves. An outside intervention like this so-called affliction is not a sustainable solution."

"I see what you are saying," the other guest said, "but the possibility of the affliction spreading across the globe could be a powerful tool to encourage world peace. Imagine no more violence in the world. After all, isn't that what we all want?"

The studio crowd stood on their feet and cheered so loudly that Bill couldn't hear the host speaking.

Bill struggled to understand how people wanted the affliction to spread. He changed the channel. Crowds were participating in a massive sit-in just outside of Bends Creek. The TV camera panned along the tents, and the number of people there shocked Bill. "Oh my God," he said out loud.

Various reporters were walking through the crowds and asking questions.

"Why are you here?" one reporter asked a participant.

The young girl, smiling, answered, "We need to accept the BCP for what it is. It's the universe trying to correct itself. And we all need to be a part of that." The people standing next to her screamed their approval.

The reporter asked another question. "What is the BCP?"

"The Bends Creek Phenomenon," the girl jumped up.

"So, how does everyone become part of the BCP?"

The girl jumped up and down again. "We become citizens of Bends Creek," she laughed.

Bill changed the channel again. This time, his mouth dropped. *Oh no...no! How could this have happened?*

There, on the TV, at the anchor's counter on one of the news broadcasts, was Elias Stout. Elias was seated with a big grin on his face.

"Mr. Stout, how are you today, sir?" the anchorwoman asked.

Elias had coveralls on and a white T-shirt underneath. He was only visible on camera from the chest up. Elias stared at the camera and grinned, "I'm great, just wonderful."

"So, you're from Bends Creek?"

"Yes, I am. I am from the Promised Land." Elias started laughing. He began bouncing in his seat as he laughed.

"I thought there was a restriction imposed on the town that no one could leave?" asked the anchor.

"Yes, ma'am, there is. But you can't keep a fox in a cage if he been raised in that cage you're keepin' him in."

Bill was still in a state of shock. He couldn't believe that Elias would do this.

The anchorwoman wore a polite smile. "That makes a little sense, I guess. Why did you leave?"

"We can't get us the internet no more, so we can't talk to people to let them know what's really goin' on."

There was a knock on Bill's office door.

Pulling away from the TV was hard. He backed up to the door, never taking his eyes off his television.

"My God, Bill, you watching this mess?" Maggie asked as she entered.

"Yeah," Bill said, his gaze still fixated on the screen. Jessica followed Maggie inside. They all sat down and continued watching the TV.

The anchor continued with her interview with Elias. "Well, here you are. So tell us what is going on in Bends Creek right now."

"First of all, let me tell you. This here affliction ain't so bad. Most of us are right happy with what's happenin'."

"Really? Why is that?"

"Because we can be who we want to be, that's why." Elias continued grinning at the camera.

"I don't understand what that has to do with the affliction."

"I can feel how I want 'bout anything and anyone. I ain't need to worry 'bout bein' judged for who I am or how I feel."

"And how do you feel?"

"Like I died and gone to heaven," Elias raised his arms.

"Are you referring to the fact that you only see white people now?"

"That's right. This is how it always should have been, and now it is."

"So, you're a white nationalist?"

"Out here, I guess I am. But I'm just another white man livin' in peace in Bends Creek."

"Since you've been outside of Bends Creek, do you still only see white people?"

Elias laughed louder. "Yes, ma'am. That's why I'm so happy. It don't matter where I go. The change stays with me. I hope it lasts forever."

The announcer raised her eyebrows, "You realize this is a very racist attitude, don't you?"

"I don't care about that no more. How can I be racist if everyone is the same?"

117

"Do I look white to you?"

"Yes, ma'am." Elias nodded.

The announcer moved her head slightly from side to side as she responded. "Well, I am African American, and I am feeling uncomfortable that you don't see me as I am."

"I understand how you feel. I do. But I feel great because I'm sittin' here, not judgin' you."

The anchorwoman folded her arms, "But you're still judging me because you see me as white, not as I am."

"True, that does seem to perpetuate a moral dilemma, now, don't it? Lemme ask you somethin'. If you could go through every day, and I mean every minute of your day, without havin' to deal with racist crap, wouldn't you want to?"

"Of course, I would. But not like this."

"Why not? Maybe this is what it takes for all of us to accept each other. Maybe we got so far gone that somethin' extreme like this had to happen. Maybe it's the only way."

Bill looked at Maggie. "I can't believe this is Elias speaking."

Maggie shook her head in agreement, "I know. He almost sounds reasonable."

The anchorwoman paused and rolled her eyes from Elias to the camera. "Well, we have a lot to think about now, right? We'll be right back.

As the commercial came on, Bill jumped up. "When I see him, I'm going to kick his racist butt."

"It wouldn't do any good," Maggie said. "You might feel better, but it won't help the situation."

"Hey, do you see what's happening here?" Jessica pointed at the television.

Bill said, "Yeah, Elias just opened the floodgates."

"No, not just that," Jessica said. "He's still afflicted. He's outside the town, and he's still afflicted. The consequences of the affliction are not tied geographically to the Bends Creek area."

Maggie looked confused. "Why does that alarm you?"

Jessica started pacing across Bill's office. "There will be some troubling possible outcomes for the town now. Man, this one incident will drive the powers that be nuts."

Bill and Maggie both looked at Jessica. "What other outcomes could there be?" Maggie asked.

"With Elias running around outside proving that there are no geographical ties to Bends Creek, it raises the question of whether this could happen anywhere."

Bill was confused now. "I don't understand."

"If Elias can go anywhere and still retain the effect of the affliction, what's to stop the affliction from going outside of Bends Creek? We know nothing about this. With this new variable, the government will ask a new set of paranoid questions. And worse, these paranoid bastards will act on their paranoia the only way they know how."

Bill replied, alarmed, "Jesus, what if the government decides to quarantine us permanently?"

Jessica looked at Maggie and Bill. "Strathern will be ticked off that someone escaped on his watch. The next order he receives, he will follow to the letter with zero compromise. He's not going to be any easier to deal with now."

Maggie had a terrible thought. "My God, Bill, what the hell is going to happen to us now? The government will take over, and we will be locked up in our town. It's going to be like a concentration camp here. I can't..."

Bill walked over to Maggie and, hugging her, said, "It's going to be okay. We'll figure this out."

Jessica looked at the two of them. Her thoughts were still racing. The lives of everyone inside Bends Creek were about to change.

15 MARTIAL LAW

As they suspected, it didn't take long before the government sent more reinforcements to Colonel Strathern's command. The governor went on TV and declared a state of martial law in Bends Creek, and the town was locked down. After receiving a reprimand from his commanding officer for allowing Elias to escape on his watch, Strathern buckled down. He ordered his troops to push back all outsiders another 500 yards. The colonel also set up street patrols within the city on a 24/7 schedule. No one was to leave or get in, and with martial law imposed, the repercussions for breaking this rule would be far more devastating.

Rayburn went on the radio, announcing what was happening and what to expect. His message was recorded and replayed every hour. The citizens of Bends Creek were finding the military occupation more like an invasion than support. Because of the affliction, the groups of protesters were even more significant than expected. It wasn't just one individual group that was angry. The whole population of the town was working together on this. Bill couldn't believe what he was witnessing. In all his time in Bends Creek, no event had brought everyone together like this. There were times when some white citizens had supported some Black citizens on particular issues and vice versa, but this was something that had never been seen or done. Everyone from the town, white and

Black, gathered together and supported each other.

A large crowd gathered in Mudwater Park to protest. Several group members were on the platform, taking turns speaking into the microphone.

"This ain't right!" the first speaker shouted into the microphone. "We can't be held prisoners in our town." The crowd responded in agreement, cheering.

"We need to message the governor that we will not stand for this harassment," another speaker yelled. The crowd was getting anxious.

Bill, Rayburn, and Colonel Strathern walked up to the platform. The crowd booed as Strathern walked up into their sight. The colonel just smiled and waved to the masses. Bill looked at the colonel as he grinned, enjoying the attention. Rayburn was the first to speak to the protesters.

"Listen up. Everyone, please. We have to calm down. We don't want to make any decisions based on our emotional state of mind right now."

"So when do we make decisions then?" someone yelled out. Others in the crowd started agreeing.

"We can't do anything rash. You have to understand the situation here," Rayburn pleaded.

"Why don't you tell us what the situation is, then? How long is this going to go on for?" People continued to shout out questions.

The mayor held his hands up, asking the crowd to quiet down so he could speak. "This situation was ordered by the governor to protect you, the citizens of Bends Creek. There are thousands of people gathering outside our town right now. They want to come here and make a shambles of our town."

The crowd was growing more restless. "What are you going to do about this? How does locking us up in our town help?"

Bill sensed that Rayburn was losing control of the situation. He started for the microphone. Just before he got to it, Colonel Strathern put his hand on Bill's chest, stopping him. "I'll take it from here, Sheriff." He smiled and stepped toward the microphone. He held his hand out to Rayburn, and Rayburn placed it in his outstretched palm.

Strathern smirked at Rayburn and spoke through the microphone. "Thank you, mayor," he said. "Ladies and gentlemen, what we have here is a failure to communicate. Sorry, I always wanted to say that." The crowd was silent. Not one person in the gathering reacted to the colonel's dry humor.

"Okay, I was trying to lighten things up a little. No takers? Let's get right to it, then. Let me introduce myself to you all. I am Colonel Strathern. I am now the man in charge of enforcing martial law in Bends Creek. The governor has declared that this town is in an emergency, and we are here to protect and serve."

"By holding us as prisoners in our town?" someone from the crowd yelled.

The audience started grumbling, growing anxious again, and the clamor grew louder and louder. Finally, Strathern began speaking at a lower volume, and the crowd immediately quieted down to hear what he was saying. They were all focused on the man with the microphone.

"Let me explain what's going to happen next." Strathern was in charge of the crowd now. "Alrighty then," the colonel said, shaking his head while smiling. "Let me explain the rules. We are here to enforce the law and protect the good citizens of Bends Creek. Anyone starting trouble or inciting a riot will be arrested and dealt with accordingly. So I suggest everyone head on home and call it a night."

Military trucks surrounded the park as the colonel finished his sentence. Two dozen soldiers jumped out of each vehicle and completely encircled the crowd.

"Let's all call it a night," the colonel repeated, his cheerful demeanor unchanged. "I need you all to disperse and head home now. Your cooperation is deeply appreciated."

The crowd, looking at the soldiers, realized they had to listen. Many group members shouted obscenities at Strathern as they left the park. Strathern waved and thanked them while smiling from the platform. As the park emptied, Strathern walked away.

Jessica Morales confronted Strathern. "Was that necessary, Colonel?"

"I made a decision, and as you can see, it was correct. We did not hurt one individual in this exercise, so I would say it was necessary. Goodnight, ma'am." And with that, Strathern headed to his tent.

Jessica, Maggie, and Bill watched the colonel walk away. Bill was visibly upset and wanted to confront the colonel. Maggie looked at Bill. "Don't even think about doing it, Bill Jackson," she said.

Bill looked confused. "Doing what?"

"Going after the colonel to confront him. He'll have you locked up, and then where would we be?"

Jessica nodded, "She's right. Now's not the time."

***

Bill was driving through Bends Creek and shaking his head at the sight of all the soldiers. Bends Creek looked more like a military base than his hometown. He headed over to the mayor's office to catch up with Rayburn. Bill knew the mayor was going to speak to the governor today. Walking into the office, he saw Morales raising her hands and voice. They were on speakerphone with the governor.

"Sir," Morales said. "I know that the presence of the military is necessary, but a show of force to grab attention? Come on. You cannot condone this kind of behavior."

The governor spoke. "Ms. Morales. I appreciate your concern and all the help you provide for the town. I do. But the colonel is an experienced soldier and has handled many of these situations."

"But sir—"

"Ms. Morales," the governor cut Morales off. "Let me finish, please. We have given the colonel our full support to do what he deems necessary to keep the peace in Bends Creek. That means everyone, especially government employees, is expected to support him."

"Yes, sir," Morales said. "I understand the protocol, but this is a small community of people that feels invaded by the military. They need to be supported as well."

"Morales, we agree completely. That's why it's up to the mayor to keep everyone calm and well-informed. I would appreciate it if you would stick to your area of expertise and let us do our jobs."

"Yes, sir," Morales said. "I apologize for causing your team any unwarranted stress at this time. It was not my intention."

"Rayburn?" the governor called out to the mayor.

"Yes, governor?" Rayburn answered.

"I expect you to also keep Bends Creek and your team in check. Understood?"

"Yes, governor, sir."

Bill and Morales were shaking their heads as Rayburn spoke with the governor. They knew this was going to get worse before it was going to get any better.

"Rayburn, the colonel, will also report to us regularly. I expect to hear good reports about how your team cooperates with him. Understood?"

Morales noticed that the governor seemed agitated when he spoke to the mayor. She assumed she'd hit a sour note with him.

"Will do," Rayburn said. "Talk in a few days. Goodbye, sir."

Rayburn hung up the phone and let out a big sigh.

Morales took a step closer to Rayburn. "I am so sorry for causing you problems with the governor."

"You didn't," Rayburn said, smiling. "You were saying what we were all thinking. It's all good. Bill?" Rayburn looked at the sheriff.

"What's up, Rayburn?"

"We need to let the town know this is only temporary. People have to know what's going on."

Bill shook his head. "Rayburn, if we lie to them, it will make people angrier. We could make it even worse than it is."

Rayburn shrugged and shook his head, "Well, what do you suggest? We have to say something. They're going to riot pretty soon. I know a lot of people are talking about escaping and getting out. They will be shot and possibly killed if they do that."

"I know. You have to get on the radio and keep at it. We can't give up. We have to keep trying. We're out of options."

Rayburn looked at Morales with sad, imploring eyes, "How long do you think this will last? What do you suggest we do to handle this situation?"

Morales lifted her head. "Mr. Mayor, I have no clue when this will end. As we all saw, Elias is on the outside and still has the affliction. So there's a good chance this will continue for a long time. As far as a course of action? I agree with Bill. We have to keep trying. They need to know that they have someone on their side dealing with the government. The information you give them may not be what they want to hear, but they can still feel comfort knowing someone is watching out for them."

"Yeah, you and Bill are right," Rayburn said quietly. "We have to let them know they're not alone in this. I'll get started with the broadcasts. Bill, please keep me in the loop if anything new comes up."

"Will do, Rayburn," Bill said. Bill and Morales turned and walked out of the mayor's office. Rayburn was left alone at his desk, shaking his head in disbelief.

***

At about two p.m., the crowd gathered at Virgil and Pete's corner for their daily sermon. As more people joined in, they threw money into the hat on the ground before Virgil. They listened to Virgil jam on the harmonica as Pete played some blues progressions. They all clapped when it was over, and Pete grabbed his box to stand on and look over the crowd. The crowd was immense today. He could sense the tension.

He started talking to them. "Well, it is so good to see you here today. I am so glad you came by."

The voice in Pete's head cut into his speech. *Do you think all this is necessary?*

Not now, Pete said telepathically to the voice.

You seem to like this.

I have to communicate with people about the importance of caring about each other.

Okay then. Have at it.

The crowd looked at Pete, puzzled. While he was addressing the voice, he seemed distant to them.

"Pete, you okay?" one man called out.

"I'm fine," Pete replied.

"Pete, what are we supposed to do about these soldiers?"

"Pete, how can we keep going on like this?"

"Pete, many of us are terrified, especially our kids."

The questions kept coming from the crowd. They weren't here to listen today; they were looking for answers.

Pete raised his hands in the air. The crowd became silent.

"Good people of Bends Creek. I am not sure I have the answers you are looking for."

"Pete, we need your help."

"There's no one else who will answer our questions."

Pete could see the anxiety in the crowd. "Look at each other. See what I see," he said.

The crowd started looking at each other, and Pete smiled at the sea of different colors in the group. Everyone was mingling in peace. It was a welcoming sight.

"You have all come together as one, just as the universe intended. You are truly all connected, and that is a wonderful thing."

One crowd member yelled, "It ain't so wonderful being a prisoner in your town!"

Another voice from the crowd asked, "Yeah, what can we do, man?"

Pete responded, "Okay, this is a difficult time for everyone. But like I said, look around you: you all are here for each other. Together, you will be able to work through this."

"How are we supposed to work through this concentration camp?"

"We want our lives back!"

Pete sensed that this situation was about to quickly nose-dive.

"Okay, I promise I will talk to the authorities and see what I can find out for you."

"Why would they talk to a homeless man?"

"Yeah, no offense, Pete, but what can you do to help?"

"Why would they listen to a homeless man?" Pete repeated. "I think you can answer that better than I can."

The crowd laughed.

"I have told you before that we are connected and part of the same universe. Unfortunately, some of us have lost our way. Maybe we can talk to the authorities and see if we can reason with them."

Before the crowd could reply, an army truck with a dozen soldiers pulled up. The soldiers jumped out and surrounded the group. The leader, a young lieutenant, pulled out his bullhorn.

"We need this crowd to disband immediately," the lieutenant announced.

The crowd became angry, shouting at the lieutenant and the soldiers.

"I will give you until the count of three to start moving away from this area."

"Or what? You going to shoot us?" someone in the crowd yelled.

Another person followed suit. "You going to gun us all down?"

"I will do what is necessary to follow my orders. We are requesting you to disperse expeditiously. If you do not, we will use force to remove you."

"Some big talk while you're holding a gun."

"Go back to your fort!"

No one was moving.

"Sergeant, begin removing these people. Throw them in the truck and proceed to lock up. I have more trucks on the way."

The sergeant motioned for the soldiers to begin arresting individuals in the crowd. Two soldiers marched forward and grabbed one man. The remaining soldiers had their weapons ready in case the group retaliated. Once the soldiers had placed the residents in the truck, they proceeded to arrest other citizens. The people in the vehicle saw an opportunity to flee when the soldiers turned their backs on them. They ran into the middle of the crowd.

The crowd started laughing.

The lieutenant did not find this action amusing. Just then, another truck with another dozen soldiers pulled up. All the men jumped out. They dropped several boxes in front of the lieutenant. In one box were handcuffs and tear gas guns. Another contained gas masks. The lieutenant ordered his men to put on the masks. Once the soldiers were armed correctly, the lieutenant spoke over the bullhorn.

"One more time: you all need to disperse immediately." The lieutenant now had a tear gas gun in his hand.

The crowd stood their ground as dead silence fell over the area. Everyone was awaiting the lieutenant's next move.

Virgil and Pete were watching everything. Virgil was scared. "Pete, this ain't going to end well."

"I know."

"These people came to see us. If they get hurt, it'll be on us, man."

Pete looked at Virgil. "I understand."

"You going to do something then?"

"What are you saying, Virgil?"

"Pete…whatever you can do to help these people, you gots to do it."

Pete knew Virgil was right. If that first canister of tear gas dropped into the crowd, chaos would break loose, and someone was going to get hurt.

Pete closed his eyes and spoke to the voice in his head. *Well, what do you think?*

The female voice spoke softly. *This isn't the preferred way, but we do not appear to have a choice.*

Finally, we're on the same page. Are we on?

The voice sounded happy. *Oh yeah, it's on.*

The terrible thudding sound of the tear gas canister shooting into the crowd shattered the silence. It appeared to have landed in the middle of the group, but didn't explode. There weren't any signs of smoke in the area. People around the epicenter slowly stepped backward, forcing others to follow. They formed a circle around one man standing with his head bowed. The man held the tear gas canister in his right hand. He continued to look down at the ground, avoiding eye contact with the lieutenant and the crowd. His hair was hanging straight down, covering his face. The lieutenant ordered his men to arrest the stranger. As the four soldiers headed toward him, he raised his head. It was Pete.

Virgil, standing on the box so he could see into the center of the crowd, yelled out, "Oh, my man, yes!" He moved the wrong way and caused the box to kick out from under his feet. He fell to the ground. "I'm okay," he yelled. But no one was paying attention to Virgil. All eyes were on Pete.

The lieutenant looked shocked as the gas from the canister was sucked into Pete's coat sleeve. It continued until the cartridge was empty. Pete dropped the canister, and it rolled away, stopping at the lieutenant's feet. Pete lifted his head and tilted it slightly as he raised both arms straight to his sides, palms facing up. The soldiers stopped advancing toward him when they saw Pete's arms begin to glow. Streaks of lightning seemed to swirl around each arm. At the center of each of Pete's palms was a round sphere made of electricity. Pete looked up. His eyes glowed bright white as if they, too, were comprised of electrical charges.

Everyone watching, including the soldiers, didn't move. Everyone stood, staring at Pete. The soldiers dropped their weapons, eyes fixed on Pete, while some people in the crowd fell to their knees. Electricity was all around Pete now. The bolts were flashing through his body and hair. Pete started to rise off the ground slowly. He stopped when he reached a higher point than the tallest person in the crowd. Pete clapped his hands together. The contact of his two hands created a force of light so powerful that everyone fell to the ground, unconscious. Pete floated back down to earth, and the electrical current stopped flowing through his body. He looked around. Everyone present was out cold.

The voice in Pete's head sounded confused. *I don't understand. Nothing in your training or my briefing said you could do anything like this.*

Pete walked over to where Virgil was lying. He shook Virgil and woke him. "Come on," Pete said. "We have to go now."

Virgil was groggy. He didn't notice all the people in the middle of the street. Pete held Virgil's arm and walked down the sidewalk toward the shelter.

Well played, the voice in Pete's head commented.

Yeah, I wish I could remember how I did it.

Pete didn't look back at the crowd when he heard some of them waking up. They began to stand up, wondering where they were. Confused, they asked each other what they were doing in the street. The soldiers didn't fare any better. Each soldier got up, reached for his weapon, and picked it up, looking at the soldier next to him in confusion. The lieutenant glanced around. There were a few people in the street looking back at him. He waved to the soldiers to get into the trucks. The soldiers followed his order, and the trucks drove off.

***

When Maggie and Jessica entered the shelter, Pete and Virgil sat at a table. "Hey, Pete," Maggie smiled.

Pete stood up. "Hi, Maggie. How are you?"

"Pretty good. I want to introduce you to Jessica Morales. She's with the CDC and is now a temporary resident." Maggie and Jessica laughed.

"Pleased to meet you, ma'am." Pete nodded.

"Ma'am? We appear to be the same age, no? I am not 'ma'am' to you. Please, call me Jessica."

"I did not mean to offend you. Sorry."

"No apologies needed. I'm just saying we're all the same, right?"

"Yes, we are."

Maggie handed Pete some new packages. "Merry Christmas, Pete."

"Christmas?" Pete turned his head slightly as he took the packages from Maggie.

Maggie continued smiling. "It's not Christmas, silly. We got you some new clothes. Why don't you shower, shave, and try them on?"

"Sure. Okay, thank you." Pete headed to the showers.

Maggie and Jessica sat down at the table with Virgil. "Virgil, this is Jessica."

"Hi," said Virgil.

"Nice to meet you, Virgil," Jessica smiled.

Maggie asked, "So, how was your day today, Virgil?"

Virgil looked a little confused by the question. He was massaging the back of his neck. "I can't say that I know, Maggie."

Maggie laughed. "You've been drinking again?"

"No. Ain't had a drop since I met Pete. He won't let me drink no more. I just ain't so sure what I did today."

Jessica sat up, "Do you remember anything at all?"

"Just Pete picking me up off the ground and heading back here is all."

Jessica noticed the concerned look on Maggie's face. She felt the warmth of Maggie's eyes as they slowly fell across Virgil's face like a mother worried her child had just suffered an injury. Jessica saw that Maggie was afraid that something terrible had happened and that Virgil was blocking it.

"Where were you?" Maggie softly coaxed Virgil.

"We were at my usual spot. I must have passed out or something."

"Did you fall?"

Virgil blinked, " I ain't sure what I did."

"This doesn't make any sense. Do you remember how you got there? Or when you got there?"

"I swear I don't remember none of it."

"Maggie pressed Virgil further, but no matter how many questions she asked, his answer remained the same. He remembered nothing or wasn't telling them what it was."

Before Maggie could ask Virgil a follow-up question, Pete walked into the room.

Jessica and Maggie looked at each other, then back at Pete. Pete was clean-shaven, save for a little shadow left on his face. His hair was wet and fell straight down past his shoulders. He wore the new jeans, sneakers, and a black t-shirt that Maggie had just purchased.

Jessica spoke first. "You clean up nice, Pete."

"Thanks."

Jessica asked Pete if he wanted to join her at the diner for coffee. Pete looked at Virgil. Virgil nodded his approval, and then he left with her.

Maggie looked over at Virgil, "Let's talk a little bit more."

16 THE BIG REVEAL

Pete walked alongside Jessica down the sidewalk. Walking with Jessica and feeling her energy generated images in his mind of him laughing with another woman. Unfortunately, Pete couldn't identify the woman's features in his head and had difficulty remembering her. The pictures flashed in and out of his mind, switching on and off intermittently. No image remained in his head long enough for Pete to analyze it.

What are you doing? The voice in his head asked.

Nothing.

It sure seems like something is happening here that shouldn't be.

How am I supposed to know what is or isn't supposed to be going on if I can't remember anything?

True. True. Carry on.

While responding to the voice, Pete moved his head slightly to one side as if he had a cramp.

Jessica noticed. "Something wrong?"

"No, not at all. I have trouble remembering things, and walking with you instantly put some images in my head. Not sure what they are."

"Hopefully, we can get more of them to pop up." Jessica smiled, turned, and walked into the diner. Pete followed her inside. They sat in a booth toward the back of the restaurant. Jessica ordered a coffee, and Pete ordered tea. Jessica looked at Pete. She liked what she saw. Pete was not only handsome; he seemed humble, as well. Of course, the fact that he looked like an adorable lost puppy didn't hurt his looks either.

"It's awesome that you look out for Virgil the way you do," she began.

"He took me in. Well, took me into his corner, that is," Pete answered as he looked out the diner window.

Jessica smiled. "Yeah, he's a sweet man."

"He's a good man with a good heart," Pete tried smiling back at her.

Jessica looked up at Pete from her coffee cup. "I heard you guys had a run-in with a couple of bullies the other day."

Pete looked away from her, back out the window. "Yes." Pete watched people walking by the diner. He saw a woman laughing while holding a girl's hand. A man in a gray suit was walking and talking to another man in a suit. Several children were on bikes being chased away from the sidewalk by a store owner. Pete got lost in the atmosphere of it all. It seemed like everyone knew who they were and where they were going.

"The sheriff said he's having difficulty figuring out what happened to you guys. Any luck remembering anything?"

Pete raised an eyebrow, "Did the sheriff send you here to interrogate me?"

Jessica shook her head. "Just my curiosity. I'm a scientist by trade. I like to solve mysteries."

"You think I'm a mystery?"

Jessica laughed. "Well, you don't know you, and Bill doesn't. So maybe I can get to know you."

There was something about Jessica that was familiar to Pete. Her demeanor? Her personality? Pete couldn't quite put his finger on what made him want to be with Jessica.

"That sounds good."

Jessica tilted her head slightly to the side and nodded. "Yeah, it does, doesn't it?"

The voice in his head quipped, *Gag me, please.*

"You know, Pete, there is a drug that I can administer to you to help you regain your memory. We keep certain drugs on hand in the event we need to use them on test subjects in the field. Enhanced memories are one of the side effects of this one particular drug. So you may get a piece back that you can build on."

Pete's eyes widened, "Really?"

The voice in his head started screaming. *No, Pete, no drugs!*

Why not? Pete yelled back.

We can't interfere with the mission. This isn't about you.

From where I'm sitting, it is pretty much all about me. I have to know. Please work with me on this.

Pete felt like the voice was stomping her feet inside his head. When the stomping stopped, the voice in his head answered softly, *Okay,*

I'll back off for now, but we have to stay focused. We are on a tight schedule to accomplish our mission.

Pete nodded. *Thanks.*

Jessica sat quietly, watching Pete stare out the window. It was as though Pete was in deep thought. She didn't want to disturb him while he was off, who knows where, and Pete looked too happy being wherever he was in his head. Pete eventually snapped out of his brief daze and looked at Jessica.

"Where did you go?" Jessica asked quietly.

Pete shrugged his shoulders. "Just talking to my better half."

The voice laughed. *Good answer.*

Jessica raised her eyebrows. "You a little crazy, Pete?"

"Aren't we all?"

"I suppose," Jessica said, putting her coffee down. "So you want to give it a try, then?"

"What?"

"The drug. Do you want to come to the office and try it? We can do it tomorrow if you like."

"How about right now?"

"Now?" Jessica seemed surprised. "Sure, why not? Let's go."

"Yes, let's go."

They both walked out of the diner toward Jessica's office.

***

Jessica turned her office lights on and invited Pete in. She walked into another room toward the back of her office and told Pete to come in. Pete closed the door behind him and noticed the office was empty. It was just the two of them.

"Pete, please come back here," Jessica called out.

Pete walked to the next room, a private office with a couch and a few chairs. On his left was a small kitchen and dining area. To the right were several locked cabinets on the wall next to a large whiteboard. Pete watched Jessica get a needle and a small bottle out of one of her locked cabinets.

"What kind of drug is this?"

"It's experimental right now. Tests have proven that it increases long-term memory in the majority of patients. But, as I said, it is experimental, so it has no guarantees. One good thing? There have been enough tests to prove no ill side effects. If there were any, I would not have suggested this."

"Okay, let's do it."

"This will cause drowsiness; you may sleep for a while, so please lie on the sofa."

Pete got on the sofa. He lay down, and Jessica put a cushion under his head. "Comfortable?"

He nodded.

She took the syringe, punctured the vial's top, and carefully measured the amount. She smiled at Pete, and Pete nodded in agreement, giving her the go-ahead. She wiped the inside of his arm with a sanitizing cloth and stuck the needle carefully into his vein.

"Feels like cold liquid going in," Pete said.

"Yeah," Jessica said. "It will take effect pretty quickly." Before Jessica could say another word, Pete was out.

***

Pete was standing in the dark. He raised his right hand and couldn't see it. No visual markers were available, so Pete didn't move. He waited patiently for something to happen. Time was nonexistent here. Hours could have passed before anything might have happened. But then, without warning, a circular light appeared on the ground, or floor, directly in front of him. It looked like a small spotlight. There was activity in its center. A little blue light became liquid as it rose from the center; the outside ring remained stationary. The liquid blue luminescence rose until it reached a height just below Pete's chin. Pete reached out to touch it, but his hand went right through it as though it wasn't there. Then, the light began turning in place, never moving outside the spotlight on the floor. The blue light was twisting and spinning faster and faster, taking the shape of a miniature blue tornado. As the liquid moved, it started making the form of a woman without a face, standing in front of Pete. There were no details on her body; he saw only the outline of her hourglass figure.

Pete reached out and touched the front of the figure where the face should be. The touch of his finger caused ripples across the face like a stone hitting water. He gently tapped where the left eye should be. Space opened to reveal an eye. Pete tapped the right side similarly, and the right eye opened. He drew a short line in the center of the face, and a nose appeared. When he came to the lips, he drew a single line to create a smile. The mouth opened.

"Oz?"

The liquid light smiled. "Hello, Pete." Her voice sounded so warm and friendly.

Pete nodded. "Oz, where are we?"

"This is where you began your journey."

"You know this place?"

"Yes. This place is where we met for the first time. It was here that the Council trained and programmed you. It's where the Council assigned me to you."

"I don't remember training or programming. All I know has come from you describing the mission to me. I have accepted that you're in my head, and there was a reason, the mission. But that's it, Oz. I don't know anything else. It seems appropriate that I am standing in the dark right now."

"Pete, you must remain calm, and I will do my best to explain."

"What do you mean, programmed me? Am I a robot or something? Am I not human anymore? I can't feel anything. I can't laugh or cry."

"You are human," Oz answered. "You are the one the Council has chosen as their herald."

"Why me? Is this why I can't remember anything? What happened to me?"

"I am going to show you, Pete. But if I reveal too much too quickly, your mind may be unable to handle it. I am not sure what will happen to you mentally."

"Show me as much as you can. I have to know."

Oz looked at Pete. One side of her body moved, and an arm rose toward Pete's face; as her arm got closer, a hand formed and touched him on the cheek in a friendly manner. His cheek started to glow blue from her touch.

"We've been through so much together, you and I," Oz smiled.

Oz pulled her hand back and turned away from Pete. She raised her hand over her head to light a small area in front of her. The light revealed a small room with a table. Pete could not see what was on the table.

"How are you doing this?"

"Every part of your training and programming has been recorded. I am accessing those recordings for you."

Pete walked closer to the table. Oz stopped him.

"Pete," Oz said, "you must realize this has already happened. You are now outside of all this, looking in. You cannot change anything here. Whatever happens, you must understand that no one can hear you."

"I get it," Pete said. "I can watch, but I can't touch."

"Well put, as usual. Ready?"

"Yeah, let's do this."

Twenty minutes had passed since Jessica injected Pete. She began to worry. Jessica had never seen someone stay under for so long with this dosage. She started to think, searching for a way to revive Pete. Jessica was looking for another drug in the cabinet when she heard a moan from the sofa. She ran to the side of the couch. Pete was sitting up, rubbing the back of his neck, a little stiff from lying down.

"Pete, you okay?" Jessica asked, concerned.

"Yes," Pete said, stretching his body a little. He was sweating, so

Jessica got him a towel.

"Thanks," he said as he wiped his face and around his neck.

"What did you see?"

Pete stared at the towel. *I was experimented on. Why can't I feel emotion? Am I human? Was I ever human?* These and so many other questions raced through his mind.

Maybe if I engaged with another human more personally, I could trigger an emotion and reset my original capabilities.

Pete slowly raised his head, "We have to talk, Jessica." Pete put his head down, shaking it slowly back and forth. "This is not going to be easy for you to understand. I may need some time to process this whole mess before I can tell you anything. I don't know."

Pete started tapping his right foot rapidly.

Oz spoke up. *Do you think that's wise? Especially with the way you're feeling right now? It would be best if you calmed down and thought this through.*

Pete answered her as he rubbed his neck. *Oz, I need answers that you won't be able to give me. I need to talk to someone who understands what being human is. A person who understands what emotions are. Maybe Jessica can point me in the right direction. For some reason, I trust her.*

Can you trust anyone? Don't you want to run some tests first? Maybe—

Pete interrupted Oz. For the first time, he spoke to Oz out loud. "I can trust her, Oz. I know I can trust her."

Jessica stood up and took a few slow steps away from the couch. "Pete, who are you talking to?"

Pete looked at Jessica. "Oh crap, you heard me."

"What do you mean, I heard you?" Jessica took another step back, away from Pete. "Have you always talked to yourself?"

"Yeah, this is going to be hard to explain. Maybe I should talk to someone else about this."

Jessica took a step toward Pete. "Just tell me you're not crazy, please."

"I can't guarantee that." Pete looked into her eyes. "I'm not sure now. I need to process this; maybe if I talk to you and hear it out loud, I can make sense of it. Maybe you can help me figure this out. That is…if you want to."

Jessica sat down next to Pete. She nodded. "Yeah, Pete. That's why we're here. Let's try."

"Thank you." Pete looked at Jessica and stood up. He started pacing. He wanted to tell her everything, but he didn't want to scare or make her think he was crazy. "Jessica, please, whatever you do, don't walk away until I explain everything. Okay?"

"You're scaring me again. Can we just take it slowly, one piece at a time?"

Pete was still pacing back and forth. Finally, he walked to Jessica's window, stopped, and stared at the evening sky. He started to speak to Oz telepathically.

I need to bring you out.

No way, Pete, we can't.

We can trust her. You must understand that the story we are about to tell is so unbelievable that she may want to lock me up. If we start this way, she will take everything else seriously.

Oz was hesitant. *Are you sure there is no other way?*

146

Trust me, Oz. This is the only way.

Pete turned from the window and looked at Jessica. His expression alarmed her, and she felt uncomfortable in her seat. She considered how vulnerable she was sitting there and started to get up.

"No, please stay seated. I want to show you something."

Jessica was sitting straight on the couch, one hand on the sidearm, ready to push herself up and run away. Reluctantly, she said, "Okay, go ahead."

Pete sat on the chair, directly facing Jessica. There was a small coffee table between them. Pete held out his hand, palm up, over the coffee table. Jessica waited impatiently. She looked at his palm and then his face. "What?" she asked anxiously.

"This," he said. A small pool of liquid blue light swirled around in his palm. Jessica's facial expression froze.

"Tell me this is a magic trick, Pete." Her eyes felt like they were popping out of her head.

The room radiated with blue light. A figure of a woman emerged from the center of the luminescence in the center of Pete's palm. Jessica's jaw dropped open, and she squeezed the sidearm of the couch tighter.

The figure's face formed, and her eyes looked directly at Jessica.

Oz smiled and waved.

Jessica's face was still frozen, and she couldn't move her mouth. She couldn't even blink. She just stared at Oz in amazement. Oz's blue aura brightened the entire room.

"Do you want me to send Oz back?" Pete asked softly so as not to startle her.

Jessica shook her head rapidly, keeping her gaze locked on Oz. She was stunned but understood that she needed Oz to remain if she wanted to know more.

Pete sat and waited patiently for Jessica to regain control of her senses.

Oz looked up at Pete. "You are handling this very well. I am impressed."

"It…she…it? She…speaks?" Jessica finally spoke, her sentences broken.

Oz smiled at Jessica. "Yes, I speak. I am inside Pete. I am his guide."

"Why does he need a guide? What are you? Who are you? Pete, where the hell are you from?" Jessica couldn't stop asking questions. "Why are you here? Holy shit! Are you responsible for what's happening?"

Oz looked up at Pete and pursed her lips, "She's taking this rather well, don't you think?"

Pete nodded. "I told you she could deal with this. Just give her a few more minutes to grasp it. She'll be fine."

Jessica got up from the couch. She started pacing back and forth across the room. Pete was still sitting in the chair, holding Oz in his hand. Jessica moved behind the couch, waving her hands in front of her.

Oz looked at Pete. "What is she doing?"

"I believe she's trying to calm down."

Jessica paced right out of the room and popped back a second later. Her pacing went on for several minutes.

Finally, she walked over to Oz. "Yes, I am trying to calm the hell down. This is how I do that. Okay? This, right here," Jessica waved her hands before her body, presenting herself to Oz. "This is how I calm down." She returned to pacing.

"Looks like you're making yourself angry, lady."

Jessica stopped behind the couch. "Where did you get such a smartass attitude?"

Oz looked back at Pete. Pete shrugged his shoulders and raised his eyebrows. "Guilty," he said.

After a few minutes of brisk pacing, Jessica finally collected herself and sat beside Pete.

"Okay," she said. "Let's try this again. Pete, I appreciate that you shared Oz with me. I think I'm ready to get some answers now?"

Jessica slowly pushed her hair to the side of her face. She took a deep breath through her nose and slowly let the air out of her mouth. "Please start from the beginning. I want to know as much as you can tell me."

Pete looked at Jessica, then at Oz.

"Oz showed up in my search and guided me to a memory concerning my mission. I still don't remember how or why the Council chose me for this mission. But now, I fully understand why I am here."

Jessica interrupted Pete. "Sorry to break your train of thought, but I think it would be better for me if you explained who or what Oz is first. It's tough to give you my undivided attention while I look at Oz, not knowing what she is."

Pete looked at Oz again. "You want to take this one?"

Oz looked at Jessica. "Would you want to hear it from Pete or me?"

Jessica let out another breath slowly. "It would be great if you told me about yourself. You mentioned you were Pete's guide?"

"Yes. I went through a process similar to Pete's. The Council chose me, along with other candidates, to train and program. After all the training, the Council chose the best candidate to match Pete's physical and mental capacities."

Jessica looked even more confused. "Okay, so you were trained and programmed by the Council? Is this Council a secret government operation?"

Oz looked at Pete. Pete nodded, indicating it was all right to answer Jessica's question.

Oz turned back to Jessica. "Are you sure you want to know the answer to that? It's a lot to grasp."

"Please go on. I want to help. I need to know as much as possible to do that."

"I am a Wen'q'rixshi from Wen'q'rixsh."

"A Wen…what?"

"I am not from this world. My home is hundreds of light-years from Earth."

"Shut the front door!" Jessica screamed. "Freaking aliens! Like outer space aliens? Oh freak, no, no, no!"

Jessica started pacing again, now rambling in Spanish. "Esto es una mierda loca. Nunca debí haber tomado esta estúpida tarea. Tengo que alejarme de este pueblo lo antes posible. No seré devorado por jodidos alienígenas."

"Jessica! Jessica!" Pete cried out. He got up and put his hands on her shoulders to stop her pacing.

"Pete, what happened to the alien?" Jessica asked Pete in a whisper as her eyes fixed on his hands resting on her shoulders.

They both simultaneously looked down at the coffee table. Oz was standing on the coffee table, waving one hand at Jessica. She closed and opened her fingers, slowly grinning sardonically.

Jessica screamed again. "I thought Oz and you were connected?"

"We're connected even when she separates from me. We are always together."

Oz laughed. "Better believe that."

"Relax, Jessica. The Wen are on our side." Pete tried to reassure Jessica to no avail.

She looked over at the coffee table, pulled away from Pete, and continued pacing. Finally, she yelled, "Pete, they always say that, man! Right before they eat your ass!"

Oz yelled, "I don't eat ass! What's wrong with her, Pete? I told you this was a bad idea."

Pete raised his hand to Oz, gesturing for her to wait a minute. "Jessica, please calm down so we can continue. Or would you rather we stop now?"

"No, I want to continue. Give me a moment, please."

Jessica left the room and returned with a bottle of red wine and an empty glass. She sat on the couch, placed the glass onto the coffee table, and poured some wine while looking at Oz. Jessica then picked up the whole glass, raised it to toast everyone, and proceeded to drink until it was empty.

She reached for the bottle to pour another glass.

"Jessica…"

Jessica raised her hand to stop Pete from talking and continued to pour. This time, she took one long sip and leaned back, holding the glass with two hands. She smiled at Oz. "Let's give this a minute to soak in…literally."

Oz looked up at Pete. "She okay?"

"I think so."

Jessica looked at Oz, then at Pete, as he sat back in his chair. "Okay, I think I am better prepared now. Please continue."

Oz continued. "As I was saying before, I am from Wen'q'rixsh. Our race exists on a planet hundreds of light-years from Earth. Compared to your most intelligent scientists, we are light-years ahead."

Jessica took a sip of wine. "Is everyone like you on your planet?"

"No. Our world consists of many diverse life forms. Each life form plays an integral part in our society. For instance, highly intelligent life forms exist to advance our technology, defend our planet, and so on."

"Do you vote on leaders to represent the different life forms?"

Oz looked confused. "I don't understand what you mean."

"How does your world go about making decisions?"

"What kind of decisions?"

"Like, who is in charge, you know? Do you vote on anyone to make a final decision for you?"

"No one person or group decides for the masses. We live in a highly intellectual society where all actions derive from logic."

"But how does this Council get to do the things they do? Are they allowed to make decisions without approval from other factions of your society?"

"Why would they need approval to do anything?"

"Without checks and balances, it becomes a sort of dictatorship. You have one lifeform making all the choices for everyone else."

"Our society is highly advanced. We do not think or exist the way your Earth does. We do not have wars, crime, or hunger. Greed does not exist because it is not logical. Hurting another lifeform to gain their possessions or to control them is not logical."

"So you all live on a huge hippie planet where everyone loves each other and is non-aggressive toward each other?"

"I don't understand what you mean by hippie planet, but the last part of your question is getting closer. We do not let emotions dictate our actions. We are a logic-based society."

Pete was sitting in his chair, listening. He knew as much as Jessica did about the Wen.

"I guess this conversation could go on forever, and it's fascinating, but we should move on for now."

Oz nodded.

Jessica's wine glass shook. "Explain to me who you are. Are you a lifeform subordinate to the Council?"

"There are no subordinate lifeforms on my planet."

"So, you volunteered to do this?"

"It's all about our purpose."

"And what is your purpose?"

"The societal faction I belong to is called the Vailens. Vailens are composed of technical elements and some biological material."

"You're a cyborg? Like the Terminator?"

Oz smiled. "I liked that movie. As part of my training, I had to go through a library of Earth information, which included movies and music."

Pete cut her off. "Oz, focus, please."

Oz continued, "The biological material in a Vailen's form lets us shape our outer shell into different life forms. This ability is helpful when communicating with different species."

"Like shapeshifting?"

"Yes."

"So, you can shapeshift into any form you choose? How about inanimate objects?"

"Inanimate objects can be broken down into many levels and compounds. A Vailen can react to any level or compound accordingly."

Jessica was still holding her shaking glass with two hands as she took another sip of wine and looked at Pete. He was paying close attention to Jessica and Oz's discussion. She realized this was new to him, too.

Jessica continued, "And what is the technology side of your form used for?"

"It allows the Council to train and program us for missions if we're needed."

"So, this Council is composed of highly intelligent Wen?"

"Yes."

"The Council trained and programmed you to do…what?"

"I was trained to be a guide for Pete on this mission."

"I know, but what specifically were you trained to do as a guide?"

"I was trained to make sure Pete understands the mission and to help him hit critical points on the schedule."

"What are you capable of doing as a Vailen? Do you have special abilities that we would consider extraordinary?"

"My tech is implanted into Pete's brain. I can enhance whatever abilities Pete has. For example, I can act like an extension of Pete's subconscious. If he feels the need to be protected, I can surround him with an energy field. If he needs help with the mission, I can replay specific instructions to help him. There are countless other things I help with, as well."

"But you can't fight anyone or hurt anyone?"

"No. That is illogical for a Vailen."

"Why the name Oz? That can't be your real name, right?"

"My name is Oskalan. As I said earlier, I have studied Earth culture. I wanted a nickname like so many humans. I loved watching The Wizard of Oz. I must have watched it more than any other Earth file. I am the wizard."

"I think you've been on this planet too long." Jessica took another sip of wine before continuing. "Okay, so let me see if I have this straight. Your planet consists of various lifeforms that serve the greater good through an encompassing logical thought process. The Council conducts missions based on logic. When they create a mission, they enlist whatever lifeform on the planet is needed to help the mission succeed. How am I doing so far?"

Oz nodded. "Your summary is very close. Continue."

"The Council trained and programmed you to be compatible with Pete. You are well-versed in Earth's history and culture. You do not have any superpowers, and all your actions and thoughts are logic-based. And all this leads us to the mission. What is the mission?"

Oz looked at Pete. "You should take it from here."

Pete took in a deep breath and let it out slowly. "Okay, Jessica, this is where everything becomes very serious. The Wen are not the only aliens involved in this story."

17 MISSION-CRITICAL

Pete looked at Jessica and began. "When you gave me the memory drug, I first saw darkness. Then Oz appeared and showed me a recording that the Council kept on file for further reference. It is one of many that the Council has logged."

Jessica asked, "So the drug didn't help?"

"It did. It took me back to my last memory. Then, it was dark, and the Wen, I assume the Council, spoke to me."

"What did they say?"

"Oz, why don't you use your playback function and let her hear the recording?"

"Yeah?" Oz questioned.

"Yeah," Pete said. "She can hear for herself firsthand."

Oz looked at Pete, then back at Jessica. "This is what Pete went through, Jessica. He was in total darkness, strapped to a table."

"You were strapped to a table?"

Pete shrugged his shoulders. "I suppose so. I don't remember."

Oz continued. "We are starting after Pete's long ordeal, when his training was coming to an end. Pete had no idea how long he had been in this position. There was no sense of time for him."

"I understand."

"The voice you hear first will be the Council." Oz glanced at Pete. "You ready?"

Pete nodded.

Oz began to play the recording, the audio coming from her body.

"J9-1-7, you were chosen for a vital task." The voice sounded huge, as if it were filling a concert hall.

"Wait, please pause it," Jessica said excitedly.

"What is it?" Oz asked.

"He called you J9-1-7, Pete. Is that your real name?"

Pete answered softly. "Not sure if it was a project name or my real name. When I found myself here, I just called myself Pete. I thought J9-1-7 would be hard for everyone to accept."

"Why the name Pete?"

"I woke up in the alley across from the hardware store. They had a sign in their window that said they were having a sale on peat moss."

Jessica smiled but held back her laughter. "Sorry to interrupt, Oz. Please continue."

The recording started again with Pete's voice, "I don't recognize your accent, sir. It's bizarre. The little sounds between each word you speak make it difficult to understand you. Do you think you can speak closer to the mic or something?"

Jessica spoke. "Damn, Pete, how did you make it through this alive? You were such a smart ass."

Oz responded, "He was lucky they didn't vaporize his smart ass."

Pete's voice on the recording continued, "And what? What task? What the heck is going…?"

"SILENCE!" The voice interrupted, louder now. Jessica jumped slightly.

"Okay, you don't have to be so rude."

"Your insolence will not be tolerated! You will listen or be terminated!"

"Okay."

"We chose you, J9-1-7, out of many others for this most critical task. We have been preparing you, and you now appear ready for the next phase of this mission."

"Alright, I'll try to control my thoughts."

"That's a wise decision. We will explain and give you some background so your human mind can ingest this information without imploding."

He said human. Oh great. Am I dealing with aliens now? Pete thought to himself.

"Yes, you are. You need to pay attention to what I am about to tell you. I will only explain this once. If you cannot comprehend this, we will terminate you immediately."

"You like using that word a lot. Why don't you terminate me and get it over with already?"

"It appears that we successfully removed all fear and emotions from within your being, but we weren't as successful with your sarcasm facility. We can only conclude that losing your other emotions enhanced your sarcasm. Interesting. I will tolerate it for now, but I will not tolerate another outburst. Remain silent or suffer the consequences."

"Did you say you erased my emotions? What about my memories? Is that why I don't know who I am?"

"Yes, J9-1-7. Your memories and emotions mustn't interfere with the mission. Memories of your past relationships with friends and family will only distract you. However, your memories of general knowledge remain. For example, memories of Earth's history, politics, and customs are clear. But if a memory involved personal interaction with other humans, we eliminated it."

"And I did not react to what you just said because you eliminated my ability to produce an emotional response?"

"Yes. Humans make decisions based on foolish emotions. Emotions are not logical."

"So I don't know who I am, and I don't know anyone. So, I am your robot?"

"You are not our robot. You are the vehicle we will use to communicate with the humans of Earth."

"Am I still human?"

"Yes. Our robots do not have sarcasm capabilities. Now pay attention."

"Yes, Your Highness."

"Man, Pete, did you want to die?" Jessica asked.

Oz looked at Pete. "I know, right?"

The voice remained silent for a few moments before continuing. "We are not of this world. We are from a planet and time beyond your comprehension. We have come here to Earth to help your planet. Refrain from all sarcasm, and let me finish. Your species must heed our warnings and accept our help."

"This is serious do-do."

"Yes, J9-1-7, this is indeed serious do-do. We are a race called the Wen'q'rixshi. I will not go into our technical capabilities because you could not comprehend the science. We are a peaceful species and do not have wars on our planet. Unlike your world, greed is non-existent because we do not need rulers or possessions. Another contrast to your Earth, which relies on religion and other spiritual entities to guide right and wrong, the Wen use logic."

"So why come to Earth?"

"It is not logical to watch civilizations perish if there is a way to help them. Therefore, we must make an effort to save as many species as possible. Consequently, it has become our mission to try to save different civilizations from total eradication by the Xanoclax.

The Xanoclax are an alien race whose sole purpose is to annihilate weaker species to become more powerful. The Xan have been doing so for thousands of your Earth years. The only rule they have is that they can only prey on self-destructing civilizations. The Xan cannot come to any planet and destroy it directly. According to their Logic Belief, there has to be justification for their actions. Following this 'logic belief' enables the Xanoclax to complete the transition."

"What transition?"

"The transition of a species' life force into themselves. The only way to accomplish this transition is to enslave the civilization and slowly suck the life force out of every living thing that inhabits the planet. Eventually, there will be no living beings on the planet. Once the Xan accomplish the transition, they move on to the next civilization, leaving behind a barren wasteland."

"So they choose a planet by what? Observing the planet's behavior?"

"Yes, J9-1-7. They have been studying Earth for hundreds of years. Their scouts have watched your planet slip through disaster after disaster. They have observed your species, waiting for you to reach your full potential for hatred before they attack to gain the benefit of all your will and power. As we speak, the Xan scouts could be on your planet, reporting back to their superiors."

"So they justify killing billions by concluding that it is inevitable that we will destroy ourselves anyway? But if we do that, they gain no benefit, so they swoop in and take advantage of the opportunity?"

"It may be hard for humans to understand, but yes. There has to be logic. They cannot gain the benefit of consuming your life force through unjustified murder. Their logic belief, what you would call religion, has them believe they are doing right by a self-destructing civilization by destroying it. They will receive a great reward by committing what the Xan deem a selfless act."

"What reward will they receive?"

"The Xanoclax will receive all the will and power each human possesses. I believe you call this your soul. They call it something different on other planets, but it is all the same. It is a life force, the most potent energy in the universe. The life force of other beings is like a drug to the Xan. Without it, they cannot survive."

"They sound like vampires."

"Throughout the short life span of the human race, humans have treated each other with hatred, disrespect, and cruelty. Yet, humans have survived all this time because the good outweighed the bad. But now the Xan have seen what they need and are waiting for the right moment to strike."

"What have they seen to make them feel it is time?"

"That is an excellent question, J9-1-7. The Xanoclax have seen the race of humans become more divided into different belief factions. These factions become increasingly self-serving at the expense of others' freedoms and well-being. Hatred of others for no other reason than the color of their skin or religious beliefs is more prevalent now than ever before on your planet. Your primitive social media system has allowed the rapid spread of hateful opinions that lead to hateful actions. The killing of individuals simply because they are different brings the Xan closer to their final date of the invasion. Time is running out for your species, J9-1-7."

"And you are here to help us do what? Fight the Xan?"

"No. Xanoclax technology is too advanced for humans to survive an all-out war."

"Why haven't they attacked your planet and tried to stop you?"

"Our technology is far more advanced than that of the Xan. We have covered our entire planet with an energy field that cannot be penetrated by any known force in our universe. They have tried many times to no avail. The only way Earth can stop them is to appeal to Xan's logic."

"And how do we do that?"

"With you, J9-1-7. You are Earth's only hope."

Jessica was beginning to lose it again. "See, I told you, didn't I?"

Pete looked puzzled. "What did you tell me, Jessica?"

"These freaking aliens are going to come and eat our ass!" She started pouring another glass of wine.

"No, the Wen want to help us."

"Not them, those other human-ass-eating freaks!"

"What is it with you and eating ass?" Oz asked sarcastically.

Pete interrupted Oz. "Jessica, are you talking about the Xan?" Pete asked. "We have a plan to stop them."

"Yeah," Oz said. "The plan is coming up. You okay with going on?"

"Yes," Jessica said, taking another swallow of wine.

Oz continued the recording.

"Me?"

"Yes, J9-1-7," the voice answered.

"So how do I do this? What is the plan here?"

"It has already begun. We have started an experiment in a small town in the southern part of your country, the United States. It is in the land we believe you call Mississippi. We eradicated the ability to pass judgment based on appearances, religious beliefs, or economic status."

"Okay, wait a minute. Why Mississippi? And how can you take our ability not to judge others away? Is everyone a robot now? What the–"

"J9-1-7, all will be explained. Although there were many similar places to choose from, we decided on Mississippi for its significant history of racial violence. Besides, we liked the name."

"Did you just make a funny? Now, who's being sarcastic?"

"In this area, you call the Deep South, committing acts of hatred toward others based solely on outward appearances seems to be the norm. We will not go into the horrific details because we know you are aware of this history yourself. Because of these factors, this is the perfect setting to conduct the test phase of our mission."

"The test phase?"

"A proven process that we have developed as an alternative to war. In our attempts to help other civilizations, we realized that common sense does not prevail. If a world refuses our help, we cannot force it upon them. Logic is reserved for highly developed species. So, we will offer a test phase to see if the planet can accept our intervention. If they can, we move on to enhancing the citizens."

"Enhance?"

"Yes. We use our technology, which binds to an individual's mind and adjusts it appropriately."

"Adjusts? How?"

"Every human can make an immediate judgment based on what you would call the first impression. Unfortunately, this ability is also what we found to be the root of all your struggles. We interfere in the individual mind at the moment of this first impression and let them see not as it is but as it needs to be to promote harmony among all people."

"Brainwashing?"

"You could call it that. If that is the term you understand, so be it."

"What exactly does the technical process do to a person?"

"Without going into complicated technical and biological details you would never understand, I will attempt to simplify. If a human is prejudiced and if the color of another human's skin evokes anger or discontent toward them, our process removes the ability to make that specific choice."

"Removes? How?"

"He sees others as he sees himself. If he is white-skinned, he sees others as white-skinned. If he is Black-skinned, he sees others so. The result is the same for every race on Earth."

"I don't understand how this is going to work. How will people adjust to this?"

"We have weighed all possible outcomes and predicted success or failure based on all conceivable reactions. Some humans will be happy, while others will feel invaded and want their choices returned. However, this process only works on humans extremely troubled by prejudice. Those humans who experience mild cases of bias will not be affected. It is human nature to notice differences between beings. Seeing differences is acceptable within parameters. It is when a specific judgment is passed based on these differences or first impressions that our process takes hold."

"You guys are brain-jacking."

"We don't understand this term, brain-jacking. But we can guarantee it is not mind control. People still have free will to make decisions and choices on their own. Only now will appearances not initiate a specific opportunity for intolerance. It is the hope that this process will bring harmony to your planet and cause the Xan to pass it over. If this attempt doesn't work, your world is doomed to be enslaved, and life as you know it will cease to exist."

"I appreciate what you are trying to do, but this could backfire and worsen things."

"We have prepared you to speak for us to explain our process. We have equipped you to represent us and bring understanding to your planet before it is too late."

"Me? If the future depends on me, we are screwed."

"We shall see J9-1-7. We shall see."

Jessica let out a loud sigh when the recording stopped. She looked at Pete, who wasn't paying attention. He had lowered his head, staring at his hands.

"Pete," Jessica said in a soft voice. "I'm glad you and Oz shared this with me."

Pete looked at Jessica. "Really? You seemed pretty freaked out about it earlier."

Oz hopped over to Pete's lap and looked up at Jessica. "Yeah, I thought I was going to have to terminate your ass. If you were a horse, we would have put you down."

Jessica glanced at Oz. "You, my dear, are so funny." She looked back at Pete. "What happens now?"

"I have to perform my duties according to my mission. I have to prepare now."

Jessica looked concerned. "Prepare for what?"

"Prepare for what happens next."

18 CROWD CONTROL

Strathern was getting more and more resistance from the Bends Creek citizens. They were scared and angry, a combination Strathern had seen too many times on other campaigns. Fear and anger led people to make crazy choices, and when they grouped up, they always felt their fear and anger were justified. So Strathern was preparing for a town-wide revolt. And as it turned out, he wouldn't have to wait too long.

About 150 people gathered and marched down Main Street toward Strathern's HQ. Strathern ordered additional soldiers into the area. The group was standing there, screaming obscenities and demanding that Strathern come out of his tent and address them. The crowd kept pushing forward, pressing against the wall of soldiers. When the protesters pushed the soldiers, the troops braced themselves and drove them back. Strathern exited his tent and walked down to the wall of people. He had a bullhorn in his hand. He had a soldier drive a Jeep behind the wall of troops. Strathern stood on the vehicle's hood, facing the crowd.

"Ladies and gentlemen, I suggest you all break this up and go home or about your business immediately, if not sooner," Strathern bellowed through the bullhorn.

The crowd responded with more obscenities.

"You need to get the hell out of our town." With each obscenity someone yelled, the crowd seemed to grow more fervent, shouting louder.

"Okay, people, you will leave us no choice but to calm this situation and disperse this illegal gathering by using force."

More obscenities from the crowd answered Strathern's warning.

"Lieutenant, gas masks!" Strathern commanded.

The lieutenant ordered the men to place their gas masks over their faces. The soldier standing by the Jeep handed Strathern a gas mask. Before placing the mask over his face, Strathern yelled, "Fire the gas!"

The canisters of gas made loud thudding noises as they fired from the soldiers' guns into the crowd. The gas formed a thick cloud of smoke, spreading quickly through the crowd. Panic set in, and the group tried to escape the gas. Terrified people trampled over a woman when she stepped into a pothole, twisted her ankle, and fell to the ground. She was kicked and run over; no one stopped to help her. Strathern ordered his soldiers to begin advancing into the mass of people. As the soldiers pushed into the crowd, several people attacked them. Some successfully pulled the masks off the nearby soldiers, causing those individuals to retreat. But more soldiers advanced into their places, knocking the attackers to the ground. Some soldiers used their weapons to beat down the attackers.

As the tear gas dissipated into a white mist, it formed a light haze that hovered over the town. Soldiers patrolling the area left their masks on until the gas abated entirely. People who could see Main Street from the safety of their homes or stores would later say that the soldiers walking through the haze looked surreal, like something out of a video game. It seemed like time had slowed for those moments, the soldiers' bodies slowly appearing out of the mist. It was frightening to watch.

As the soldiers cleared the streets, Strathern walked in behind them. He slowly walked up to the woman lying on the ground, unconscious. He ordered one soldier to call an ambulance for her. Next, he walked over to a man who had been beaten by a soldier for attacking them. The man was lying on his stomach, barely breathing, his head facing to the side. Blood was pouring out of several wounds on his head and spilling out of his mouth, causing him to cough and choke. Finally, Strathern stopped his boots in front of the man's face. He looked down at the man and sighed, observing all the carnage.

"Now, was all this necessary?" he asked the man. He squatted down and whispered, "You were lucky this time." Then, he stood up and commanded, "Get another ambulance here. Let's clean this mess up!"

Strathern walked down the street and saw a man lying face down, motionless, on the road. He ordered two soldiers to turn the man over and check his vital signs. The man was breathing, just unconscious. Strathern looked at the heavyset man and shook his head in disbelief. The man lying on the ground must have weighed at least 300 pounds. It was Rufus. He must have slipped, fallen, and been trampled by the crowd. Strathern looked at Rufus's bloody face. "Looks like a good reason to join Weight Watchers, don't it, son?" Strathern smirked and walked away.

Bill, Maggie, and Jessica were watching from Jessica's office window.

"I should have been down there," Bill barked.

"And what? Ended up getting tear-gassed and beaten by Strathern's men?" Maggie said.

"I could have done something," Bill lowered his head as he looked out the window.

Jessica spoke up. "Bill, we both know there was nothing you could do. You would have involved your men, who may have gotten hurt too."

Jessica looked at Maggie and Bill. "I called you guys over here because I have something you need to see."

"What is it?" Maggie asked, turning away from the window.

"You both need to sit down and listen to this," Jessica said as she placed a USB drive into a PC on her desk. As per Pete's request, Oz had made a copy of the recording for Jessica to show Bill and Maggie. So they both sat down, and Jessica assumed Oz's position as narrator.

After they finished listening, they just sat there, stunned looks on their faces. Then, finally, Jessica removed the drive from the PC and said quietly, "Look, guys, I know this is a lot to take in, but it explains everything."

Bill looked at Jessica. "So you're saying…what? That we are dealing with an alien invasion? And that's supposed to explain everything?"

Jessica was sitting at her team's table when Pete walked in. He closed the office door behind him.

"Bill," Jessica replied. "I know this stuff is hard to swallow. Pete can tell you I freaked out all over the place last night while I heard the recording."

Bill looked at Pete. "Why are you telling us? Why tell us anything? Why don't you do what you have to do if all this is true?"

"Because I am having difficulty understanding how to deal with the responsibility of Earth's survival. Maybe together we could talk about how I should feel about this. I didn't ask for any of this."

Maggie looked at Pete. "Pete, I'm sorry, but you don't hear this kind of news every day. I mean, it's not discussion material for the breakfast table."

The noise from the riot grabbed Pete's attention. He walked over to look out the window. Thin smoke from the tear gas canisters rolled over the streets. People were screaming and running away from soldiers. Several ambulances pulled up to the corner of the road.

Bill clenched his jaw, "I feel you could have stopped this."

Pete kept looking out the window at the carnage. "Yeah, most likely."

Bill raised his voice. "Then, why didn't you?"

"It's not part of the mission, Bill. It wasn't time for me to go public."

Bill stormed away from the window. "What does that mean? You say this is a mission to help everyone, yet you stand by and let this happen?"

"You must understand that the result we are trying to accomplish goes way beyond Bends Creek."

"But you chose Bends Creek for your damn experiment! So now you're just going to toss us aside for the greater good?"

"I am about to go public with this, Sheriff. As a friend, I wanted to tell you beforehand so you could be ready for repercussions."

Bill walked over to Pete, "I know you mean well, Pete, I do. And I am grateful that you are on our side of this mess. But we can't let innocent people suffer and die because of this. When you go public, people will look to you for guidance. When they see what happened here, they won't think your plan is a great idea."

Pete turned around and faced Bill. "If I had the answers, Bill, I wouldn't need your help."

Maggie finally stood up and joined the conversation. "Look, guys, we must put our heads together and figure this out."

Pete looked at Maggie, "I'm in. But you all have to realize that once the time arrives to go public, I do not have a choice. I am not in control of when this hits the fan."

Bill looked at Pete. "Man, that ship has sailed. It's already on the fan."

"Let's come up with a plan of action that makes better sense than tossing stuff at a fan," Jessica suggested. Everyone looked at each other and started laughing.

"I think we need to involve Oz in this, Pete," Jessica said.

Pete sighed, "I don't know; I don't like her being outside and exposed to too many people."

Oz spoke to Pete. *Do I have a say in this?*

"No," Pete said out loud.

Maggie looked at Pete. "No need to be rude, Pete. Jessica was just making a suggestion."

Jessica smiled at Maggie. "He wasn't talking to me, Maggie."

Maggie's eyes opened wide. She looked at Bill, who was equally confused.

Bill asked, "Wait, there's more?"

Jessica snorted facetiously, "Oh yeah, there's much more."

Bill looked at Pete. "You know, if you want us to help, you have to give us all the information so we can make the right choices here. You can't hold back anything, Pete. We have to know everything. If you and Jessica ask us to believe what you're saying, then we need to know what you know."

Pete, if you trust these guys, what's the problem?

"I don't know, Oz," Pete replied out loud. "I can't do this without you. I can't let anything happen to you."

Aww, Pete, I would cry if I could shed tears.

Pete laughed. "Smartass."

I learned from the best.

Meanwhile, Maggie and Bill were staring at Pete with eyes wide open, neither blinking nor saying a word.

Pete looked at them. "Sorry, I was just talking to Oz."

Bill looked at Jessica, "Really?"

Jessica responded, "Bill, wait a minute, please. And you'd better sit down for this."

Pete held out his hand like he had when he first showed Jessica. Then, Oz came out and got the same jaw-drop reaction from Bill and Maggie as she had from Jessica.

Jessica looked at Bill and Maggie, holding back her laughter, "You guys, okay?"

Maggie and Bill gasped while nodding, not saying a word. Jessica introduced Oz to them. "Bill, Maggie, this is Oz. Oz, Maggie, and Bill."

Oz smiled. "Pleased to meet you guys."

Jessica couldn't hide her massive grin as she watched Maggie and Bill's reaction. They were so busy staring at Oz that they overlooked Jessica. They sat frozen in their seats.

"Look, we can figure all this out and help Pete and Oz. I know we can. Our hearts and heads are all in to help the town. So let's get started."

Maggie and Bill could only manage a short, quick nod. Bill's jaw was still wide as Oz walked across the table and flicked her finger into his jaw. Bill's mouth closed with a popping sound, and Bill looked over to Maggie, his eyes popping out of their sockets. Maggie laughed.

Oz smiled, reached her arm around her back, and patted herself. "Yup, I'm the world's best icebreaker."

19 THE ELEPHANT IN THE ROOM

Jessica asked Oz to explain who she was and provide more details about the Wen to Maggie and Bill. Oz proceeded to describe the Wen, the Vailens, and the Xanoclax as she had for Jessica. When Oz finished, everyone sat in silence for a few minutes. You could hear a pin drop.

Maggie was the first to speak up. "I understand what the Wen are trying to do, but isn't there another way they can do this?" She directed her questions toward Oz. "I mean, you're all supposed to be part of this highly evolved intelligent community, and the best you could come up with is mind control? Couldn't you figure out how to come to the planet and diplomatically get everyone to realize the importance of getting along?"

Bill looked at Maggie. "I don't agree with this either, but look at the trouble we have communicating with each other about racism. It's a very emotional subject, and we can't get past the first five minutes of a discussion without a loud argument breaking out."

"We don't argue all the time."

"No, we don't, but when we come to an impasse in a conversation about racism, you tend to either get real defensive or very political."

"And you don't?" Maggie was visibly starting to get irritated.

Bill approached Maggie, who had risen to stand behind the couch. "Listen, I am not saying you are wrong, or that it's your fault when it happens. I'm just saying it's not an easy subject to talk about, that's all. And maybe the way the Wen approach this is the only way that will work?"

"So, you agree with mind control?"

"No, I'm not saying that. I think human beings need help right now, which might be the only solution."

"I don't like it."

"Neither do I, but what's the solution then? Speaking as a white person and not for anyone else, it's hard for me to communicate with Black people about the subject of race."

Maggie took a few steps back from Bill. "What's that supposed to mean? That Black people don't want to resolve this?"

"No, that's not what I'm saying. But, Maggie, it's hard for a white person to talk about racism because they don't know how to approach the subject. There's a certain amount of fear that we will say something to offend someone. With all the politically correct jargon today, expressing yourself without walking on eggshells is hard.

White people don't see other white people the way Black people understand each other. There is solidarity among Black people that white people do not have or advertise."

"What's that got to do with anything?" Maggie's voice level rose a little. "Seems to me that Elias and other groups like his are all on the same page."

Bill shook his head, "This is the big problem. Everyone focuses on the Elias Stouts of the world. All the extreme racist groups get so much publicity, which makes it look like all white people feel the same extreme way. But that is the furthest from the truth as it could be."

Bill shook his head, "This is my theory: white people do not have a bond with other white people that Black people have with each other, which makes communication that much more difficult to achieve. It's logical for African Americans to assume that all races have this same bond, but they don't. When Black people talk about race issues, they group all white people as a single force that agrees on all issues. But that is not the case."

"That sounds ridiculous. African Americans don't agree on everything. The issues that we do agree on are rooted in fundamental justice and equality. Being treated decently and with respect."

"But not all white people are bad. I believe that the majority of white people want what African Americans want. But grouping them in with the racists will only push them away."

"How else should we get everyone to understand that doing nothing is making a choice? You have white cops mistreating and even killing my people. White politicians are telling people of color to go back to where they came from if they don't like it here. You want more examples?"

Bill raised his voice. "How many times have you heard a white person say 'my people'?"

Maggie straightened her shoulders, "Elias says it all the time."

Bill curled his lip, "See? You're quoting extremists. The non-racist white people have to be included in all efforts to combat racism. African Americans can't fix this by segregating themselves from all white people. Not all white people are racist. And by communicating that we are all racist, it makes us feel that there's nothing we can do to help."

"African Americans do not group all white people as racist."

"When I see African Americans on social media saying white people be like this and white people be like that, how am I supposed to interpret that? Comments like that push white people who want to help eradicate racism away. They don't become racist; they become passive and not proactive."

"You do realize I see the opposite, right? I see white people being hateful to black children for no good reason. I've seen police grab an older woman from a car and throw her on the ground. The examples are endless."

Bill moved slowly toward Maggie, his eyes soft and caring. Bill quieted his tone, "I know, Maggie, it's awful. Social media is probably one of the most unsocial places in the world. I know that different races can get along in this country. I've seen it. But we never see posts of people helping each other or being happy together. As long as we stay on our own side, and you stay on your side, we will never change anything. Maggie, I want to help change everything."

Maggie quelled her anger. She knew Bill was a good person. His openness reminded her of why she was falling in love with him. Her eyes widened, and a tear rolled down her cheek. "You've never told me this before."

Bill wiped the tear from Maggie's cheek, "I am always afraid to bring it up."

Bill paused a moment and continued, "All I know is that the inclusion of all races is paramount to the success of this fight. Racism needs to be dealt with and eliminated by all Americans. It shouldn't be African Americans' battle to fight alone."

Maggie hugged Bill tighter, saying, "We should talk more about this again."

"I agree. Thank you for hearing me out, Maggie. I can't imagine your pain regarding the horrible acts of racism against African Americans. Unfortunately, what I deal with is the result of those acts. If there were something I could do to help change the way people treat each other, I would. You know that."

Oz spoke up. "Excuse me, will you please allow me to say something?"

Maggie walked around one side of the couch, and Bill walked around the opposite side. When they both reached their chairs, Oz began.

"The Wen did not choose sides when they developed this plan for Earth. After all their research, they concluded that human beings quickly pass judgment on one another. Judgments are not logical and only hinder social justice because they cloud the evaluations of social issues.

The Council has based its conclusion on historical facts and logic. Logic states that other measures must be considered if a civilization cannot help itself."

Maggie spoke up. "We are trying to help ourselves."

"Yes, there are many good people on this planet. That's why the Wen wants to help. The problem is that humans are not resolving this issue quickly enough to avoid the Xan invasion. As Bill pointed out, racism is a very personal issue that is difficult to have open discussions about civilly. Look at the two of you. You know each other, trust each other, and care about each other. Even so, it was difficult for you to discuss."

Maggie and Bill looked at each other, and both nodded slightly.

"As a Wen, I can assure you we do not want to control another species. Using what you call mind control does not serve any purpose for us. It is the only logical solution to get everyone on this planet to change together at one time. Like flipping a light switch on the planet, turning on the nice light."

Maggie looked at Oz. "If there were enough time, what would be a logical approach to solving this problem?"

Oz looked at Maggie and smiled. "The logical approach is not to fight and argue about it. Promoting racist acts in the media and on your social networks only provokes rage."

"What's happening is wrong, and those hateful acts must be exposed."

"Yes, it does, but what is the expectation from the publicity of a racial act?"

"To end racism."

"But it doesn't end, does it?"

"No."

"It is illogical to expect that racism will end with the proliferation of negativity. You can't right a wrong by committing other wrongs."

"So, what is logical? Just let it happen and hope it goes away?" Maggie was upset by Oz's response, and her eyes began to water. Bill squeezed her hand.

"Maggie, if you were teaching a class of five-year-old children, and two of these small children were fighting and arguing, how would you handle it?"

"I would pull them aside and explain fighting is wrong."

"If they did not agree and kept fighting, would you give up trying?"

"No. I would keep explaining to both that it is important to get along with everyone."

"Until adults can show this type of patience toward each other and listen with the intent to understand each other, racism will always prevail," Oz spoke in a softer tone now. "Maggie, the end of racism is a difficult task to take on. Unfortunately, in every free and democratic society on Earth, racism exists. Until humans evolve to a higher level of intelligence, racism will always be a part of human life."

"So, there's no logical hope?"

"The most logical path to eliminate racism is to concentrate on specific occurrences. For example, you mentioned the police commit racist acts?"

"Yes, all the time."

"You have publicized these acts, yet they continue?"

"Yes."

"Then, the current approach is not logical. You must concentrate as much energy as possible on the specific location and eliminate the racism."

"How do we do that?"

"By approaching the source with great numbers and demanding change."

Maggie's eyes widened, "Protest?"

"Protesting was the most effective weapon in your country's past. Looking over your history, I found it fascinating that in the 1960s, people communicated with each other a lot more easily than they do today. In the 1960s, no texting, cell phones, or the internet existed. But hundreds of thousands marched into Washington, DC, to listen to Dr. Martin Luther King."

"Our technology has made us complacent."

"Yes. Everyone complains about racism on individual social media pages. However, it's not just racism; political leaders and other current events are persecuted on social media platforms and contribute to the overall segregation of people. Why? So that their few hundred friends will agree with them? How does that further the fight against racism or encourage political change? Everyone should be using social media to get together and fight this common enemy, not each other."

Maggie looked at Oz with tears running from her eyes.

Oz apologized. "I didn't mean to upset you, Maggie."

"It's not you. It's just so painful seeing people of color get treated like they don't belong in a country they helped build. Children are dying for no other reason than the color of their skin. It's unbearable."

Oz responded, "But now the Wen has found a way to turn on the nice switch."

There was a moment of silence, then Jessica spoke.

"Maggie, you okay?"

"Yeah. Sorry if I overreacted."

"No apologies needed. In this room of friends, we should be able to share our thoughts without judgment or apology."

"Thanks, Jessica. I'm good. Let's move on, okay?"

"Okay, then what's next?" Jessica asked. "What should we focus on first?"

Pete responded, "Well, eventually, the Wen will start spreading the affliction, as you've all named it, across the country and the world. They believe there is still time to save the planet if we follow their schedule. But this reaction from the town and military brings up a huge roadblock."

Bill shrugged, "What do you mean?"

"The idea of using the affliction is to promote peace and harmony, so the Xan will see that Earth is not killing itself. But if the next step after the affliction is to cause even more violence, then the plan will be scrapped, and the Wen will leave us to our fate with the Xan."

Bill was still looking at Oz. "Pete, what is your next step in all this?"

Pete looked at Oz, as well. "My guide is supposed to release that information as needed as the plan moves forward."

Oz moved her arms forward with her palms up, "Before you get any ideas, I only receive Pete's orders in small chunks. Then, once he succeeds with one order, they send me another when ready."

"So you don't know what happens next?" asked Bill.

Oz looked at Maggie and joked, "Wow, you broke the bank with this one, huh? He's right on top of this, isn't he?"

Bill threw his hands up, "I was just playing sheriff."

Oz apologized. Bill just smiled and kept silent.

Maggie asked a question. "If you don't know what is coming next, how can we help?"

Pete tilted his head, "I don't know, Maggie."

Jessica said, "Maybe we should focus on Bends Creek right now. How can we improve this and possibly show the Wen that everything is okay?"

Pete cast his gaze around the room. "The whole idea of this experiment is to see if this approach will save humanity. I believe we must decide whether we agree with this plan. I'm not too fond of the whole idea of brainwashing people, but I have to admit I am not sure there is another way to go about this. If we believe the Wen that the Xan are coming, we must ensure that this experiment works in Bends Creek."

Bill joined in. "I don't like what they're doing, Pete. I'm big on free will. I know there are a lot of idiots out there, but we don't get to decide who gets protected. We protect everyone in the same way, both good and bad. So let's make this work."

Jessica and Maggie agreed to help, as well. Maggie stood up and asked, "So, how do we protect the experiment and ensure it's a success?"

"Thank you for your help," Pete said gratefully. "This situation is going to get worse with all the military here. The town will eventually erupt as more and more people band together."

Bill said, "So, my friend, we have a dilemma, don't we? If you interact with this situation, the military will react, and this will get more intense. But if we do nothing, we may lose the opportunity to save our planet because of the military intervention anyway."

Oz spoke up. "Damned if we do and damned if we don't."

"What do you suggest?"

Oz glanced at Pete, then out at everyone else. "Violence begets violence. Nothing good comes from anger, but I am unsure what peaceful remedies we have available."

Jessica agreed with Oz. "She's right; what are our choices here? Pete, you have to do something. What are you thinking?"

Pete lifted his arms while shrugging his shoulders, "I don't know. I am not sure what is appropriate."

Bill leaned forward. "What if we make the military's presence go away?"

Pete looked at Bill. "How?"

Bill developed his idea as he spoke. "Well, from what you have said about the Wen, their tech is far more advanced than ours, right?"

Pete nodded his head in agreement.

"They must have something to help us make the military want to leave. Oz, what can you tell us about what may be available?"

Oz looked at the sheriff. "I'm just a guide. I don't know very much about bio stuff."

"Aren't you a Wen?" Bill pressed.

"Yeah, so?"

"You can speak their language. You can communicate with the Wen."

"It's not like they're on my speed dial list, Bill."

"Maybe you can ask for something that can help? What if they could expose the military to the affliction?"

Pete looked interested. "What outcome do you think that would bring?"

"I am not entirely sure, but they may consider the town contagious and pull the troops out at least."

Jessica became excited, "Pete, this could work. The violence would stop, and the Wen mission would proceed as planned."

Listening to the discussion made Oz apprehensive. She began

pacing back and forth on Pete's leg.

Bill asked Oz, "Don't you report to them?"

"Duh," Oz stopped pacing, dismissing his comment.

Pete looked down at Oz. He picked her up and brought her up to his face. "Oz, there has to be something we can do. You need to let us know if anything is available to us."

"You realize that if I ask the Council questions, they will know we are exposing the plan, right?"

"We can tell them I thought we needed to try to expose the plan a little to ensure its success. The Wen want this to work as badly as we do."

Bill spoke up. "If the Wen want this to work, they should be receptive to this plan, right?"

Pete answered, "Bill, the Wen are highly intelligent lifeforms. They have set events into place that were logically created. These events have predictable outcomes. They rely on that predictability for success."

Oz looked at Pete and lowered her head. Then, in a soft, concerned voice, she asked, "What if I lose you, Pete?"

Pete looked at her. "Look at me. No way that's going to happen. I don't want to be part of this if I can't have you as my guide. Understood?"

Oz nodded, "Thanks, Pete. You're the best."

"I know."

Oz punched Pete in the shoulder. "Damn, you're insufferable." She then addressed the room. "They will be contacting me tonight. We talk, well, I listen, and they talk. Then, after our meeting, I report to

Pete with their instructions."

Pete nodded. "This is good, Oz. That information is excellent. You must tell them I need to speak to them, that it's urgent. Tell them I fear the experiment is in danger."

Oz looked concerned. "You know how they are. Any deviation from their plan is illogical for them."

"I know."

"Okay. It's your butt."

20 FIRST CONTACT

Initially, the Wen placed Pete in an alley and disguised him as homeless as part of their plan. While the mission was developing, Pete would be inconspicuous until he needed to go public. It was logical to keep Pete out of the spotlight until he was needed. Therefore, contacting the Council from a nondescript location they approved was reasonable.

Pete and Oz found a secluded spot in an alley familiar to Pete. He sat in the alleyway against a dumpster tucked in toward the back. Oz told Pete that the Wen expected her to contact them once Pete fell asleep. He made himself comfortable, lodged between the dumpster and the side building. There was a gentle breeze blowing through the alley. Pete thought it seemed like the perfect spot until he caught the smell of rotten fish. The alley was quiet, except for maybe a few stray cats wandering around some trash cans. Finally, he closed his eyes and tried to fall asleep.

Pete wondered if the Wen found him in an alley like this. He always contemplated the same questions every night before falling asleep.

Maybe I was chosen because I had no ties to anyone? No one would miss me.

These thoughts weighed heavily on his mind and would somehow help him fall asleep. He stretched his arms outward and started yawning. He was careful not to inhale too deeply to avoid getting the rotten fish odor in his mouth.

Pete woke up in his dream just a few hours later. He was standing in the dark again, just like the first time he had gone under with Jessica's help. Pete stood still, waiting patiently for what was to come next. He was hoping Oz would appear again. He wondered if this was a dream or if the Wen were summoning him.

"So far, this is bull."

"Your sarcasm is still at one hundred percent, J9-1-7."

The familiar Wen voice caused Pete's mouth to twitch. He caught himself before attempting a sarcastic comeback. He had to pay attention to what he was thinking.

"It's been a long time," Pete answered. He didn't see anything; he stood there talking to the darkness.

"What is so critical that it demands our attention? Contacting us is not part of your mission procedures."

"We need to tweak the plan a little."

"What is this tweak?"

"Tweaking is a human term for making a slight adjustment."

"Why would we need to make any adjustments to the plan? All possible scenarios were analyzed and tested."

"Well, you may have overlooked one possible scenario."

"Impossible."

"Alright, don't get your panties in a bunch. It's human nature we are dealing with here. The possibilities for us to screw up are endless."

"What are panties?"

"That's just a saying; it's not important. My fault. I was sarcastic again. I digress."

"What is this one possibility we may not have seen?"

"Military intervention."

"We considered that. We examined the possibility that the military may desire to weaponize what humans call the affliction, causing unneeded stress."

"Well, there's a little bit more to it."

"What do you mean?"

"With military intervention, the afflicted are going to retaliate and riot. More violence will occur, and people will die and get hurt. If you release the affliction on a global scale, this could result in violence escalating instead of being hindered."

"We have considered this outcome and have determined that global acceptance would outweigh the calculable global violence."

"But we are just beginning the mission. If the test results in violence at this level, there's a chance that the violence will be greater during the next phase of the mission. Around the Earth, different countries will be alerted and prepare for retaliation because we will have incited it."

"I see your point. We trained you well."

"Are you actually going to take the credit for this?"

"What do you propose we do to…tweak this situation?"

"We need to expose the military in Bends Creek to the affliction immediately."

"How will that help?"

"It may cause them to vacate the town, relieving tensions until we take the next steps."

"We will consider your proposal."

"Don't take too long. People are already rioting. The innocent are getting hurt."

"We will get back to you on the next step."

"Wait, this must be at the top of your to-do list. Hello? Hello, Mr. voice alien? Hello…"

"Pete. Pete, wake up." Pete's eyes flew open to see Oz standing on his chest.

"What? They just left. No hint of when or if they will help with this." Pete stood up and kicked an empty trash can.

"They're going to think about it. That's what they do. The Council never rushes into a situation without considering all the possible outcomes."

"Yeah, I know. I guess I was just hoping."

"You understand that hope is not a logical concept for the Wen, right?"

"I know, I know. But I am not a Wen."

"You were trained to think and act like one. So the sooner you succumb to it, the better."

"I'm afraid to lose who I am. I already feel like my humanity is slipping further and further away. I can't remember anything. I feel like I'm just floating through each day without a sense of being. I have no history to recall. I can't believe the universe has chosen this for me."

Oz hopped up onto a trash can. Pete lifted his face to the sky and yelled, "There has to be more!" His body started to energize and glow. The entire alley lit up as the light intensified.

Oz shouted, "Pete! Get a grip! You have to calm down."

Pete fell to his knees. The light slowly dimmed. Pete placed his two hands on the ground before him as he knelt there. He stared down at the ground, never looking up. "Why am I being punished, Oz?"

Oz replied, "Well, you know what I think about this, right?"

"What?"

"When life throws you lemons, you make iced tea!"

Pete turned to the side to see Oz, "You know that's not how it goes, right?"

"Yeah, but it sounded too corny the other way. Needed to change it up a little to make it interesting."

"I don't know what I'd do without you, Oz." Pete leaned back against the trash cans, staring at the night sky.

"Let's hope we don't find out, okay?"

21 WORKING IT OUT

Everyone met back in Jessica's office at the team table the next day. Bill was the first to ask if Pete had a chance to talk to the Council. Pete said that he did and that they would get back to him.

Bill began to grow excited. "Did they say when? So this is a good thing, right?"

Pete shrugged, "They didn't give me a time, Bill. And yes, this is a good thing. They are considering our proposal. I believe they listened because human behavior is a paradox to them."

Bill looked puzzled. "That's a good thing, right?"

"Yes, I believe it is. Human behavior is unpredictable, so the Council understands they must revisit their analysis."

Bill remained positive, "I guess that's something then. We're a little better off than we were yesterday, anyway."

Maggie was curious. "So the Wen that contacted you. Did they look like Oz?"

"I was in the darkness again. I just heard the same voice you heard on the recording."

Standing on the table, Oz explained, "Wen do not have similar shells as humans or other species; we are highly evolved life forms consisting mainly of energy. We assume a shell to communicate with different beings."

Maggie lifted her eyebrows, "How do you procreate?"

"Logically."

Maggie just shook her head. "Yeah…turns out I don't want to know."

Bill laughed at Maggie, kissed her, and walked toward the door.

Maggie asked, "Where are you going?"

"I have to help keep the peace. We need to talk to people and try to prevent them from organizing another riot."

Bill closed the door behind him. Jessica smiled at Maggie. "The town is lucky to have him here."

Maggie sighed, "Yeah, he's one of the good ones."

Maggie stood up. "I must head to the shelter and ensure everyone is okay before I go home."

"Please tell Virgil I'll come by later," Pete said.

"No problem. See you guys later." Maggie walked out and left Jessica and Pete alone.

Pete stood at the window, staring out at the town. Jessica recognized his distant look.

"What's bugging you, Pete?"

"I'm just struggling with a few internal things, that's all."

"Well, why don't we head down to the diner and talk about it?"

"I appreciate you wanting to help, but I don't want to burden you with my mess."

"Stop being a wimp." Jessica smiled. "Let's go." She grabbed Pete's hand and walked out of the room together.

Oz said to Pete, *I really like this girl.*

Pete focused on the hand that Jessica was holding while they walked to the diner. She was talking, but he wasn't listening. He was concentrating on her grip. He knew this gesture meant something, but he couldn't remember what.

Am I supposed to have a feeling about this?

The Council took away all your emotions, Pete. So it would help if you didn't try to see more into this gesture than what it is.

Maybe if I think about it, something will come back to me.

I don't have an answer for you, Pete. But I know you will become unstable if you don't try to accept what the Council has done to you.

The Council eliminated all memories that dealt with emotions, so Pete could not be distracted from his mission. Did holding Jessica's hand imply that there were feelings between them? Whatever the meaning of the gesture was, Pete knew it had to be good. He held Jessica's hand as long as she allowed it. He only let go when they separated to sit across the table from each other in the diner.

Jessica smiled at Pete. "Let's just try to enjoy the moment, okay?" Let's not talk about the Wen or the military or anything else that's going on outside."

"Sure."

The waitress approached their table, and Pete asked for a burger, fries, and a soda. Jessica started reading the menu and speaking Spanish. "Nunca tienen una buena comida picante. Me encantaria un taco picante o un burrito en este momento."

The waitress frowned, "Ma'am, please, I need your order in English."

"Lo siento. I mean, I'm sorry. Sometimes I don't think about it. I'll have what he is having. Thank you."

The waitress put on a fake smile, turned, and walked away with their orders.

"Okay, where were we?" Jessica asked Pete. "Let's start with you and what you are internalizing. Maybe if we talk about it, it will make you feel a little better."

"I guess we can try." Just as Jessica was reaching for Pete's hand, they were interrupted. A burly man strode up and pounded his fist onto their table. The salt and pepper shakers and the metal napkin holder bounced up and crashed onto the tabletop. Jessica jumped back. Pete took his eyes off Jessica to look at the man. He was taller and broader than Pete, but his head was a little small for his body.

"You the piece of crap that put my brothers in the hospital?" The man snarled.

"I assure you I didn't put anyone in the hospital who didn't deserve it." Pete looked away from the man and back at Jessica, ignoring the brute.

The man pounded his fist on the table again, harder than the first. Jessica looked at the man. "Why don't you just return to your coffee and leave us alone?"

The man took his eyes off Pete to glare at Jessica. He leaned in toward her. His frightening stare caused her to pull her hand away from Pete and lean further into the booth.

"Why don't you shut your mouth, Miss Taco?" The man raised his voice at her, laughing in her face. Jessica could smell the tobacco and coffee on the man's breath, making her nauseous.

Before the man could look away from Jessica toward Pete, his feet slipped back from the table. The man's head hit the dining table top with a horrible thud. It sounded as though someone had slammed his head into the table. For a split second, the man's head was on the table; he made eye contact with Jessica, his mouth agape. Jessica's mouth dropped, and her eyes opened wide.

"Whaa–" was all she could say as the man's head bounced off the table. It all happened so quickly. She looked at Pete. He never left his seat, and his eyes never looked away from her throughout the incident. She looked at the man on the floor and back at Pete several times in complete disbelief. She finally calmed down and focused on Pete.

She whispered, "Did you?" She rolled her eyes at the man lying on the floor.

Pete never looked down, still staring at her. "You okay?"

"Pete. Did you do that?" Jessica whispered again, a little more anxious for the answer.

"Wasn't I subtle enough?"

Jessica looked down at the man again and noted that he wasn't moving. He was out cold. Moreover, several people in the dining room were talking and pointing at their table. She stood up and threw a twenty-dollar bill down on the table. She grabbed Pete's hand and pulled him to the door.

"We have to leave now," she said to Pete as they stepped over the man toward the door.

"But what about your coffee?"

"Pete!" Jessica barked in a loud whisper. "Screw the coffee; we need to go. Now."

They stepped out of the diner, walked a few feet, and stopped.

"Why are we stopping?" Pete asked.

"I forgot something at the table. Wait here. I'll be right back," Jessica said as she returned to the diner.

The man was still out cold in front of their table. She looked down at him and then kicked the man several times in the side, yelling, "Taco this, you redneck idiot!"

She looked up at the other people in the diner, straightened herself out, smiled at them, and said, "Have a nice day."

She left the diner and grabbed Pete's hand, "Let's go to my place for coffee, okay? It may be a little safer."

She laughed.

Pete looked at Jessica as they started walking, "Feel better?"

She didn't look at Pete; she continued to stare down the sidewalk in front of them. Finally, she smiled and said, "You know it."

***

Jessica brought Pete a cup of green tea. He was sitting on the edge of one bed. Jessica returned to the desk's coffee maker to start her coffee. There wasn't much in her hotel room regarding food or drinks, but she was glad they had the coffee machine. She walked over to Pete and sat on the edge of the other bed.

"So…you want to tell me how the hell you did that?" she started.

Pete sipped his tea. "I just thought about it, and it happened."

Jessica was curious, "What, you have superpowers or something?"

"I don't know what I have," Pete seemed baffled. "When I want to do something, somehow my mind wills it. It's like I leave my body when it happens."

"What do you mean? How?"

Pete got up and put his cup on the desk. He turned to Jessica, "I thought we weren't going to talk about this stuff?"

"Pete, what you did brings a whole new variable into this. We should try to understand as much as possible to know what we're dealing with here. Then, maybe we will find some answers."

"I'm beginning to feel like I'm one of your assignments you need to figure out."

"No, Pete, I promise you it isn't like that."

"What is it like, then?"

Jessica walked over to Pete slowly. She gently touched his face. Their eyes met. She leaned in toward him and gently pressed her lips to his. Pete's eyes stayed open as they embraced. She slowly pulled away and looked at him. He couldn't take his eyes off her. Her face seemed to glow as she stood before him, smiling. He couldn't respond. He didn't know how to.

Jessica stepped back. She wasn't sure what to make of Pete's reaction. He just stood there, staring at her, not saying a word.

She spoke first. "Pete? You okay?"

Pete did not respond. He was internalizing the moment.

Has this happened before? He asked himself.

Oz spoke up. *It's what you humans call déjà vu.*

What is that?

It's when you feel like you were in the same scenario in the past.

Do I remember a kiss?

Maybe.

Jessica just looked at Pete, who seemed distant. She sighed, "Are you discussing this with Oz? You know that's rude, right?"

Pete snapped out of his trance. "Sorry. Old habits, I guess."

Jessica touched Pete's hair, "You can talk to me, too."

Pete looked at her. "Yeah, I know. It's just, well..."

"What?" Jessica flirted.

"Can we do that again?"

"Absolutely," Jessica laughed and pulled Pete close to her. This time, the kiss was more passionate and lasted a little longer.

Jessica opened her eyes and looked into Pete's. "Was that okay?"

All he could do was nod.

She kissed him again. This time, Pete instinctively put his arms around her and squeezed her tightly. Pete felt amazing. He wasn't sure what it was, but it felt warm and relaxing. He couldn't explain or grasp what he was feeling.

"I don't understand," he finally said to her.

She stayed in his arms, holding him tightly. Her cheek rested on his chest.

"What don't you understand, Pete?" She felt a warmth through her body that she had never felt before. Her mind seemed to have left her body. She was light as air. She didn't want to open her eyes and have this feeling end.

Pete pulled himself away from her slowly. She was still in a relaxed state, and she moved slowly. Jessica's eyes were closed as she tilted her head back. He had to guide her to the bed and sit her down. She sat there and swayed ever so slightly back and forth, her face maintaining the glow as her lips parted slightly. Pete sat on the other bed, facing her. He watched her.

Oz, what is happening?

Oz seemed perplexed. *I don't understand human emotions, Pete. Maybe she is having what they call an orgasm?*

Pete looked at Jessica and said aloud, "I'm not sure what this is. But she appears happy."

Jessica stopped swaying, looked at Pete, and batted her eyes several times. "What happened?"

Pete looked at her. "I was hoping you could tell me."

"I kissed you, and when we embraced, I felt this warm energy run from your body into mine. It was unbelievable. I was totally relaxed, without a care in the world. I have never felt this way before."

Pete stood up. "Is this a bad thing?"

"Hell no. This is good, man!" Jessica laughed, got up, and stepped toward Pete.

Pete looked at Jessica with a confused expression on his face. "Jessica, I can't feel anything. I have not encountered any feelings for as long as I can remember. So I don't know how to respond to your kiss." Pete looked over Jessica and over her again. "The Council removed my ability to feel any emotions."

"I know. That's terrible."

"But it serves the mission. I can't allow any emotions to impede my judgment. You saw what I did to that guy in the diner, right?"

"Yeah, you put his racist ass down."

"But I did it without any emotional baggage whatsoever. I just sensed a threat and acted immediately."

"What's so bad about that?"

"I didn't do it because he insulted you. I didn't do it because he was a racist. I wasn't defending your honor. I just did it."

"How do you know? You said you have never felt anything before. How do you know you didn't react in a very human way?"

Pete was confused. "I don't understand the sensation…maybe it was a feeling. Oz mentioned déjà vu. I don't know. I don't even know if it's a feeling at all."

Jessica turned Pete toward her. She put her hands on his arms and looked into his eyes. "Pete, just let it happen. Don't try to figure it out. The answers will come to you."

"I'm not sure I understand."

"Maybe the Council only took away your ability to feel emotions based on previous experiences."

"What do you mean?"

"Maybe you can learn how to feel based on new experiences that are not a product of your memory."

Oz sighed. *Humans never want to give up and accept the inevitable.*

That is what we call hope, Oz.

Jessica pulled Pete toward one of the beds. She gestured for him to lie beside her. He lay on his back. She went to the other side of the bed and lay down next to him.

"What are you doing?" Pete asked.

"Just relax," she said. "Just lie here and relax. Don't think about anything. Just be with me right now." She snuggled up to him, lifting his arm and putting it around her. She rested her head on his chest.

Pete lay still. He didn't know what to say or do. Instead, Pete felt Jessica's warm body heat as they lay on the bed, fully clothed, and closed their eyes.

***

"Jessica! Jessica, wake up." Oz was pulling on Jessica's shirt.

"What is it, Oz?" Jessica asked, starting to wake up.

"You need to leave the room now!" Oz sounded excited.

"Why?" Jessica got up as Oz, now the size of a full-grown woman, pushed her toward the door. She looked back at Pete, who was still asleep on the bed.

"No questions. Please just leave!"

Jessica left her room and went down to the lobby, heading outside. That's when she noticed the fire alarms were going off, and people were evacuating the motel.

Just as she saw the firetrucks pulling up, she heard a loud explosion inside the motel. She watched as the roof exploded straight up into the air. A fire started immediately, and the firefighters went to work.

Jessica stood there in the crowd, bewildered. Questions began to run through her head. *What just happened? Was that Oz? She was as tall as a full-grown woman. What happened to Pete?*

She began to panic. *Did I somehow cause this to happen? Did I somehow hurt Pete?*

Smoke engulfed the motel. No one could see the building through the thick, black clouds. Someone in the crowd pointed toward it and screamed, "Look, someone is coming out!"

It was Pete. He walked out of the smoke with only a towel wrapped around his body. He looked like he had just come out of the shower. He walked toward Jessica.

Pete leaned forward, holding his towel, "I think I had another memory."

Jessica hugged him. "I am so glad you're okay. What happened?"

"I don't know; maybe Oz can help explain it."

Jessica took Pete's hand and started leading him toward her car. Jessica spoke to Pete as they walked, never looking directly at him. "Yeah, we need to talk about Oz. She ain't so little anymore."

Pete followed Jessica to her car. "Yeah. She doesn't just shapeshift into small objects or beings. Oz can reshape her outer shell to different sizes as needed."

"Let's get you some clothes. Then we can figure all this out, okay?"

"Good idea."

Jessica drove off, leaving the motel and the chaos in her rearview mirror.

It was about a five-minute drive to Maggie's house from the motel. Jessica didn't say a word to Pete as he stared out the car window. She could tell he was trying to figure out what had just happened. Jessica decided to let Pete start the conversation when he was ready. She glanced over at him and caught herself smiling. Jessica turned back to the road. She was happy he was okay.

They rang Maggie's doorbell. Maggie opened the door. She tilted her head, "Do I need to know what happened to your clothes, Pete?"

Jessica rushed Pete into the house. "Can we borrow some of Bill's clothes until we can go to the store?" Jessica asked, standing next to Pete in Maggie's living room.

"Sure. Come on up to the bedroom and pick some out."

As Jessica went through Bill's clothes, Maggie asked Pete, "Is there something I need to know?"

"Well, the motel is on fire right now–"

"What?!" Maggie interrupted. "Are you responsible? How bad is it?"

Jessica answered from inside Maggie's closet, obscured from Maggie's view. "Well, it kind of blew up."

"Kind of what? What happened?"

Pete looked at Maggie. "Everyone is okay. Nobody got hurt."

"Okay, that's a good thing," Maggie answered Pete. She raised her voice and spoke to her closet door. "Are you going to tell me what happened?"

Jessica came out with a flannel shirt and a pair of jeans. She looked at Pete. "You may have to roll up the jeans a little, but this should be okay until we get to the store."

"Jessica!" Maggie raised her voice.

"Qué?"

"Are you going to answer me?"

Jessica handed the clothes to Pete, and he went into the bathroom to change. Jessica looked at Maggie. "Let me tell you what happened."

"Thank you." Maggie sat on her bed. Jessica was standing a few feet in front of her.

"Pete and I were in my motel room, lying in bed."

Maggie pulled her head back, "Excuse me?"

"No, we didn't have sex. We were sitting on the bed, fully clothed. We kissed a few times and decided—well, I decided—we should go to bed."

"Jessica, you need to slow down because this sounds exactly what it sounds like to me."

Jessica was pacing. She was still coming down from the gamut of extreme emotions she had just experienced: the ultra-high being next to Pete and the ultra-low, when she thought he was hurt, were difficult to digest.

"Yeah, I need to calm down a little," Jessica agreed and sat next to Maggie.

"What's going on?"

Jessica looked at Maggie. "We were just lying on the bed, fully clothed," Jessica repeated, ensuring Maggie understood. "We fell asleep, and it was so wonderful."

Maggie could tell Jessica was drifting off. "Honey, stay with me. We can do the girl talk later. Please tell me what happened to the motel."

Jessica laughed. "You're right, sorry." Jessica relayed the story to Maggie, pausing to answer Maggie's questions. Jessica also revealed to Maggie that Oz's capabilities are not limited to her size, as she previously thought. "That's how she could drag me out of bed."

Pete walked in, dressed now in Bill's clothes. "Everything burned in the fire. I was lucky enough to grab a towel on my way out."

Maggie stood up and looked at Pete, then at Jessica, then back at Pete. "So now you're saying you're...what? Fireproof?" She looked at Jessica. "Did you know about this?"

Jessica leaned back onto her elbows on Maggie's bed, "No way. I just found this out myself."

"So, now what?" Maggie asked.

Jessica asked, "Can we crash here until we figure out where we can stay?"

"So, it's *we* now?" Maggie turned and looked at Pete.

He lifted both hands to his sides, his palms facing up, and shrugged.

"Yeah, I have a spare room. I also have a couch that opens into a bed if needed."

Jessica laughed. "You're playing mommy now?"

Maggie looked at the two of them as they stood side by side. "You guys have to be careful, okay?"

Jessica asked why, and Maggie continued, "Look, I'm not saying you two being together is bad, but you don't even know if that's possible. Am I right, Pete?"

Pete looked down at his feet, took a moment, and looked at Jessica. "Maggie is right. We need to figure all this out."

Jessica took Pete's hand. "We will, I promise. But I want to be able to help you figure it out, okay?"

Pete nodded. Maggie walked out of the room, and they followed her. They went to the kitchen and sat at the table. Maggie started to boil some water.

"So now what?" she asked as she put their cups on the table.

Pete sighed. "To be honest, I'm not sure. I want to ensure the town is okay and the plan is moving forward. The mission should be the only priority for me right now."

"Why do I feel like there's a 'but' coming?" Maggie asked as she stood by the stove, waiting for the water to boil.

Pete went on, "But... I am beginning to understand what I'm going through."

Maggie looked surprised. "Really? That's good."

"I'm not sure if it is or not. Jessica sparked something inside of me. I can't determine whether it's older feelings or a new experience. But I believe I returned to the beginning when we fell asleep."

"Beginning of what?"

"I think I was where the Wen first began their project on me."

"Wow, that's good! Did you recognize anything?"

"Just the darkness."

"I don't understand." Maggie looked puzzled.

Jessica said, "The Wen kept Pete in total darkness the entire time. I can't even imagine what that could have been like."

Maggie stood up, went to the stove, and picked up the kettle. "Pete, are you having trouble remembering because you're afraid to revisit that experience?"

Pete watched the hot water as it poured into his cup. He stared at it, then looked up at Maggie. "I'm not sure. I can't feel emotions."

Maggie finished pouring Jessica's hot water. "Oh yeah, sorry. That's what we heard on the audio, right?"

"Yes. But when Jessica kissed me, I had what Oz called déjà vu."

"Did you remember something?"

"Not a specific place or person. I had what I thought was a feeling I must have felt before the Wen did this to me. I don't know how to explain it. I don't know if it was a feeling or a reaction from my training."

"What about the dream?"

"Well, it's coming to me in pieces." Pete looked at Jessica. "You are helping me. I've never had this dream before."

Jessica smiled and nodded.

Maggie wanted to know more. "Pete, what happened after your dream? Did you have anything to do with that explosion?"

Pete looked at Maggie. "I think so."

"How?"

"I'm not sure since this has never happened before."

"Can we ask Oz? I think you need to understand the consequences of trying to reawaken your memories."

Pete held out his hand, and Oz solidified from the blue liquid.

Jessica and Maggie both greeted Oz, who waved up at them.

Pete asked Oz, "Can you explain what happened?"

Oz hesitated. Pete looked at her. "What is it?"

Oz was visibly nervous, "Well, the more we talk about it, the more dangerous it gets for us, Pete."

"I told you we will always be together."

"Not if the Wen Traa'zels find out. They can end the whole mission."

Jessica raised her eyebrows, "Traa'zels? Who are they? What will these Traa'zels do, Oz?"

"They are the actual scientists responsible for this mission. Together, they are referred to as the Council. If they abort the mission, they will assimilate me back into Wen society."

"What would happen to Pete?" Jessica grew restless.

"He would be terminated permanently. The Traa'zels do not take failure very well."

"What the hell, Pete?!" Jessica yelled at him. "Did you know about this?"

Pete looked at Oz and then at Jessica. "I knew that if I didn't complete the mission, there would be uncertainties regarding what would become of me."

Jessica was irritated, "Doesn't that worry you?"

Pete looked at Jessica. "I am not sure if it does or not."

"Sorry," Jessica apologized, "I should have been more sensitive to your situation."

Oz pleaded, "This is why there can be no emotions involved. Look at you. You're like, what is it called? A basket case? Yeah, that's it. A freaking basket case."

Jessica nodded. "I get your point, Oz."

Oz glared at Pete, "Look, if the Traa'zels figure out that we have been sharing our knowledge with anyone external to the mission, they will pull us out immediately. So we have to be careful, Pete. Do you understand?"

Pete shrugged, "Oz, the only way they will find out is if you tell them."

"They can find out anything they want from me without me agreeing to tell them. Hello? Wen technology, remember? Pete, you have to call for me now. I have shut you out, so I don't hear what's happening. The less involved I am, the better." Oz snapped her finger and disappeared.

What was that? Pete asked Oz.

Do you like that? I learned that from my studies on Earth magic. It was cool, right?

Yeah, Oz, it was cool.

Jessica asked Pete if he could explain the explosion.

"It has to do with Wen technology. They may have some alarm set up."

"Like a burglar alarm?"

"Yes. If I am immersed in memory too long, energy builds up. It explodes, damaging my sensors and preventing me from remembering what I just discovered."

Jessica was perplexed, "But you remembered. How is that possible?"

"It was Oz; she redirected the energy so that it exploded in the room instead of inside my head."

Maggie got up from her chair and walked to the sink.

"Jessica, we need to talk, please." Maggie walked out of the kitchen and into the living room. Jessica followed.

"What's up?" Jessica asked.

Maggie looked back at the kitchen and watched Pete sipping his tea. She softly addressed Jessica, almost whispering, "Jessica, listen to me. You have to leave Pete alone."

"Why?"

"He is very dangerous."

"What do you mean by that? He wants to help us."

"I don't mean dangerous in a bad way. But he's capable of stuff we could never understand. Hell, Jessica, he's not even sure if he understands it."

"He wants our help, Maggie."

"We can help him by not getting too personal with him. Honey, he needs to be communicated with on a technological level. At the very least, we should let people who know more than we do about technology connect with him."

Jessica frowned, "I won't turn my back on him."

"I'm not asking you to turn your back on him. But what if someone dies the next time Pete has an experience with you? Will you be able to live with that? What happens after that?"

Jessica lowered her head, "I don't know." What Jessica did know was that Maggie was right.

Pete knocked on the kitchen wall before walking into the living room. "Can I join?"

Maggie said, "Of course, Pete."

"Look, I think you're right, Maggie."

Maggie raised her eyebrows, "How much did you hear?"

"Everything," Pete said. "You know, alien technology and all."

"You see, Jessica?" Maggie shook her head. "This is what I'm talking about. Pete can hear through the walls. This is way beyond us. He needs to talk to people who can give him answers based on tech."

Jessica looked at Pete. "Pete, do you want to meet with anyone from the tech community? Maybe that's part of the mission anyway. You must explain what is happening to the world soon, right?"

Pete noticed Maggie and Jessica had concerned looks on their faces. "Look, you have been involved way beyond what you should have. Why don't I return to the alley and await my next orders?"

"Pete, we don't want to abandon you. We just want to ensure you get the right help," Maggie reassured Pete.

"I know, Maggie. You all mean well. I don't have any receptors telling me otherwise. But Oz was right; if I continue to include you guys, the Wen may think the mission is compromised and terminate it."

Jessica felt helpless, knowing it was useless to disagree, "So, what now? What do you want to do now? Go back to sleep in the alley?"

"That was part of the plan. I was to be homeless. That way, no one would pay attention to me, and we could focus on the mission. Besides, we should get an answer soon about how to proceed with the military issue. I don't want anyone getting hurt because of me."

Jessica knew Pete was right. She didn't like it but knew she had to let it go for now.

"Okay, but can we at least go to the store and get you some new clothes? I'm sure Bill won't appreciate you sleeping in an alley while wearing his."

"Sure."

Pete and Jessica started to leave. Pete left first; as Jessica moved to walk through the front door, Maggie grabbed her hand. They looked at each other, and Maggie hugged Jessica.

Maggie spoke softly into Jessica's hair, "It's all going to work out. It has to."

"Thanks," Jessica nodded and caught up to Pete.

After they spent some time getting Pete's clothes, Jessica drove to Pete's alley. She parked a few blocks away. "Will you be going to the shelter later?"

215

Pete opened the car door. "Most likely. It's the logical progression that the Wen would expect."

"Pete, please let me know if there is anything I can do to help, okay?" She reached over and hugged Pete. That same warmth she felt before was still there.

Pete waited a moment, thinking Jessica's gesture would cause some kind of reaction within his mind, but nothing happened. He sensed he should return her kindness, but didn't understand how. Pete didn't feel anything, not even Jessica's intentions. After a moment, he pulled away slowly. Pete got out of the car and closed the door behind him. He leaned down to the open window and looked in.

"Jessica, you will always be the first human being I will think of if I need anything." And with that, he walked toward the alley.

Jessica watched Pete walk to the alley before making a U-turn to drive back to Maggie's.

22 TEAMWORK

Pete met Bill, Maggie, and Jessica the following day in the team room. They were all anxious to hear what Pete had to say about his meeting with the Wen.

Pete was walking through the door when Bill ambushed him. "Did they come up with something to help?"

Maggie shouted at Bill. "Damn, Bill, give the man a chance to get his tea and sit down."

Bill stepped back from Pete, "Sorry, Pete. I'm just a little nervous, that's all."

Pete sat at the table across from Jessica. They looked at each other, and he turned to Bill. "Yes, I have some news."

Pete sipped some of the tea that Maggie put in front of him. "Thanks, Maggie." He put the cup on the table and looked at Bill.

Without expression, he said, "I am not sure you will like their response."

"Give it a shot, please."

"Okay. The Wen agreed to impose the affliction on the military as we requested."

Bill was getting more anxious, "Nice. So far, so good."

"After they are afflicted, I am to stay away from them."

Jessica was surprised. "What? Why?"

Pete explained, "I cannot be involved with manipulating this project's outcome in any way."

"It has to be a natural transition," Maggie reasoned. "The Wen will not be here forever. They want to see if we can take this process on our own."

Pete looked at Maggie. "Have you been talking to Oz?"

"Of course not. It's just a logical assumption," Maggie smiled, sipping her tea.

Pete continued, "This will happen later today. I am telling you this ahead of time so you can prepare. I am not supposed to be here; I must return to where the Wen expects me."

Jessica followed Pete out. Standing outside the building, Jessica asked Pete, "You doing okay?"

Pete answered that he was and turned to walk away.

"Pete," Jessica called to him.

Pete turned around. "Yes?"

Jessica shook her head. "Nothing, never mind. Talk to you later."

Pete turned back around and left, never looking back. Jessica watched him walk down the sidewalk until she couldn't see him anymore. She went back up to the team room. After Pete's non-reaction to her calling him, keeping her emotions in check was challenging. Jessica knew the Wen took away his ability to feel her intentions, but knowing that didn't make it easier.

As Jessica walked into the team room, Bill was pacing.

Maggie looked at Jessica. "Can you please help me calm this man down?"

"What's up, Bill?" Jessica asked.

"Guess I'm a little anxious. I'm not sure what I should do right now."

"We must let this play out, so why don't you sit down and relax? We're all anxious but don't know anything yet, so we can't act."

Bill continued his restlessness, "Yeah, I know. I want this to go well, that's all."

"We all do, Bill," Maggie said. She gestured for Bill to sit down, and he reluctantly took his seat.

"And do not tap your feet or shake your damn leg, please," Maggie barked.

Bill sat briefly before getting up and walking to the window. He turned around, holding his hands up and palms facing Maggie. "I'm okay. I'm just looking."

Maggie walked up next to him and looked out the window as well. He put his arm around her shoulder, and she put her arm around his waist. They stood there together, staring out the window.

Jessica watched them. She was missing the warmth that she felt when she had hugged Pete. She closed her eyes and thought about lying with Pete on her bed. It brought a smile to her face. She got up and walked to the other window.

None of them realized an hour had passed as they stood there, staring out the windows in silence. Then, finally, Rayburn ran into the room and startled everyone. He looked concerned.

"Bill, thank God I found you."

"What's up, Rayburn?" Bill looked surprised.

"I think we're in deep. The affliction has struck again. Strathern and the soldiers are all part of this now. The soldiers are freaking out. Some are deserting, and others are, well, damn, Bill, come see for yourself."

Bill looked at Maggie and Jessica, and they all nodded. Bill left with Rayburn. Maggie turned to Jessica. "Let's keep our fingers crossed."

"We have to hope the military sticks to its protocol. God forbid they decide to have a conscience now," Jessica replied.

Bill walked down to Strathern's tent. It was empty. Bill motioned to Rayburn that Strathern wasn't there. They started to walk toward the Main Street gate, hoping to find Strathern, when they heard a mob of voices.

As Bill approached the gates, he saw hundreds of soldiers clustered in a confused mass. Bill and Rayburn made their way through the swarms of soldiers. They came to a Jeep in the center of the chaos. On top of its hood stood Strathern with his bullhorn.

"I need everyone at attention, and platoon leaders take control of your men, now," Strathern spoke in a nonauthoritative tone, not his usual harsh, commanding voice.

Bill was shocked to hear Strathern speak as if he were surrendering his position. He noticed that no one heeded Strathern's command. Every soldier was talking and ignoring him: some were scared, some were kneeling, praying, and others were celebrating.

Bill noticed that the soldiers acted precisely like the townspeople did the first day the affliction started. He immediately looked for the group that was just as confused as he had been. He wanted to gather all the non-afflicted soldiers first, as they had done in town that first day.

He found one lieutenant who was standing in shock. "Lieutenant," Bill grabbed the lieutenant by the shoulder. "What do you see?"

The young lieutenant looked confused as he turned to Bill. "Sir, I see soldiers acting confused and scared."

"Do you notice anything about the soldiers physically that has changed?"

"No, sir. They're just acting strangely."

"Okay, now listen to me. If you want to make sure no one gets hurt, we need to gather the soldiers who see what you see."

"Sir?"

"What color is my skin, lieutenant?"

"You're white, sir, same as me."

Bill pulled the lieutenant over to an African American soldier, "And this soldier?"

"He's an African American, sir."

"Okay, but what color is his skin?"

"Black, sir."

"Alright, let me give you the quick and dirty soldier. Your men and commanding officers are afflicted. The same thing happening in town is happening to everyone out here."

The lieutenant started to panic. "What do we do now, sir? What happens next? Is it contagious?"

"Calm down, soldier, get a grip. We're going to help everyone get through this. I need you to find everyone else who is like you—not afflicted. Can you please do that?"

"Yes, sir."

"Good. We need to separate the non-afflicted from the afflicted. Bring all the non-afflicted soldiers to the field over yonder. Spread the word and get the non-afflicted soldiers to help you gather the others. Can you do that?"

"Yes, sir. I'm on it."

Bill and the lieutenant separated. Bill headed toward Strathern. He was now sitting on the hood of the Jeep. Strathern looked worn down and lethargic, shaking his head. The bullhorn was sitting on his lap. Bill felt sorry for the colonel but knew he had to act quickly.

"Sir, we need to get you into the tent. Rayburn? Please escort the colonel to his tent and wait for me there."

Rayburn took Strathern by the arm and escorted him to his tent. The shocked look on Strathern's face affected Rayburn. Gone was the stoic, confident stone face. In its place was confusion and fear. Rayburn felt sorry for Strathern.

"Colonel, it's going to be okay," he told Strathern as they walked. Strathern looked at the mayor. They stopped walking. He turned back, then looked at Rayburn again. His confidence, his true strength, was diminished. Strathern just nodded, and they continued walking to the tent.

Bill stood on the Jeep's hood and spoke through the bullhorn. "Listen up. If you calm down and listen, I can explain what's happening."

The crowd of soldiers began to quiet down a little. Bill spoke again, "Yes, please, that's it. Calm down now."

One soldier yelled out angrily, "Did we catch this crap from your town?"

The other soldiers became restless again. Bill knew he needed to deflect the blame away from the town. If the soldiers believed Bends Creek was responsible, they might get violent. Bill looked over toward the other side of the barricade. His deputies and some other part-time sheriff's department volunteer deputies had gathered, awaiting his orders.

Bill picked up his radio and spoke to Randy. "I need you guys to walk through the crowd and gather all the weapons. Don't draw any attention to what you're doing. I don't want them to get paranoid."

"Got ya, Sheriff, we're on it."

As Randy and the other deputies waded through the crowd, picking up weapons, Bill began to speak to the soldiers. He wanted to get their full attention. It would make it easier for his deputies to confiscate the guns.

"Look at me, soldiers," Bill demanded. "I am a vet. I served two tours in the Middle East. You can trust me."

The crowd of soldiers started to calm down again. The majority were fixated on Bill now.

"I will not lie to you. I will be straight with my brothers." That got a cheer from the crowd. "This thing you are experiencing is not fatal. It is not contagious; you cannot catch it from each other or from anyone else."

Bill had their attention now.

"Listen, there are some of you who are not afflicted. The non-afflicted are gathering in that field over there."

Bill saw some of the soldiers from the crowd head over to the field. The numbers moving to the area made Bill feel better. The crowd that remained was going to be a bit more manageable now.

One of the afflicted group soldiers yelled at Bill, "What are we supposed to do now?"

"We all need to step back and try to work with this. It takes a little while to adjust. I give you my word that you will be okay. Several agencies and scientists from all over the world are working on this. We will figure this out."

Bill felt a little better as the soldiers started to understand the situation.

"You should all now return to your tents and await orders from your colonel. He is talking to DC now, and I am sure they will have a plan."

The soldiers started to disperse and head to their tents. Bill noticed that a few still held onto their weapons. Randy looked at Bill and pointed to the soldiers who remained armed. He was asking Bill if he should retrieve those weapons as well. Bill shook his head and waved Randy and the other deputies off.

Bill walked over to the field where the non-afflicted soldiers were gathered. The lieutenant walked up to Bill.

"I believe this is all of us, sir," he said.

"Thank you, lieutenant. What we must do next may be difficult for all of you to grasp."

"What's that, sir?"

"By the looks of it, the non-afflicted outnumber the afflicted right now."

"Yes, sir, it looks that way."

"Lieutenant, you know all the men far better than I do. You need to look at this situation and decide what we need to do. I can't tell you or your men what action to take next. That has to come from you."

"I understand and concur, sir." The lieutenant saluted Bill.

Bill saluted back and nodded.

The lieutenant did an about-face and ordered his men to file into place.

Bill turned and walked away. As he walked toward Strathern, Randy intercepted him. Bill advised him to take the military truck they had used to store all the guns into town and place a 24/7 guard.

Bill walked into Strathern's tent. He was sitting at the table with his head buried in his arms. Bill looked at Rayburn.

Bill strode to the chair in the corner of the tent and picked up Strathern's gun belt from it. He handed it to Rayburn and told him to give it to Randy.

After Rayburn had left, Bill addressed the situation with Strathern, "Colonel, we need to talk."

"What about?" Strathern's voice sounded muffled as he spoke directly into the table.

"Sir, we need to call your superiors and get new orders on how to deal with this."

"You haven't called DC yet?" Strathern asked, his voice still obscured by the table and his arms.

"No, sir. That's not my place or anyone else's. This is your command, sir. It has to be you."

Strathern lifted his head and looked at Bill. "I thought you people would get some satisfaction from all this."

"No, sir. No one benefits from this mess." Bill looked at Strathern as the colonel stood up. He walked around the table and came face-to-face with Bill.

"Once a soldier, always a soldier, eh?"

Bill stood a little straighter. "Sir, yes, sir."

The colonel smiled at Bill. "I'm lucky you're in charge of this mess, son. I need a soldier I can count on to help me weather this storm."

"Whatever I can do to help, sir."

"Thanks, Bill. I guess we head to the mayor's office and get the Pentagon on the phone."

"My thinking exactly, sir."

They both walked out of the tent. Strathern stopped and straightened his uniform.

"Sheriff?" He looked at Bill.

"Sir?"

"Good move on confiscating the weapons." Strathern smiled at Bill. He turned and headed to Rayburn's office. Bill just nodded and walked beside the colonel.

***

Strathern and Bill walked into Rayburn's office. Jessica and Maggie were there, talking with Rayburn. They stepped aside to let Strathern make his way to the mayor.

Strathern proceeded to address him. "Sir, we have a situation that I am sure you are aware of."

"Yes, Colonel. I was down there," Rayburn responded.

"I need to call Washington immediately on our secure direct line. Please type the code into the phone lock device for me."

Rayburn went over to the secured phone. The phone was enclosed in glass and didn't have a keypad. It reminded Rayburn of the Bat Line in Commissioner Gordon's office from the Batman TV show. Only this phone was black and not red. There was a small keypad lock on the side of the glass case.

"I need the code, Colonel."

The colonel looked at Rayburn. "It's J917."

Maggie, Bill, and Jessica looked surprised. Jessica gasped a loud, hard gasp that caught the colonel's attention.

"You okay, ma'am?"

"Yes, sir, I am. Thanks for asking." Jessica walked over to where Bill and Maggie were standing.

Bill whispered, "Not now."

The colonel picked up the phone as it rang at the general's office. Strathern put the general on speakerphone and explained the situation.

"My God, Grant. Are you afflicted as well?"

"It appears so, sir."

"What the hell am I supposed to do with this crazy mess?"

The general's angry voice was getting louder. Bill thought the speaker was going to blow. He felt he needed to say something in support of Strathern.

"General, this is Sheriff Jackson. If you can give the colonel a little more time to adjust to the situation, he may be able to figure this out."

"Sir," the general spoke. "I appreciate that you want to help, but this situation needs immediate action."

"Yes, sir; the colonel has separated the non-afflicted and afflicted soldiers. They are patrolling the perimeter and helping the other men to adjust, sir."

"Grant? Why didn't you say something?"

Strathern looked at Bill. "Sir, this has been a little overwhelming, and I guess I didn't feel it necessary to mention it now. My apologies, sir." Strathern never took his eyes off Bill. Then he nodded, and Bill nodded back.

The general was still on fire. "Well, let me speak to the CDC representative. Is she there?"

Jessica moved closer to the phone. "Yes, sir, I'm right here."

"Can you tell me how long you think this will last?"

"No, sir. Our department has not found anything out yet."

"Good God, Almighty!" the general screamed out. "Does anyone know what the hell is going on?"

Rayburn spoke up. "General, I do not believe we can afford to let the military stay inside the town."

"I am sure this is the freaking mayor speaking, am I right?"

"Yes, sir."

"And why can we not afford to let the military stay inside the town?"

Before Rayburn could answer, Strathern spoke up.

"Sir, the Pentagon will not send more troops for fear the new troops will also be infected."

"What's your point, Grant?"

"General, we must concentrate all our efforts on our troops' adjustment to this situation. I am unsure if we will have enough non-afflicted men to do both tasks. I do not want weapons in the hands of the afflicted soldiers until they are fully adjusted. Right now, they blame the town for what happened to them. The soldiers need to stay away from the citizens of Bends Creek."

"Your point, quickly!"

"I believe we can hold the outside perimeter and care for the afflicted soldiers with what we have right now. We already have men deserting in fear. We need to spend time with the remaining troops to help them adjust so they will stand their ground. I believe the CDC will be willing to help with this, sir."

Jessica nodded her head in agreement.

"For God's sake, Grant. Get this started and get me an update by 0800 tomorrow."

A big popping noise burst through the speakerphone when the general slammed his phone to hang up. Bill thought for sure the speaker had blown out.

Everyone stood in the room and looked at each other without saying a word. It was a quiet and awkward feeling.

Maggie spoke first. "What just happened?"

Strathern looked at everyone, "I guess this was us working together. You know, you always remember your first time."

They all laughed. Strathern shook everyone's hands and thanked them for their support. He asked Bill to walk him out of the office. When they reached the lobby door, Strathern spoke.

"Sheriff, I appreciate what you did for me in there."

"Once a soldier, always a soldier, sir," Bill replied.

"I'm going to give the order to pull out of town. I'd appreciate it if Morales could have her team down at the external camp in a few hours to get started."

"She'll be there, sir."

"Thanks again," Strathern said as he walked out the door and headed back toward his tent.

Bill returned to Rayburn's office and saw Rayburn, Maggie, and Jessica with glasses in their hand, ready for a toast.

Maggie brought Bill a glass. "Let's toast to our first time."

They all sipped at their glasses and started laughing.

When they finished the first glass, Rayburn started pouring everyone another. Bill looked at Jessica.

"You'd better hold off. The colonel wants your team to be at the camp in about two hours. He's very anxious to get this started."

Jessica put her glass down. "Absolutely." She walked out the door to gather her team.

Bill looked at Rayburn and took the glass from him. "Rayburn, we're done celebrating. We have to tell people that the troops are leaving town."

Rayburn walked around his desk, heading toward the door on his way to the radio station to make the announcement. He grabbed the bottle of liquor that they had been drinking off the coffee table and hugged it with both hands. There was no way Bill was getting the bottle away from him. Rayburn headed out of the office.

Maggie looked at Bill. "Holy crap! Bill, our plan is working."

Bill smiled at her. "So far, no one has been hurt. So yeah, it's a great start."

"You sound like you're not sure our plan will work."

Bill narrowed his eyes, "It's not that. I'm just cautious, that's all."

Maggie giggled, "Well, you can be cautious for both of us. I feel terrific about this."

Maggie hugged Bill. While they embraced, Bill looked out the window at Rayburn, walking down the street toward the radio station. Bill allowed himself a smile when he saw Rayburn skipping along his way.

23 ON THE OUTSIDE

Unsurprisingly, the internet blew up with the news about the Bends Creek soldiers. The world's curiosity swelled, and everyone from around the globe wanted answers. Online discussion forums were popular, but people everywhere wanted to hear about the affliction from those afflicted. In addition, everyone wanted to know what it was like to be in Bends Creek.

The military decided to hold Elias Stout for questioning and observation. Pressure from various scientific and political groups to allow Elias to speak publicly got the president's attention. The military received a direct order from the White House to escort Elias to various public speaking forums. Their instructions included protecting Elias and always keeping him in their custody.

Elias thought he was the most important man in the world, as a whole military escort accompanied him to an auditorium at the local university for a special broadcast. He was seated on a stage with various people, including scientists from all around the world. People from everywhere were watching this event as it streamed across the internet. Elias Stout had never felt this important.

Here he was, Elias Stout, a poor white Mississippi boy who was suddenly now the center of the world's attention. He was excited that people were paying attention to him. People in the audience shouted Elias' name, and he waved back. Everyone wanted to hear what he had to say; he was enjoying his moment in the spotlight.

Questions from the panel on stage and the audience were numerous. They even allowed people from across the globe to ask questions online. The discussions went on for a few hours. After the time was up, while everyone exited the auditorium, two soldiers escorted Elias to a military vehicle. People outside were screaming at him as he walked to his car. He felt like a celebrity. Elias Stout entered the car and waved at the crowd from inside it.

After they pulled away, he sat back in his seat. He only then noticed that a military man was sitting next to him.

"You a general or somethin'?" he asked.

"Yes, sir. I am General Robertson. I am here to escort you personally to your next stop."

"Next stop? I thought we were goin' to my hotel room?"

"No, sir. We have one more stop to get to."

"Okay," Elias smiled. He poured himself a glass of the bourbon inside the car. "Want a drink, General?"

"No, sir, not while I'm on duty." The general smiled.

Elias laughed. "Okay, then. More for me." Elias poured more into his glass and raised it, saluting the general. The general nodded.

The car drove off, and Elias Stout was never seen in public again.

24 REVELATION

Strathern and his men were adjusting quickly. Jessica's team had worked with them over the past two days and was already seeing progress. The men started accepting and learning to live and work with the affliction. Strathern seemed to have the most difficulty.

"I never saw myself as a racist before," he confided in Jessica. The two of them were alone in his tent. "I mean, I never supported supremacist groups. I'm not saying these groups didn't approach me to join because they did. But I never accepted, didn't believe it was right."

"Colonel," Jessica responded carefully, "this affliction doesn't mean you're a racist."

"What else could it mean?" The colonel asked, confused.

"Maybe it's just taking your ability to judge others away. Maybe when we look at someone, we form an opinion based on what we see instead of understanding who we see."

"That still sounds like racism."

"Well, I have been the victim of racist assholes all my life. I have come to learn there is a difference between a racist and somebody who doesn't understand a person who is different than themselves."

"I guess I am as dumb as I look," the colonel laughed. "I need to be educated on this subject."

"Well, a racist individual thinks his race is superior to another. Therefore, other races are inferior to him, no? He believes that people who are dissimilar in color and religion possess characteristics or abilities specific to that race of people, right? So, they focus on these characteristics and distinguish them as inferior. Their sole purpose is to eradicate or control other non-similar individuals."

"I still don't think I see the difference."

"We all notice differences in each other, Colonel. We are human. I notice you're white. You notice I'm Hispanic."

"Not anymore."

"You know what I mean," Jessica went on. "It's how we handle those observations that make us racist or not."

"Please go on."

"Okay. If I look at you and I feel like Hispanics are better than you just because you're white, that would be considered racist. But suppose I notice you are white and I observe you are confused about how to deal with me because I am Hispanic. In that case, that's what I consider understanding the differences."

"It's all about thinking I'm better than someone else?"

"Yes, Colonel. Noticing differences is okay, but judging someone on their appearance is not. We need to celebrate our differences, not condemn them."

Strathern shook his head, "So I guess I screwed that one up, huh? I'm paying for it now."

"Colonel, you are not alone in facing this sensitive subject. Judgments have become cemented into the foundation of our society. Our social foundation allows individuals to benefit from a racist society without being racist. Over the past few hundred years, systematic racism has controlled our social makeup and identity. The processes and rules put into place have benefited like-minded individuals. For example, people in positions of power, such as hiring future employees, have hired individuals who look like themselves and believe the same way they do. This dogma has been in place for a few hundred years or more. It will require everyone to unite and get this country on the right path."

Strathern tilted his head and pressed his lips, "So my white privilege is that I have benefited from a system constructed to promote my race and hinder others?"

Jessica nodded, "Basically, yes. As a military man, you must notice the disparity in the number of white officers to officers of color."

"Yes, I notice."

"And has that bothered you?"

Strathern lowered his head, "No, I can't honestly say it has."

Jessica smiled at Strathern, "Colonel, your honesty is like a breath of fresh air."

Strathern smiled back, "A lot of good it's doing me now."

"It's a start, Colonel. It's a great start. The main thing here is that we all must understand each other to make this a better world. It's not that hard, actually."

"Easy for you to say."

"Colonel, I believe things will work out for you and everyone else."

"Why is that?"

"Because they always do." Jessica smiled and walked out of Strathern's tent.

25 MOVING ON

Pete was in the alley with Virgil just after sunrise. Pete sat with his head buried in his arms, resting on his knees. Virgil looked at Pete; he was worried there was a problem because Pete was not talking at all.

"Something wrong, Pete?"

Pete didn't answer.

Virgil looked crushed, "You mad at me? I do something?"

Pete raised his head and looked at Virgil. "No, Virgil, I don't think I could ever be mad at you. I wouldn't know how anyway."

Virgil was confused. "What does that mean?"

"Nothing, I'm just talking."

"So what's goin' on? You seem like you ain't even here today."

"Yeah, I know. I've got a lot on my mind."

"Oh, man," Virgil clapped his hands. "You got girl problems."

"No, that's not it."

"What then? Girl problems always mess up a man. If not that, then what?"

"I have to leave Bends Creek tonight and don't want to go."

Virgil looked down at Pete. His eyes began to fill. Tears ran down his face, "Then don't go, man. You can always stay here with me. I don't want to lose you, man. You're my friend, Pete. You're my brother."

Pete stood up and looked at Virgil. Pete wanted to feel Virgil's pain, but he couldn't. Pete put his hand on Virgil's shoulder and sensed the innocence in Virgil's eyes. Pete knew he should respond emotionally, but he couldn't. Pete felt he should show Virgil something out of respect and let him know he was hurting, too.

"I know, Virgil. That means a lot to me. But there's something I have to do."

Virgil didn't understand why his new friend had to leave or wanted to go. He took a few steps back, wiped his tears away with his coat sleeve, and sniffed a few times. He kept shaking his head like he didn't understand what was happening.

Virgil kept rubbing the back of his neck. "What's so damn important that you need to leave your family?" Sniff. "You got a lot of folks here that be supportin' you. Why do you need to go now? What you got to do?"

Pete looked into Virgil's eyes, "I've got to save the world."

***

The plan to get the military out of Bends Creek was a success. Strathern kept his word. He pulled out all the troops and concentrated on the external perimeter of the town. Finally, the town seemed to accept its new role as the world's epicenter of change. Individual citizens of Bends Creek seemed excited about the attention.

Bill was driving around town again; it was business as usual. The stress levels dropped quickly with the military presence removed from inside Bends Creek. People were walking around and carrying on as if nothing had ever happened. It was a good feeling. It seemed like he and everyone else had their town back..

It was almost dark when Pete walked up to Maggie's house just as Bill pulled his cruiser into her driveway. Pete waited for Bill to leave his car before walking to the door.

"Hey, Pete," Bill greeted as he closed his car door.

"Hey."

They shook hands and walked up to Maggie's front door. Bill knocked, and Maggie opened the door. Bill waved Pete in first and followed behind him. When they entered, they saw Jessica sitting on the sofa.

"Hi, Pete," Jessica said, smiling, happy to see him.

Pete looked at her and waved. Maggie asked Pete to take a seat, and he sat down next to Jessica. Jessica was a little concerned that Pete did not look directly at her. He just sat there, watching Bill and Maggie sit down.

"Is there something wrong, Pete?" she asked him.

"I need to talk to you all about something." He waited for Maggie and Bill to get comfortable.

"What is it?" Bill asked.

"It's time for me to leave Bends Creek."

Jessica had a concerned look on her face. "But we just fixed everything. Why now?"

Pete turned to look at her. He could see that she was getting upset. Her eyes were beginning to water the same way Virgil's did.

"The test that the Wen conducted on Bends Creek was a success, and the Wen want to move forward now."

Maggie nodded her head. "It seems like the next logical step to take."

Jessica was still upset. "Why is that the next logical step? Why not try to improve what they accomplished here? Why no—"

"Jessica," Pete interrupted. "If the test runs too long here, new problems may arise, especially with all the uproar outside of town. Also, the Wen are on a strict schedule to complete this project. So now is the time to spread the affliction while people accept and understand it."

"So, now what? Where do you go next?"

"The Wen will release the affliction on a larger scale. Once the full extent of the affliction is complete, I must appear before the world's leaders and explain what's happening."

Jessica started to shake, "Pete, what if they don't accept your idea? Or worse, what if they don't accept you?"

"I have to try. It's my mission. If I can't get the leaders of this world to understand what their future holds, then I fail. The Wen will leave Earth to the Xan."

Maggie spoke up. "Pete, we understand and appreciate what you did here for us."

Bill shook his head. "Yeah, Pete. I am glad you were here with us."

Jessica's body drooped. "Will we see you again?"

Pete looked at the three people he trusted during his brief stay in Bends Creek. They were sitting there, looking at him with concerned expressions. Pete was in the same situation when he said goodbye to Virgil. Only this time, Pete felt something, making his chest heavier. Pete was confused. He didn't understand what he was experiencing. He sat silently for a few seconds, trying to grasp the sensation.

Oz spoke to Pete telepathically. *Pete, are you okay?*

Pete wanted to yell to relieve the pressure in his chest. *Oz, I don't understand. What is this?*

I think this is what a human emotion feels like, Pete.

This sucks, Oz. Make it go away, please.

I can't. This is beyond my protocols. You weren't supposed to be experiencing emotions, remember? There's no solution to this. Maybe Jessica was right; perhaps you can relearn how to feel with these new experiences. This may be a good thing, Pete.

Pete knew Oz was right, but his chest felt like it would cave in. Emotional reaction or not, it was still uncomfortable to bear. He waited to see if the heaviness would disappear. It didn't.

Pete's three friends sat silently, watching Pete stare at the floor. No one said a word. They were accustomed to Pete zoning out and knew to wait for him to snap out of it. Jessica reached over and gently touched Pete's hand without saying a word. She gave his hand a slight squeeze, and Pete started blinking. He looked up at Jessica like he had just woken up.

"Pete, are you okay?" Jessica asked softly.

"I am. I didn't realize leaving all of you would have such an effect on me. All of a sudden, I sense this heavy weight inside my chest. I don't understand what this is. Oz said it might be a human emotion."

Jessica smiled. With a tear falling down her cheek, she said, "Sadness, Pete. You are feeling sad because you are leaving the people that you care about and trust. Sadness is what we're all feeling as well. Goodbyes are sad, Pete. We don't like to let go of people or things that are meaningful to us. Not all human emotions make us feel good; sadness is a strong human emotion. You need to embrace it and hold on to it."

"I feel this weight in my chest because I am sad?"

Jessica noticed the innocent look on Pete's face. He almost looked like a child as he asked her these questions. She continued to speak in a soft, understanding voice. "Yes."

Pete stared into space with wide eyes, "But I have to leave to accomplish my mission."

Jessica wiped the tears from her cheeks. "Yes, Pete, you have to complete your mission. You need to leave us now."

Pete stood up and walked to the center of the room. He looked at his three friends. "I will be keeping in touch. You three are the only people I have to openly talk to about what is happening. I respect your opinions."

Jessica strode over to meet him. "Will I be able to get in touch with you? Or will I have to wait and hope you communicate with me?"

Pete nodded, "Jessica, we will always be able to talk to each other. I will be closer than you think."

Pete moved to shake Maggie's hand. Maggie pulled him close and hugged him.

"Pete, thanks for everything," she said.

"You're welcome."

Maggie went behind the couch and picked up a large plastic bag. She smiled and handed it to Pete.

"What's this?" Pete asked.

"I wasn't sure when you were leaving, but I knew from Virgil that you were because Virgil came by the shelter this morning and was upset about it."

Maggie sighed, and a few tears fell down her cheeks. "It's a going-away present. Something I hope helps you to remember us. Virgil pitched in with some money you guys made on the street corner. Virgil picked this out from the store and was adamant that we get you this as a gift."

Pete opened the bag and pulled out a trench coat. He stared at the jacket for a moment. Pete looked at Maggie and put the trench coat on. He then lifted his arm to his nose. The suede smelled brand new; the odor was agreeable.

Bill approached Pete and said, "Listen, I have something you'll find interesting." He handed Pete a sealed manila envelope.

"What's this?" Pete asked.

"I think you know what it is," Bill smiled. "The reason you purposely left your fingerprints on the glass in my office."

"You found something?"

Bill smiled. "Yeah, it's not a whole hell of a lot, but it may help."

Pete shook Bill's hand. "Thank you."

"It's the least I could do."

Pete looked at Jessica. "Did you see this yet?"

"Bill showed me just before you walked in. We'll be working on finding out as much as we can."

Pete looked at his three friends. "Thank you for all you've done and have tried to do."

Pete put the file inside his new trench coat as his friends watched. Pete lowered his head and closed his eyes. A bright light absorbed him, and within a few seconds, Pete disappeared.

Jessica looked at Bill and Maggie. All three stood with stunned expressions on their faces.

Maggie spoke. "Wow, something new there, huh? I didn't know he could do that."

Bill laughed. "Yeah, that was nuts."

Jessica just stood and stared at the space where Pete had been standing. She missed him already.

26 GLOBAL CONNECTION

It had been two weeks since the Wen spread the affliction across the globe. Throughout the world, different cities and towns went through the same experience as Bends Creek. Many people were traumatized by the affliction and sought psychiatric help. Some were happy that the affliction materialized in their areas, and others showed indifference. However, the spread of the affliction forced people around the world to bring their daily routines to a halt. Everyone around the globe was dealing with its effects twenty-four hours a day, seven days a week.

Although various cultures dealt with the affliction differently, a common theme began to evolve among the many countries in conflict with neighboring nations. Multitudes of like-minded individuals were gathering at the borders between countries. Most of these groups were refugees who wanted to return to their homelands. They knew the affliction confused the soldiers patrolling and protecting the boundaries of their home countries. When these soldiers refused to engage with citizens who appeared to look similar, thousands of people rushed through the protected borders and integrated back into their home nations. Helicopters with news reporters filmed these massive caravans storming the once military-protected borders. Anyone could witness these events on television or on their phones. Now that everyone looked the same, conflicting boundaries fell, and people rejoiced and embraced each other.

The Wen experiment succeeded in accomplishing peace throughout the world. World leaders became enthralled with finding a solution and placed their ongoing political agendas on indefinite hold. Countries that once dealt with animosity toward each other now had little time for conflict. It became increasingly complex to single out an opposing force based on race. The current interaction trend made it evident to the public how unnecessary all disputes were. No world leader could justify why the conflict had existed in the first place.

Reporting on the affliction consumed the internet and television. All the cable and streaming channels broadcast 24/7 coverage of reactions across the globe. The most densely populated cities received the most attention and coverage. New York City, Los Angeles, and Chicago won the bulk of attention in the United States. Local television was kept busy reporting on the events in their communities.

Most of the public still called Bends Creek the Promised Land because, in their minds, Bends Creek was where the affliction was born. Many citizens of Bends Creek began to take advantage of being called the first of the afflicted. They set up websites and made money from advising people on how to deal with the affliction daily. Podcasts were created by several citizens to monitor live Q&A sessions. Because the affliction spread so quickly worldwide, these sites and services received millions of hits. The people of Bends Creek took advantage of being the first in the world, and now that notoriety was paying dividends.

The atmosphere in the camp areas outside Bends Creek changed quickly from a free-spirited party to widespread chaos. Most of the campers became afflicted and had to deal with it themselves. Some people panicked, while others embraced the change. There was a sense of urgency to get back home and see who else was afflicted. Thus, the mass exodus away from Bends Creek began. The area emptied as quickly as it was populated. Colonel Strathern volunteered to remain in Bends Creek with fewer troops to continue protecting the town.

Leaders from various nations contacted each other and tried strategizing to combine efforts to cure the affliction. Many of the world's leading scientists and disease experts became involved. At the center of all the heated debates was the White House. World leaders were looking to the United States for answers. After all, the affliction had started in the United States, so it made sense that the United States would have a head start in finding a solution.

Cries for answers from inside and outside the U.S. pressured the Oval Office to solve this puzzle. As a result of this global tension, the government put all other issues on hold. It focused its resources entirely on developing a solution. The president called for an emergency meeting with the country's top scientific minds. He clarified that an immediate solution to the affliction was vital to maintaining world peace. Moreover, he insisted that the answer originated from American scientists, not external organizations.

"But Mr. President, it would benefit all if we worked together with scientists from other countries," one scientist argued.

The president met with top scientists in a secure room in the White House. The meeting was in its second hour, and the president appeared frustrated by the answers, or lack of solutions, he was receiving from the scientific assembly. Whenever he asked a question or commented, the scientists reproved him.

"I understand what you're saying, and I do not disagree," the president responded. "As a world leader, the U.S. needs to resolve this first. We must show the world that the U.S. is technologically advanced enough to take this on and win."

"Sir, this isn't a contest or a competition. We all benefit from the solution, no matter who discovers the answer."

"You, sir, are right again, but let's put our minds together and try it before we ask for help. What do you say?" The president gave the scientist a stern look.

The scientist pushed the bridge of his glasses against his forehead, "Yes, sir."

"Good." The president smiled and got up from the meeting table. The scientists at the table rose as the president left the meeting with his advisers and security team. When they reached the elevator, his Secret Service agent pressed the up button.

While they were waiting for the elevator, the president turned to one of his advisers and said, "Fire that asshole immediately. I want him replaced. I need team players right now."

The adviser nodded. "It will be taken care of immediately, sir."

The president smiled back at the adviser and stepped into the elevator.

27 TROUBLE LETTING GO

Bronson Pike was the leader of the largest known white nationalist group in the country, which called itself White for Right. The group had chapters throughout the southern and midwestern states. Their membership had grown at a rapid rate over the past several years. White for Right was not known for peaceful demonstrations or their capacity to carry on intellectual debates. Whenever they organized rallies and protests, violence erupted. White for Right was the most feared racist group in the country.

Bronson Pike was an intimidating figure. He was about six feet four inches tall with a muscular body. He was bald and sported tattoos, including on his head. He had a ring hanging from his nose and wore sleeveless shirts to show off his swastika symbols and other hate-related tattoos. His arm muscles were impressively large and daunting. He was always in jeans and army boots. He had a small chain connected to a loop on his jeans, with the other end attached to the pocket knife he kept stuffed in his pocket. Most of the time, he wore a sleeveless jean vest over his black t-shirt. The White for Right logo was sewn on the back of the vest like a biker club patch.

He utilized the internet to produce videos preaching hatred against all people of color. His online rants helped strengthen the organization, making everyone who joined believe they were part of a vast family network. He encouraged the chapters to reclaim America.

"We need to get our country back!" was always his message. The membership's growth proved that he was not alone in his convictions.

When the affliction hit, Bronson, like everyone else in his organization, was excited that everyone was now white in their eyes. He went on the internet and preached that America was white again. But after a short time, he came to a realization. If everyone was white, there would be no need for Bronson Pike or his organization anymore. The membership numbers and video views started spiraling downward at a rapid rate. After so many years of being the center of attention and feeling powerful, Bronson was now just another ordinary white man.

"This ain't right, man!" he yelled from the podium of a nationalist meeting.

One crowd member yelled, "What ain't right, brother?"

"This affliction is making us see what ain't there!"

"Who cares, man? Everyone's white now." The rest of the audience cheered.

Bronson jumped off the stage and onto the member who spoke up. He began beating him ferociously. Blood flowed from the member's head like a faucet had just opened. It took three prominent members to pull Pike off the man. Bronson was wide-eyed and crazed, holding up his blood-covered hands. The three men pushed Bronson back toward the stage. Two of the men picked up the limp, bloody man off the floor and carried him out.

Bronson was onstage at the podium again. He just looked over the crowd. Pike lowered his head and shook it from side to side. He began to speak into the microphone in a softer voice.

"I apologize to my brother for that outburst. I apologize to all my brothers. We shouldn't be fighting each other." The audience cheered in an uproar.

Bronson straightened his shoulders as if he were standing at attention. He screamed into the microphone, "It's all a lie, man! What we're seeing ain't real. This affliction is making us believe that everyone is white. But they ain't! We've been tricked, man. We are celebrating when we should be purging."

A crowd voice yelled, "How are we gonna do that, man?"

Bronson looked across the stage at two members standing to the side and gestured for them to come to the podium with one bloody hand. The men had another member between them. The man they were escorting had his hands handcuffed behind his back. Bronson put his arm around the shoulders of his prisoner. The blood from his hand dripped onto the captive's vest.

"A lot of you know our brother here. His name is Cougar. Cougar here is a little different than you and me. My man Cougar ain't afflicted. He can see people as they are. They ain't all white to Cougar like they are to you and me."

Another member yelled out, "So what?!"

Bronson laughed. "So what? I'll tell you so what. My boy Cougar can point out to us all the non-white people. Then we can continue with our mission."

The crowd started screaming and chanting, "White for Right!"

Bronson raised both arms up in the air as if he had just won a significant battle. He turned to Cougar, who was still standing there in handcuffs. He spoke lowly so the microphone wouldn't pick up his conversation.

"So here's how this is going to work, brother Cougar. If you help us, I won't tell everyone here that you're an undercover cop, and they tear you apart."

Cougar looked at Bronson. "Screw you. Brother!"

Bronson laughed. "You will come with us to DC, and you will point the non-white people out to us, or we will go to your home in your little suburbia, rape your wife, and drag your little girl behind our bikes."

Cougar screamed, "I'll kill you if you touch them!"

"The choice is yours. Just one day, brother. We just need you for one day."

Cougar spat on the floor and then nodded.

"I can take those off you if you promise to help, brother."

Cougar nodded again reluctantly, and Bronson removed the cuffs and threw them into the crowd. This gesture made the crowd roar louder.

Bronson held his hands up to quiet the crowd. "In a few days, we all march on DC! We show this country that this crap does not fool us, and we are here to stay!"

The crowd cheered as Bronson left the stage. Cougar followed, escorted by two of Bronson's bodyguards.

28 MEET THE PREZ

One Secret Service agent walked ahead of the president as his entourage approached the Oval Office. The two advisers came in, followed by a second Secret Service agent. Pete made sure nobody noticed him sitting in the president's chair with his feet on the president's desk until they were all inside the room.

"What the hell?" the president yelled, surprised as the Secret Service agents pulled him back toward the door. Before they reached the door, it slammed shut and locked. When the agents turned around to face Pete, every door and window in the room closed and locked simultaneously. The agents stood between Pete and the president, forming a human shield. Both agents had their guns drawn and pointed at Pete.

One agent barked an order to Pete. "Sir, you must get up and slowly come out from behind the president's desk, now! Keep both hands in the air where we can see them!"

The president was still confused. "How the hell did this guy get in here?"

The agent addressed the president. "Sir, we will figure that out shortly. Please remain still and calm behind us."

Pete looked at the small group of individuals in front of him. This meeting was part of his mission. He needed to get all the world leaders together on the same page. Pete had to talk to them, tell them that aliens were the cause of the affliction, and explain how it worked and why it affected certain people. There was so much to discuss, and Pete figured this was as good a place to start as any. Pete looked at the president, who was shaking behind the agents.

Pete shook his head slowly and thought, *This is going to take some time.*

"Sir, for the last time, please come around the desk slowly with your hands in the air," the agent's hand visibly trembling.

Pete rose slowly from the chair and walked around the desk. He raised his hands in a surrendering gesture. Pete observed the agent who had spoken, still pointing his firearm at him. He noticed the agent's trembling hand holding the gun.

Pete tilted his head and raised an eyebrow, "Look, I need you to put those guns down before someone gets hurt."

The agent tapped his left foot. "Sir, we are protecting the president. We will not stand down until you are in handcuffs."

Pete's hands were still raised, and he answered sedately, "That's not going to happen, so drop your weapons. Let's calm down and listen to what I have to say."

"Sir, if you do not get on the floor face down, you will leave us no choice. So please, do not step any closer."

The president was getting irritated. "Just shoot this son of a bitch so we can get on with our business! That's an order!"

"Yes, sir!" yelled the agent.

Both agents opened fire. Each agent shot six shots directly at Pete; he did not move or flinch as the projectiles approached. The bullets moved in slow motion as they advanced toward him, and they stopped just before hitting him. They disappeared slowly into the invisible force field of transparent gel surrounding Pete. Each bullet hit the forcefield and gradually vanished, leaving tiny ripples in the gel-like substance where they hit. Pete never took his eyes off the men.

The agents stared, dumbfounded, at Pete. Their jaws had dropped wide open, and they were staring at the bullets, watching them disappear one by one into the barrier. The agents lowered their weapons deliberately.

The president yelled at the agents, "What the hell are you doing?"

"Sir," the lead agent replied, "he has an advantage over us. We need to see what he wants."

Pete smiled. "Wise decision, agent. Please, I am not here to cause anyone harm. I need everyone to take a seat. I have much to explain, and I need your full attention."

The two advisers sat on the couch, and the president moved to his chair. Pete looked at the two agents. "I need one of you to stand outside the door and ensure the president isn't disturbed."

"I'll go," one agent volunteered and went to the door. Pete waved his hand, and the door unlocked. The agent left. Pete repeated the wave, and the door locked again.

Pete looked at the other agent. "Sir, you can stand wherever you want to protect the president."

The agent approached the president's chair and stood close to him.

The president fidgeted nervously in his chair. He rubbed his chin several times and clenched his teeth, "What the hell do you want?"

Pete stared at the president, "I want your full attention, sir. What I must say is very important, and we don't have much time."

The president insisted on resisting the stranger, "You could have done this through the proper channels instead of scaring the bejesus out of us."

Pete shook his head, "No, I don't think so. Appearing before you like this was the best way to get your attention."

The president pursed his lips, "Okay, well, you have my attention now. What do you want?"

"I am here to explain the affliction to you."

"What the hell do you know about it?"

"I can tell you why it's happening."

The president chuckled, "Give me a break. Our scientists are working on this around the clock and can't figure it out. Why should we believe you?"

"Because the affliction is not of this world."

The men looked at each other. The president started to laugh. "So what, you're an alien? You make bullets disappear, and that makes you a spaceman? I've seen some of the world's best magicians, son. I know a magic trick when I see one."

Everyone was laughing now.

Pete spoke to Oz. *I told you this was going to take a while to explain.*

The president was still smiling. "So, Mr. Alien, what planet are you from?"

Everyone was still laughing.

"Me? I'm from Earth," Pete answered.

Everyone started to laugh harder now. Pete's eyes widened, and he laughed with everyone. Pete looked around the room at the four men, and he could tell they were no longer feeling threatened by him. It was apparent they felt Pete was insane. Pete lowered his head a little and raised his arms outward.

The president laughed and pointed at Pete. "So, what now? You're going to call your alien buddies to come in here?"

Pete didn't look up. "Screw it," he said.

Pete's hands became engulfed in white energy. As the heat started to move up Pete's arms, surrounding them, everyone stopped laughing. All four men were silent as they stared, shocked, at Pete.

The room began to tremble as though they were experiencing an earthquake. The trembling became stronger, causing everyone in the room to hold on to a piece of furniture to keep from falling to the floor. Pete was stationary, never moving, while the president and his two advisers bounced up and down. Finally, the room's walls started to make a loud cracking noise like they were splitting apart. The sound caused by the deep, striking vibration was almost deafening. The whole place was waiting to explode.

The advisers shouted and screamed for help, and Pete began to raise his hands slightly. All at once, the trembling stopped, and the advisers smiled with relief. But before anyone could get comfortable, the room started to rise in sync with Pete's hand movements. The men looked out the window in terror. The president's office began to levitate. Everyone heard the loud, horrifying sounds of wood ripping through nails and concrete breaking and crumbling away as the room rose higher.

The president was the first to yell over the noise to Pete, "Please, sir, stop this. We will give you our undivided attention; just stop whatever you are doing."

Pete did not answer, and the building kept rising higher. The air was getting colder, causing the men to scream louder because they could see their breath in front of their faces. The room finally stopped and came to rest on a group of clouds. Pete had the clouds act as a foundation, supporting the room to keep it from falling.

The four men looked to where Pete had been standing. He was gone. They panicked and started yelling at each other.

"Where the hell is he?" one adviser screamed.

The president's eyes widened, "How should I know? He was just right there."

The men never stood up. They were afraid to move. As they screamed at each other, the agent pointed out the window.

"Look," he screamed.

Everyone looked out the bay window at the same time. Pete was floating outside the room and hovering above a cloud; both arms extended to his sides. His hair and trench coat moved in the direction of the wind. He turned his wrists slightly and began floating toward the window.

As he got closer, one adviser screamed, "He's going to crash into us and send us down to our deaths!"

When Pete got to the window, he passed through it without hesitating. His body appeared to melt into the glass and slowly reappear inside the room. He floated to the spot where he had initially been standing. As he slowly drifted down to the floor, he raised his head.

"Gentlemen," Pete said. "We need to talk."

The president pleaded, "Yes, yes, let's talk. But can you take us safely down first?"

Pete raised his hands, and the room started to free-fall from the clouds. The president and his advisers were screaming as they crashed into the ceiling. The descent to the ground was so fast that no one could move or gain an advantage to brace themselves for a crash landing. Everyone was stuck to the ceiling helplessly. Everyone except Pete, who stood on the floor, unfazed.

One adviser cried out, "We're all going to die!"

As the room descended toward the ground, Pete noticed the agent showed little emotion. Instead, the agent kept staring at Pete while the room fell and appeared undaunted by what was happening. Pete thought the agent must have paid close attention during his crisis training.

The room stopped suddenly, forcing everyone inside who was on the ceiling to drop to the floor. However, the room appeared not to have changed from its original state once the noise subsided and the walls settled into place.

The president and his advisers began laughing uncontrollably.

"We made it! We're okay!" yelled one adviser as he hugged the other. He pointed down at his crotch, and the other adviser laughed, "You pissed yourself?"

"I did!" The advisers laughed louder and hugged each other until tears rolled down their cheeks.

The president was helped up by the Secret Service agent and walked back to his desk, "Thank you," he said, wiping a few tears from his eyes. "You have our full attention now."

Pete began to speak, "I know this information is quite overwhelming, but you need to comply with the utmost urgency."

All the men nodded their heads in agreement. "Yes," the president said.

Something was still troubling Pete about the agent. He spoke telepathically to Oz.

Oz, run a scan of everyone in the room. Just a quick analysis before I continue with the president.

Even the president?

Yes, everyone.

Oz started scanning the advisers sitting on the couch. *Nothing unusual about the two whiners on the sofa.*

She then turned her attention to the president. *The big kahuna seems okay, too.*

When she got to the agent, she seemed startled. *Pete, the agent, isn't human.*

Pete cut her off. *I know.*

How did you know?

I don't know—something in my gut.

You don't have any feelings, remember?

Does it matter what you call it? Can we discuss this later?

Whatever.

Pete looked at the agent. "Sir, please, I need you to come away from the president."

The agent looked at the president and then back at Pete. "I cannot leave his side," he said.

Pete looked at the agent, and their eyes locked. They stared at each other for an eternity without saying a word.

Pete spoke first in a more demanding tone. "It's not an option, and

I'm not asking."

The president stood and defended the agent, "Please hold on a minute. Jack has been with me for over six years. He's practically family."

Pete took his eyes off the agent for a split second and looked at the president. That split second was enough for the agent to grab the president. The agent held the president between himself and Pete, using him as a human shield. He moved from behind the president's desk, one arm around the president's throat, pressing tightly under his chin, and his hand restraining his head. His free hand grasped the president's arm firmly.

The president's eyes almost popped out of his head. "Jack, what? What are you doing, man?"

Jack didn't say a word and kept looking at Pete. Pete took a step toward the president. Jack smiled, and the hand lying across the side of the president's head turned into a bright yellow sword. When the hand changed, it clinked like metal hitting metal. The president screamed when the blade cut the side of his head. Blood started to drip onto the metal from the president's cheek.

"That's going to need a few stitches," Jack snarled.

Pete was calm. "What is it you want?"

"You know who we are, don't you?"

"Yes."

"The Wen trained you well, human. I am guessing your guide didn't even notice."

Holy crap, he's a Xan?

Yes.

Where did they get the cloaking tech? They know we're here, Pete.

That is obvious, isn't it, Oz?

Jack went on, "I know you two are communicating right now, so let me assure you I will be one step ahead of any actions you decide to—"

Before Jack could finish, he dropped his hand and let go of the president. The president ran to the couch where the two advisers were sitting. The president looked down at the sofa, saw a wet spot, and moved away. Jack dropped to the floor.

Oz yelled at Pete. *What did you do?*

I stopped him from killing the president. If he succeeded, our mission would be over. You know that, right?

Yes, but no one ever kills a Xan.

Pete looked down at the Xan, lying face down on the floor. A hole the size of a golf ball was in the center of his head.

Oz was confused. *How did you do that? I didn't sense your movements at all.*

I just have to think about what I want to do and visualize it. Then I can make it happen.

Pete, we need to conduct some diagnostics soon. You can do things without our systems communicating with each other. I do not sense these actions, and I have no data to support how these events are possible.

That's not a problem; maybe you can figure out what's happening later. I need you to focus on our current situation.

Okay, but we'd better keep this quiet, Pete. If we tell the Traa'zel, they may put you back under the knife.

Well, I wasn't going to tell them. Can you keep a secret?

As long as they don't ask, I guess they don't have a reason to do so. So, yeah, no problem, man. I've got your back.

I know, Oz.

Pete was grateful he had Oz. He knew he was never alone, which made him more confident in his decisions. Oz was dependable, but most of all, she was a friend.

Pete walked over to the Xan, sprawled in a pool of green liquid. Pete had never seen a Xan. There was no training associated with the Xanoclax. Pete noticed the human skin slowly disintegrating, revealing the true Xan underneath. As the surface deteriorated, Pete turned over the body. The Xan was in dark green, almost black, metal armor. The Xan's helmet resembled a closed medieval helmet. A thin metal blade followed the curve of the helm from front to back. Pete cut his finger as it slid over the blade's surface.

The visor of the Xan's helmet was a dark, metallic black. It felt hard and solid when he touched the dead Xan's helmet. He tapped on other helm areas with his knuckles; it made a metal thud sound with each hit. The eye openings were tiny red slivers cut into the metal. The eyelids looked like small, horizontal metallic doors. Pete raised one of the eyelids, exposing more of the red eye.

The mouth was open and revealed three rows of pointed teeth. The more prominent teeth were toward the front and grew smaller as they extended back inside the mouth. The Xan's tongue was hanging off to the side. It was dark olive green with many small bumps all around its surface. It looked like a Goya bitter melon.

Pete wanted to keep exploring and inspecting the Xan, but he had to pull away and continue with the mission. The timeline was critical to its success, and the Traa'zels were prompt.

The president and the advisers were sitting in shock. The president placed his hands on the couch to hoist himself up. He looked at one of his hands and frowned. It was a little wet, and he wiped his hand on the adviser's suit.

The president stared wide-eyed, "Jack, was an alien this whole time?"

Pete looked at the president and tried to explain. "There is no telling when he seized your friend's body. It could have been years ago or just today. There is no way to calculate the time of the infiltration."

Pete walked over to the door and opened it. The second agent was still at attention. Pete asked the agent to find a replacement and come inside to assist the president. Pete returned to the president, and the agent came in and stood at the president's side.

Oz, scan this one, please.

All clear.

One adviser asked the agent, "Did you feel the room crash down?"

The agent looked puzzled. "No, sir. Everything was quiet."

The advisers looked at each other in disbelief.

The president wasn't paying attention to the advisers. He was still looking at the Xan that had once been Jack. "What happened to Jack?"

"Unfortunately, I believe Jack is no longer alive."

The president could not ignore the dead Xan, "Oh, my God. This is happening, isn't it?"

"Yes, Mr. President, and we have to act quickly. Time is running out. They know we're here to help you. They possibly have other spies on this planet."

The president's head twitched as he looked at Pete, "What do we need to do?

Okay, Oz, it's showtime.

Pete took a few steps back from the president and the advisers. He held out his right hand, palm up. Pete lowered his head, and the blue liquid appeared in his palm. The fluid illuminated the room as all eyes were on Pete's hand. Oz slowly emerged from his palm.

Oz looked up at the president. "So you're the big cheese, huh?"

Everyone was silent. Their eyes were wide open, and no one dared to blink. Instead, they stared at Oz as she hopped off Pete's hand onto the president's desk. The president flinched and pushed his chair back from his desk.

"I'm not going to hurt you, so just cool your tools, man," Oz said to the president. "My name is Oz. It's nice to meet you."

The president stared at Oz. "I'm…I'm…"

Oz cut him off. "Yeah, I know who you are. I'm here to help explain what's going on. Are you interested or not?"

"Yes, please explain," the president nodded quickly.

Pete took a painting down from the wall. Oz waved her hand slightly, and a transparent visual display hovered unattached over the blank wall. Oz waved again, and all the lights turned off, causing everyone to look around the room, confused. She clapped her hands to get everyone's attention and explained the mission.

"Sir," Oz started. "I am from a planet outside your galaxy. My race is known as the Wen'q'rixshi, or Wen for short. I have a direct link to our Council of Traa'zels. They are the scientific members of our society. Please listen. We can discuss it after I show you. Are we ready?"

Everyone in the room nodded without saying a word.

Oz began the transmission. The wall was completely black, and then a voice began speaking. It was a commanding and confident voice. The sound filled the president's office and demanded attention.

"Am I addressing the leaders of planet Earth?" The screen was still dark.

The president spoke up. "I am the President of the United States." He looked at Oz. "I can't see him."

Oz addressed the president. "You will, sir. Please be patient."

The voice continued, "I am Krix'x. I am one of the Wen'q'rixsh. I am here to help save your planet from an impending invasion from the Xanoclax. You must heed my warning and take action to avoid the imminent Xan invasion!"

As Krix'x finished his sentence, he showed his face. The face on the wall caused everyone to jump back a little in their seats. It was the first time Pete had seen a Wen other than Oz. Pete walked closer to the wall, and the others didn't notice him move. Pete could recall hearing this voice before. Pete's eyes locked onto the face on the wall. Something inside his mind was telling him that he knew this Wen. But, as of now, he couldn't figure it out.

Krix'x's face was almost human. There were no tentacles or amphibious traits like the many representations of alien physicality conceived in science fiction. He didn't wear metallic armor like the Xan lying on the floor. His eyes were expressionless and completely black. Within the chasm of those lifeless eyes, Pete saw what appeared to be a galaxy of stars. Krix'x had no eyebrows or visible eyelashes. Every few seconds, his flesh would change color. His face would shift across a wide range of hues as he talked. It started with a deep blue color. As he spoke a few sentences or finished a thought, his skin would change to a light brown. These changes went on throughout his speech.

Pete kept staring at the wall. He didn't say a word as Krix'x spoke.

The president interrupted and responded first. "Sir, this is quite a lot to take in. You say you're from a distant galaxy and are here to help us. But we do not know you and can't help but consider if you want to invade us. How can we know who you are? Are your intentions honorable?"

Krix'x nodded his head. "That is a fair question. Let me assure you that if we wanted to invade your planet, we could have done so many times over hundreds of your years. Our technology is far more advanced than you hope to achieve within the next thousand Earth years. Your planet, as you say, is ripe for the taking."

The president nodded. "I understand that you could do all these things, but how do we even know what you say about the Xan is true?"

Krix'x almost looked upset. The layers of extra skin over his eyes seemed to tighten up.

"I will say this only once, and then you can decide whether you want to proceed with our help. We cannot force you to accept our help. Our Logic-Belief only allows us to offer assistance. It is up to you to accept our help. It is up to you to decide your fate.

I will explain how we intend to help your planet by simultaneously addressing all the Earth's leaders. Alert all the world leaders and have them come together in three Earth days. I will present our plan to all of you. I will explain who the Xan are in greater detail then."

The president spoke again, "Sir, it will take…."

"Enough!" Krix'x shouted, cutting off the president. His voice startled everyone in the room.

Pete now recognized the voice.

Krix'x is the Wen that always yelled at me during my training, he thought.

Krix'x had been the Wen in control of Pete's transition from human to…whatever he was now. Krix'x was the voice that was in charge of taking his memories. Pete's mind started reeling. He had so many questions he wanted to ask Krix'x.

Krix'x continued. "Three days. That's all you have to arrange for all the world leaders to convene. If you do not comply, I will terminate this mission and leave you to your fate."

Pete watched Krix'x do something that seemed impossible. His face slowly pushed through the wall toward the president. Pete was in awe of this face without a head that was slowly moving toward the president. Pete had never seen anything like this before. By the look on the faces of the other men in the room, neither had they.

The face left a dark void in the wall as it moved away from it, and a trail of liquid blue light emerged, appearing to originate from the opening. The irradiating blue light stretched from the abyss while remaining connected to the back of Krix'x's face. His inscrutable countenance progressed from the wall and stopped short of the president's nose. There was barely a millimeter of space between Krix'x's nose and the president's. His vacuous eyes turned fire-red. The president's eyes had become distended, and it looked like they would pop out of his head at any second.

Then Krix'x spoke in a mellow tone. "I realize this is a lot for your human brain to comprehend. But this is a one-time offer. We can only offer our services. We cannot force you to accept them. If you do not comply, we will not return. Then, Mr. President, you will all eventually become enslaved and terminated by the Xanoclax."

The president was afraid to move. He whispered, "How will we get in touch with you when we have all the leaders assembled?"

"We have left you our herald, J9-1-7. He will guide you and communicate with us when you are ready." Krix'x's face slowly retreated into the wall.

As he passed the Xan lying in a pool of green blood, he stopped, hovering over its body. "What is this?" Krix'x sounded alarmed. He turned to look at Pete. "J9-1-7 report!"

Pete froze; this was the first time he had come face to face with a Traa'zel.

Oz spoke to Pete. *Answer him already!*

Pete stared at Krix'x as he answered, "This Xan had taken over a human body and infiltrated this government."

"How did he meet his demise?"

"It was me. I killed the Xan ."

"This is not good news at all. This discovery means that the Xan have sent spies and may know of our plan to help. Time is not on our side; we need to act quickly."

"Yes, I know. We will gather the leaders and await your presentation," Pete agreed.

Another blue ray of light came from the void in the wall and consumed the Xanoclax warrior on the floor. The beam lifted the Xan off the floor and pulled him into the void behind Krix'x. Everyone watched as the Xan slowly disappeared. Krix'x started fading back into the opening, not taking his eyes off the president.

"Three days." And with that, Krix'x and the void slowly collapsed, and he was gone. There was no trace that he was ever there. The lights in the room came back on.

There was silence. No one spoke. Everyone looked at each other several times, expecting someone to say something. The president shifted his chair closer to his desk.

Then the president spoke. "Okay! Okay. We have to figure this out."

The president's adviser spoke up. "Sir, what do you mean?"

The president looked shaken. He kept moving his hands across the table in circular motions. Everyone stared at the president as he acted like he was concentrating on cleaning his desktop. He was staring at his hands the whole time he spoke.

"We have to decide what to do with the information we just received from an apparent alien race." It was clear to everyone in the room that the president was bewildered.

Pete approached the president's desk and said, "What do you mean by 'apparent'?"

The president stood up and looked at Pete. "How do you propose we approach the world with this information? We just say we need a meeting because an alien called for it? Who the heck is going to listen to us? The world leaders will think we've lost our minds!"

Pete gave the president a sharp look. "Sir, you have to convince them. There's no time to discuss or challenge this information."

"Okay, Mr. Alien Herald, how do we do that?" the president asked, his voice sarcastic.

"Ahem. Excuse me," Oz spoke from atop the president's desk.

Pete looked down at Oz. "What is it?"

"I think I know how to grab the world's attention with a single gesture."

The president looked at Pete as he pointed at Oz. "No disrespect, but we don't have enough time to parade Minnie Mouse around to get everyone's attention."

"Sir, you can't call her Minni–"

"What?!" Oz's scream cut Pete off. Her hand energized and

discharged a powerful beam of blue light, destroying the president's bust on a plinth in the corner of the office. The statue shattered into hundreds of pieces. "Can Minnie freaking Mouse do that?" Oz screamed.

The president began breathing quickly, and he was more scared than before. He looked at Oz's angry face. "Sorry?" He shrugged his shoulders.

Pete looked at Oz. "Was that necessary?"

"Hell, yes! Humans trust nothing. They automatically assume everyone else is wrong and don't listen to anyone else's ideas. I've seen so many different cultures across different galaxies, and no culture disrespects each other more than these awful humans! Everyone wants proof. And even when you provide proof, they don't want to believe it. Why? Because it doesn't agree with their point of view. What? Really? Is it more important to have people agree with you even though you're wrong? Aargh!"

Oz walked across the president's desk and looked at him angrily. "No one reacts or considers another way of doing things unless someone gets hurt or killed. What is wrong with you people? The Xan may favor the universe by ending this planet's pathetic existence."

The president looked down at Oz and spoke to her softly. "Please, we need your help. How can we move this forward in the time we need to?"

Pete looked at Oz. She was still angry and not responding. "I thought anger was illogical?"

Oz looked at Pete. "Must be something in the air."

"Come on, Oz, you know we need to hear what you have to say. Don't make anyone beg for it."

Oz turned her gaze from Pete to the president. The president was nodding his head and smiling.

"Okay." She turned away from the president and looked at Pete. "I was looking through your history and came up with an idea."

"What is it?" the president asked.

Oz turned back to the president. "*The Day the Earth Stood Still*," she replied.

The president looked confused, "I don't understand, the movie?"

"You see it?" Oz sparked. "I thought it was awesome. Kinda dragged in some spots, but overall, it had a great message. The original, I think, was better than the Keanu remake, but both were pretty good."

"Oz," Pete interrupted. "We're serious. What are you talking about?"

"Did you even see it?"

"I don't remember if I did."

"Oh yeah, right. Sorry."

"It's okay…just tell me why this movie."

The president spoke up as if a light bulb had gone off in his head. "Of course!" he shouted.

Pete looked confused. "What am I missing?"

The president looked at Oz. "May I explain?"

Oz smiled. "Please do."

"The ship lands in DC!"

Oz yells, "Yes!"

The president laughed and gave Oz the tiniest of high fives.

Pete looked at the two of them incredulously, "What ship?"

The president walked over to Pete and put his arm around his shoulder. "Your ship, my boy."

Pete twisted his lips. "We don't have a ship."

The president looked at Oz, "I thought all aliens had a ship?"

Pete narrowed his eyes, "Oz, we don't have a ship. Do we?"

Oz lowered her eyes and glanced up at Pete. "We never really talked about that, did we?"

Pete sighed, "No, Oz, we didn't."

"Well, we have a ship that's cloaked if we need one in an emergency."

Pete raised his voice. "We have a ship?! Where the hell is it?"

"It's orbiting the planet."

"Great, we have a ship now. So what's the plan?"

The president took over the conversation. "Simple. Like in the movie, you land the ship on the National Lawn, and the world sees your arrival. Then there will be no discussion about whether you're aliens."

Pete looked at Oz. "You're okay with this?"

"It's the quickest way to show the world, Pete," Oz replied excitedly.

Pete was confused because Oz was exhibiting human emotions. She had never been excited or angry in the past. But now she was acting differently.

The president continued with his plan. "Once you land, I will come out to greet you. And do not disintegrate my ass, either. I am not taking one for team Earth here."

Oz laughed. "Never thought of that. That would be a great way to get attention, though."

The president lifted his head, "Not funny. Anyway, you come out, and we start talking. I take you into the White House, where we contact all the world leaders for an emergency meeting."

Pete folded his arms. "Sounds too easy to me."

29 REUNION

Jessica had not spoken to Pete in a few weeks. She wanted to tell him about her decision to stay in Bends Creek for a while longer. She had convinced her boss that she could do the most good in Bends Creek since it was a controlled environment. The president had put pressure on the CDC to get answers. That pressure put the organization on edge, considering all their options. Jessica's staying in Bends Creek was a logical step.

Jessica still couldn't stop thinking about Pete. *I know he's busy.*

She thought about him and wanted to call him many times, but didn't want to interrupt him. She continued her daily business, trying to stay busy because non-work time had become thinking-about-Pete time. She was excited and surprised when he finally called her.

"Hello?" she answered her cell.

"Hi, Jessica."

"Pete? How are you?!"

"I'm the same," he said, his voice unemotional and monotone.

"So tell me: did you accomplish your next phase? It's crazy now that the whole world is afflicted."

"So far, we're on track. I met the president last night."

"Wow. How did that go?"

"He's different. Not anything like you, Maggie, or Bill."

Jessica laughed. "Well, he's a politician. They're all buttheads."

"I don't know if 'butthead' is the right word for what I saw. But the president is an unconscientious individual. It took some convincing, but he's on board now."

"Yeah, politics is a cutthroat business to be in."

"It would probably help if he had strong advisers around him instead of yes men. It seems that knowledgeable advice from different points of view would aid in making sounder decisions."

Jessica laughed. "Wow, Pete. It sounds like you had an educational visit to DC."

"Maybe. At least we accomplished what we set out to do."

"Cool. So what's the plan? Are you going to get to visit us anytime soon?"

"Well, I would like to come by and try that drug again. You know, the one that helped me remember a little?"

Jessica tried to keep the excitement from her voice. "Sure! When?"

"Now, if possible."

"Yeah! I'm at my new place. Do you need directions?"

"No, I'll find you."

Jessica hung up the phone and jumped up and down. She yelled a "Yes!" as she put the phone in her pocket. Jessica turned around, and there was Pete. Again, she screamed, this time in terror.

"Sorry," Pete apologized, "I didn't mean to startle you."

Jessica was trying to catch her breath. "Man, Pete! How long were you standing there?"

"Just a few minutes. I followed your phone signal here."

"So, you were still talking on the phone while standing behind me?"

"Yeah."

"Okay, well, I'm embarrassed now."

"Don't be. If I could react as you did, I would, I think."

Jessica smiled, walked over to Pete, and hugged him. His energy calmed her down. She looked up at his face and kissed him. The kiss seemed to go on forever, but it still didn't feel long enough to her.

Pete stepped back and lightly said, "We have to use the drug; I can't chance lying next to you and blowing your place up."

Jessica laughed. "I agree. How's Oz, by the way?"

"She's fine. She says hello. She's not with me; she's preparing for the next phase of our mission."

"Where is she?"

"Getting our spaceship ready."

"Shut the front door! You have a spaceship?"

"Yes, I do. Oz informed me about this in DC. It was the first time we ever talked about it."

"You didn't know you had a spaceship?"

"No. I guess that information was on a need-to-know basis only."

Jessica told Pete to sit down while she went to her medicine cabinet. She returned with a syringe, ready for Pete.

Jessica smiled, "I brought a few doses to my apartment in case you wanted to try again."

Pete took off his trench coat and lay down on Jessica's couch.

Jessica smiled. "I guess you do know the drill." She administered the drug into his arm. "Okay, here we go. Good luck."

"Thanks," Pete said and closed his eyes.

***

Pete woke up from this session without Jessica's help.

"How long?" Pete asked Jessica.

"This one was a lot shorter," she said. "Only about seven minutes. Maybe you're starting to control this process better?"

Pete rubbed the back of his neck, "I'm not sure."

"What did you see?"

279

"Just more of what I went through in that dark place. This time, I saw a light coming from behind a door."

"Was there anything there?"

"No. Just the light. When the door fully opened, the bright white light swallowed me up. So now, instead of being blinded by darkness, I have moved on to being blinded by the light."

"Do you think you remember everything in a certain order?"

"Maybe."

"Sounds like you may be getting closer to some answers. But maybe the answers are beyond that door?"

"Maybe."

Jessica put her hand on Pete's and squeezed it softly. She was trying not to become too emotional. Jessica noticed that keeping her emotions in check each time she saw Pete was more challenging. Jessica wanted to express what she felt, that Pete was making her feel warm and secure. And to jump for joy and tell him how great he made her feel. But Jessica knew their focus was on helping Pete now and that, hopefully, there would be time for expressing her emotions later. For now, she would play the role of his friend and confidant.

"I'm so sorry it's not happening quickly for you, Pete."

Pete looked at her. "No, this is good. If anything, I recall that I'm human every time I remember these pieces of what happened. These visits remind me that I was a human before I became what I am now, which is very important to me."

Jessica looked at Pete as he was talking to her. She didn't want him to leave but knew he had to. She knew this drug was the only reason he had come to see her, and now the experience was over.

She needed to be strong. "So, I guess you need to go now?"

Pete was still looking at her. "Yes, but…Can I stay for a little longer?"

Jessica smiled. "Of course, you can." She was excited that he wanted to be with her.

Pete spoke in a soft voice. "I don't understand what happens when I'm around you. I don't know what it is. But, frankly, I don't want to think about it. I only want to be around it. Is that okay?"

"That's nice to hear, Pete. Thank you."

"No, Jessica, I should be thanking you. You are a strong, intelligent human being, and I am lucky that I had the chance to meet you."

Jessica hugged Pete without saying a word. They sat on the couch in each other's arms. Neither wanted to break the silence. They just sat together, enjoying a peaceful moment.

It was early in the morning when Jessica awoke. She sat up in her place on her couch alone. Jessica looked around and realized Pete was gone. She looked at the coffee table in front of the sofa and saw a single red rose lying on the table. She smiled, lay on the couch, and went back to sleep.

30 MOVIE TIME

It was noon when the event that would shock the world began. Pete asked why Oz chose noon. She shrugged her shoulders and said, "Theatrical effect?"

Pete looked at her and said, "You are watching way too many movies."

Oz and Pete found a secluded alley to await the ship's arrival.

"I'm curious to see what a Wen spaceship looks like."

"Yeah, it's pretty cool." Oz smiled and laughed under her breath.

"What's so funny?"

"Oh, nothing, nothing at all."

Oz set up a metal pad that resembled a laptop on the lid of a nearby trash can and opened it. A slight humming noise emanated from the pad as it powered up, and a bright blue display screen hovered in the air directly above the unit. Pete did not recognize the markings or writing that lit up the outside of the display. He watched Oz manipulate the controls by touching the screen.

Oz contacted the ship, removed its cloaking device, and had it start flying through the Earth's atmosphere. Oz plotted a course for the spaceship that would cover most of the globe before landing in DC. She wanted to ensure that human sightings would cause excitement, so she gave the spacecraft a recognizable cloak. A familiar image that humans could relate to.

"Come on! Are you serious? A flying saucer?" Pete asked Oz.

The ship was now bright silver and was rotating in circles while it passed through the sky. She programmed it to weave slightly every few hundred miles to look like someone was piloting it. The vehicle made a sound similar to the effects of an old sci-fi movie as it passed over land. Oz was happy she had found this soundtrack to one of the classic Earth sci-fi movies. She remembered this particular movie for its primitive special effects. The strings holding up the spaceships always made her laugh.

"I'm so retro," Oz said, winking at Pete and laughing like a mad scientist who had just created life for the first time.

Radar systems picked up the saucer in every country it flew over. When the spacecraft flew over populated areas, Oz had it fly at the same speed as a passenger plane. Slowly, enough to catch anyone looking up's attention. Then, it would speed up again until it approached the next populated area.

In the next few moments, news stations from all over the world began reporting the UFO sighting. Live streaming on the internet and cable TV permeated every household and business. People from around the globe captured the saucer's movements through their skies using cell phones. The whole world was talking about the flying saucer. Pete was monitoring the internet reactions on his phone.

Pete was impressed by Oz's plan. "Looks like you were right," he said to her.

"You should never doubt me."

Pete was concerned about Oz's behavior. Her attitude and personality were changing. She no longer seemed like the logical, emotionless Wen'q'rixshi he had first met. Instead, her expressions were full of emotion and vigor. It wasn't that Pete didn't like Oz this way; it was simply odd, making him wonder if she was physically and mentally stable.

"Oz, I need to ask you something."

"Okay, what?"

"What's going on with you?"

"What do you mean?"

"You're acting strangely. I don't understand."

Oz was controlling the spaceship while talking to Pete. "Explain, please."

Pete sighed, "Well, you became angry in the president's office. I thought you were devoid of feelings?"

"Yes. Anger is not logical."

"Then how do you explain your outburst?"

Oz tilted her head. "Honestly? I don't remember the outburst."

Pete shook his head, "How can you not remember it? It just happened."

"Pete, I don't know. I have difficulty remembering my actions when I'm on the outside."

Pete looked more closely at Oz. He noticed an alteration in her blue coloring. "Oz, do you realize your skin isn't as bright as before?"

"Yes. I ran some tests on it," Oz said, unconcerned.

"What did you find?"

Oz's eyes, locked into the display, never left the screen as she controlled the ship. Finally, she responded, "We accounted for all the elements of your atmosphere, but we ignored the trace elements because… they were trace elements."

Oz twisted her body quickly to the left as if she were playing a video game, trying to get her video game character to move to the left. She giggled and turned to the right.

"In your atmosphere, these trace elements are tiny in volume. So they should have had zero effect on me."

Pete frowned, "But, these trace elements do affect you?"

"Yes. My tests concluded that the neon gases are the culprit."

"What's the solution?"

Oz rolled her eyes, "Try to stay out of the atmosphere as much as possible, duh."

Pete sighed, "What happens when your outer shell is exposed to long to the neon gas in the atmosphere?"

"As you see, discoloration occurs. When discoloration occurs, it affects my tech."

"How?"

"You know how, when a turtle gets placed on its back, it eventually dies?"

"Yes."

"It's like that."

Pete raised his voice, "You're going to die?"

"My tech starts trying to adjust to the changes. But, unfortunately, when it adjusts one area, it takes something from another area: robbing Peter to pay Paul."

"What area is it taking from?"

"It appears to be affecting my logic circuitry, which could explain my sudden outbursts."

"How can we remedy this situation?"

"After this part of the mission, I will return inside, run diagnostics, and repair. After that, I should be fine."

"What happens in the meantime? Will there be more outbursts?"

"I'm afraid so. It's unpredictable. I've never been through this before, so I apologize beforehand."

"No apologies needed. Make sure you take it easy, okay?"

"You've got it."

Once Oz directed the craft to all the countries in Asia and Africa, she led it through the Middle East, Russia, and Europe. When the spacecraft crossed the Atlantic and approached the United States, two military F-15 fighter jets rode alongside it. They were sending live video transmissions to the Air Force Command Center. They tried hailing the spacecraft.

"This is the United States Air Force transmitting to the unidentified spacecraft. Please respond."

Oz could hear the audio and ignored the call.

"I thought you worked out all the details with the president? Why are they threatening us?"

"We have to make it look authentic. So, we decided to let the Air Force do its thing. I told the president we wouldn't be in the craft anyway."

The Air Force repeated the call several times. After each attempt to contact the spacecraft failed, they issued a warning. "This is the United States Air Force to the unidentified spacecraft. You are about to enter a restricted no-fly zone. Please respond."

The saucer automatically detected the jet's audio transmission. Pete looked at Oz.

"Are you going to answer them, Oz?"

"Nah. Let's step up the suspense."

Pete just shook his head. "You are enjoying this way too much."

Oz nodded and laughed.

"This is your last warning. Please redirect your course from the restricted area, or we will shoot down your ship."

Oz did not respond.

The two jets slowed and positioned themselves directly behind the spacecraft. One F-15 fired a single Sidewinder missile at the spaceship. It was on a confirmed direct-hit course when it exploded before hitting the spacecraft. The Pentagon, watching the failed strike attempt, immediately ordered both jets to open fire. They released their missiles together. Even though each rocket was on a confirmed direct-hit course, they all exploded before touching the spacecraft.

The command center ordered the pilots to physically redirect the saucer away from its present course. When one jet came close, the flying saucer dropped below the fighter jets and came up behind them. Oz just started laughing. She had complete control, access, and direct control of the spacecraft. She was having a good time playing with the pilots. Pete told her to stop.

Oz responded, "No way! This is the most fun I've had since I was assigned here. I am having me time now."

Pete looked at Oz. "You look like a crazed person. You need to stop this."

Oz turned her head around quickly from her control unit and growled at Pete. "Back. The. Freak. Off!" She then whipped back around to her control unit, laughing intensely like a megalomaniac.

Pete raised his hands. "Whatever."

The saucer was now trailing the two jets. The pilots maneuvered their aircraft alongside the flying saucer again. Finally, one pilot was able to get his jet to fly directly under it to help avoid the same maneuver from happening. The pilot, alongside the flying saucer, slowly started to fly closer. Just as it reached within a few feet, the spacecraft darted forward, leaving the two jets alone.

Pete watched Oz as she controlled the ship while giggling like a child. She enjoyed playing with the two pilots every minute, jumping up and down while she toyed with them.

"Man, this is so cool," she said as she shook her head from side to side.

The two pilots flew after the saucer but could not find it. It disappeared from their radars. While communicating with each other and their base, one pilot looked over to the other. He pointed his finger straight up. When the pilot looked up, he was startled by the sight of the saucer floating directly above both jets, flying at the same rate of speed.

Pete had had enough. "Oz, cut the crap and get the ship here now!" he said, his tone demanding.

Oz lowered her head. "Fine, spoil all my good times."

Oz cloaked the saucer again so that the pilots and radar systems couldn't see it. It reached the Washington, DC airspace within a few seconds. Oz released the cloaking device and let the saucer hover about a hundred feet above the National Lawn.

"We need to let it sit in the air here for a little while," Oz said as if she had done this before.

Pete knew not to question her since her plan was working.

The military wasted little time reinforcing the area. The Pentagon deployed troops and tanks to the National Lawn from Fort Belvoir, Virginia. Two AH-64E Apache Guardian helicopters, fully armed with missiles, surrounded the spacecraft. The on-site army commander ordered troops to seal off the ground directly underneath the saucer. Soldiers set up barriers along the tree lines on both sides of the National Lawn. They installed temporary steel walls roughly 250 feet from the center of the field where they determined the saucer would land. Pete and Oz phased into the saucer. When they were inside, Pete looked around.

"This is it? Wen tech is so advanced, and this is all there is here?"

Pete was referring to the lack of technical equipment in the saucer. The area inside the craft was barren—there was no sign of advanced technology, only space and naked steel walls.

"I thought I would see some highly technical consoles and gadgets. But this, this looks like terrible special effects from a bad movie."

Pete saw one console installed against the wall. There was only one chair there. The controls on the board looked like they came from an old TV station from the '60s, just analog displays mounted on the control panel. The display meters were circular, with needles fluctuating inside the glass. Different colored lights were set up in rows and flashed continuously on and off in a randomized pattern. Pete thought the lights were annoying.

Pete looked at Oz. "You did this, didn't you?" Pete pointed at the console and the lights. "This isn't the real interior, just like the saucer isn't the real exterior."

Oz touched her index finger to her head. "Man, you're a smart one."

"Wiseass!"

"Learned from the best," Oz laughed. She was now standing at the makeshift control panel. "This whole redecorating the interior thing is just a precaution in case you want to impress a chick and show her your saucer."

"You just keep getting funnier all the time."

"Yeah, it's a gift. But in all seriousness, if somehow anyone other than us gets in here, our actual technology will not be exposed."

"Obviously."

"There's the smart butt I know and love."

Pete looked over at Oz as she sat at the control panel and pressed a switch. A crack appeared in the center of the wall in front of the control panel. Then, each side of the break began sliding in the opposite direction from the other. As the two sides finished separating, they exposed a large screen that looked like a window. The display stretched across the entire length of the wall above the console. The display played a visual of the National Lawn directly in front of the spaceship. Pete could see the military barricades and the troops waiting for something to happen.

Pete kept looking at the screen, asking Oz, "What happens now?"

"We wait for the president to show up, and then make our grand entrance. But, first, we need to lower this puppy and freak everyone out."

"Why are you talking like a creepy mad scientist?"

Oz shrugged, "I don't know. It works in old movies. I guess it's appropriate."

Pete narrowed his eyes, "So, you're not going to remember acting like an idiot after you do repairs?"

"Not likely."

"That's convenient."

Pete just ignored her and watched the reactions of the crowd that had gathered around the National Lawn. They were pointing up at the ship and taking pictures. Some of the troops had difficulty keeping them behind their barricades. Many people were excited, and Pete noticed children jumping up and down. Some people were on their knees, crying and praying.

The saucer started to descend slowly. Pete observed Oz as she took it slow, giving the onlookers below plenty of time to get out of the way. Oz pressed a few buttons, and the saucer started to spin faster. The wind from the spinning grew more forceful as it came closer to land, making it difficult for people to stand in one spot to watch the ship land on the National Lawn. The people in front of the crowd were blown back into the people behind them. Dresses blew around, and hats flew off many heads. The powerful winds blew dirt through the air, and people had to cover their mouths and eyes. Pete didn't want to act like he noticed because he didn't want to give Oz the satisfaction of acknowledging her skill in creating the windstorm.

The flying saucer landed, and the area around the ship seemed to settle down. Oz kept the saucer spinning while it rested on the ground. The spinning made an unusually high-pitched humming noise. As the spinning slowed, the humming frequency became lower and lower. The spacecraft rotated slowly enough not to create any wind issues. The crowd was still and quiet. The soldiers stared at the slowly spinning saucer and did not move. Everyone on the ground was in awe of the ship. They were waiting to see who, or what, would come out and greet them. Even from inside the craft, Pete could sense the tension building outside.

"There!" Oz pointed to the screen. It was the president, surrounded by Secret Service agents. The agents made a path through the crowd so the president could get through. Pete and Oz watched the president closely. He came out onto the National Lawn and stopped. He was waiting to ensure sufficient media coverage before hailing Oz and Pete to come out.

"He's good at this," Oz said.

Pete stared at the screen, watching the president's movements. "This is working, Oz."

Oz rubbed her fingertips from her right hand, raised her hand, and blew on the fingers. "Yeah, I'm amazing like that."

Pete put his hand on her shoulder. "Yeah, you are."

They continued to watch the president. There were political and military advisers arguing with the president. They were trying to convince him to stay behind the line where it was safe. But instead, he insisted that he come out and greet the visitors.

"Man, Pete, I did not expect him to do this well."

"It's all part of the show."

The president insisted that he walk closer to the ship. He received resistance to that idea from his advisors and the Secret Service agents. Then, finally, his frustration got the better of him. He pushed his advisers to the side and strolled onto the National Lawn.

Oz tapped her fingers rapidly on the console. "Please let me fire a warning laser at his feet, please! I want to watch him soil himself."

Pete sighed. "Oz, please try to take this seriously. Your plan is working well. No matter how innocent, any irresponsible action will freak everyone out and ruin it."

Oz's body drooped in her chair. "I know."

Oz and Pete made the president wait for about 15 minutes. They couldn't let the world see them react too quickly.

Pete looked at Oz. "Okay, what now?"

Oz rubbed her hands together. "Well, we need to decide what we want the world to see when we open the door."

Pete agreed. "True. We have to decide what we want to look like to them."

Oz looked at Pete with a big smile. Pete knew that whatever she was thinking wouldn't be good for him.

"I think you need to come out dressed in a spacesuit. Just like the movie." She was getting more excited at the thought of recreating the movie scene.

"No, that's a bit much," Pete raised his hands.

"Well, you can't go out there in a trench coat. What will the humans think if Detective Columbo walks out of a flying saucer?"

"Colum…who? Alright, okay, make me an outfit. But no fish bowls on my head!"

"Cool," Oz grinned. "I'm thinking all black with some fluorescent blue touches. We can make your gloves flare out in a cool spike design. And your boots could match your gloves!"

"No spikes."

"We need a cape."

"What? No. No cape."

"Not a cape like a superhero, one that covers one side of your body. It will add a regal touch."

"Okay. But no hats!"

"Okay, party pooper." Oz winked at Pete. "What do you think?"

"About what?"

Oz pointed to the opposite side of the ship. "Over there."

Pete walked in the direction she pointed and looked at the wall. The wall had a mirrored surface so that Pete could see his reflection. The suit that Oz had described was already on him. The clothes fit Pete perfectly. The uniform was tight and felt like part of his skin. He looked down at his hands and felt his chest. Pete couldn't sense the outfit; it was so light that it felt like he wasn't wearing anything. When he touched his chest, he could feel his skin. The clothes looked strange, like leather, but the material was something else.

"I guess this is okay," Pete reluctantly agreed as he turned around, still checking out his new clothes.

"It has a certain look that says 'cool alien.' Besides, it's laser-proof, so it's safe."

"Okay, I've got it. This will do fine. What about you?"

"I'll be where I always am." Oz smiled playfully, "But..."

"But what?"

"We must leave a sentinel outside the ship to stand guard."

"Why?"

"Because that's what the humans will expect."

"Okay. But nothing dangerous."

"It has to be able to defend the ship!"

"But not on its own. We have to order it too, understood?"

"Yeah, yeah, I've got it." Oz looked at Pete. "You ready?"

Pete took a deep breath and exhaled. "Let's do this."

The flying saucer stopped spinning, making the sound of a gigantic machine winding down. The crowd stepped back a little. There were screams from the gathered people.

"This is it! They're coming!" Silence fell over the area as the anticipation grew.

The part of the saucer facing the president made a low-sounding vibration, and part of the craft's lower surface started to separate from the ship. The top metal of the separating segment extended out and began moving straight up, away from the spaceship. This separation created an opening in the saucer. From the opening, a long, silver-colored metal plank began extending out. The metal plank stretched from the flying saucer across the National Lawn and stopped approximately fifty feet from the opening.

Pete took a deep breath and walked out of the opening created by the saucer door. He strolled out and stood straight, trying to exude confidence to all who could see him. He stopped at the top of the opening and stood there for several minutes, giving everyone in the crowd time to digest what they saw. Finally, Pete raised his arm, his palm facing the crowd. He turned slightly from left to right to gesture to everyone there.

Okay, I waved like you told me to. Now what?

Isn't this cool? It's just like the movie.

Oz! Come on. What's next?

Step slowly down the plank and keep waving.

When Pete reached the plank's end, he watched the president and his agents come to greet him.

What happens now?

You have to say it. Oz laughed in excitement.

No way. I don't want to sound ridiculous.

Pete, they are expecting you to say it, so do it. Please! Please, for me.

Oh, alright, Pete gave in. He released a big sigh and spoke loudly, "I come in peace!"

Yes, yes, yes! Oz jumped up and down in her seat.

Calm down. We have to focus. What now?

Okay, okay. Hold out your other hand and offer the president a gift.

What gift?

Just raise your hand. I've got this.

Pete raised his other hand, and a small object shaped like a pyramid materialized in his palm.

What is it?

It's a rock. I shaped it into an object they could effortlessly identify. It's cool. It opens when you touch the side, and our planet's blue atmosphere lights it up.

That's not bad. I thought you weren't going to expose any Wen tech?

It's Earth water with Earth food coloring. I just added a little brightness to it. Now, step toward the president and offer him the gift. You touch the side of the rock, and the blue light pops out. Then...

Then what?

You get shot.

What the...?

Sorry, that was a bit much.

Pete stepped onto the grass. The ramp pulled back automatically into the ship.

Pete stood there on the grass in front of the ship. He waited for the president to reach out and greet him. While he was waiting, he surveyed his surroundings. The eyes of everyone present were on him. No one was making a sound. It was deathly silent. After a few moments, the people who could see Pete began screaming.

One man yelled, "I knew they were Black!"

Another yelled, "What the heck are you saying?! He's a white man!"

An Asian woman was screaming in Chinese, saying the alien was Asian.

It continued: every ethnicity in the crowd saw Pete as they saw themselves. The affliction was doing its job.

Oz encouraged Pete. *Just cool your tools, negative Nancy. It's going as planned.*

Cool, my what? Negative who? You need to get off this planet.

Pete began to move into place. His outfit started to itch, and he desperately wanted to scratch himself.

Oz, I need to scratch my butt. This suit is itchy.

Pete, do NOT scratch your backside! Oz yelled in his head. *You're an alien, and aliens do not scratch their asses! Of course, some aliens don't have an ass to scratch, but that's beside the point—just stand still.*

Pete was doing his best to fight the itch. He finally couldn't hold back anymore and started to scratch his butt. *Ah, that feels so good.*

Pete, you didn't!

Yes, I did, and I liked it.

Everyone in the crowd, including the troops, began to laugh.

Pete tilted his head. *I don't understand.*

Oz released an exasperated sigh. *Well, an alien just walked out of a flying saucer and started scratching his ass. He's just standing there and digging in. Don't you think that's funny?*

I don't know. Is it funny?

Oz rolled her eyes. *I don't know why I bother.*

While Pete was scratching his backside, the president walked over to him.

The president looked at Pete and whispered, "You going to take all day there, son?"

Pete stood straight and whispered, "Sorry, this suit is itchy."

The president smiled and said, "Nice outfit, good touch. I like it."

Oz raised her chin. *See, I told you.*

The president came to attention, surveyed the crowd, and spoke loudly, almost yelling. "On behalf of the United States, we welcome you to our home."

The president extended his hand to shake Pete's. Pete shook his hand, surveyed the crowd like the president did, and yelled, "Thank you."

"I have a gift for you," Pete shouted.

He held his hand, and the pyramid-shaped rock appeared before the president. Pete pressed the side of the rock, and the top began to move. Then, blue light started to escape from it.

Someone in the crowd yelled, "It's a weapon! A laser!"

The Secret Service agents ran over and made a human shield around the president, coming between Pete's hand and the president's.

Pete looked around and noticed everyone was starting to panic. "What…?"

Oz gasped. *They don't understand our technology and are starting to freak out. You may want to close the rock.*

Before Pete could do so, the president yelled at his Secret Service agents. "He's friendly, damn it. Holster your weapons."

The president swatted the gun out of one of the Secret Service agents' hands. His weapon hit the ground and fired—the bullet launched straight toward Pete's body. The projectile stopped just before hitting him. The shot disappeared into the invisible force field that surrounded Pete.

Oz was excited. *No way!*

What is it? Pete asked.

It's just like the movie, except the alien gets shot. We needed to let the bullet hit you.

I don't think so—enough of this damn movie. Let's get this back on track already.

Just then, the saucer's top door opened. Pete turned around in response to the noise. *What now?*

A giant metal robot made of solid silver was walking out of the saucer. Its design was simple, just one solid piece of metal with arms and legs. The sunlight reflected off its metal body. It stood eight feet tall and was terrifying the crowd with its presence. Its head was a separate piece of metal, and a thin visor covered the area where its eyes would be. The metallic visor stretched across the front of its face from one side to the other.

When the robot took a step, its heavy metal foot made a loud, powerful boom sound, hitting the metal of the saucer. Boom, boom, boom, boom—each time, the sound made people in the crowd gasp and scream. It stopped right at the edge of the upper part of the ship. It started slowly, panning its head from side to side without moving its lower body. It analyzed all the data that the current situation provided. When the robot saw the troops and the weapons, its metal visor opened slowly, moving upwards, revealing a thin slit. Within the slit, a red light dotted the center of the opening. The dot irradiated brightly and resembled the light of a laser. The dot flicked on and off, intensifying with each pulse.

Pete yelled at Oz out loud, "Turn him off, Oz! He cannot fire into the crowd."

Oz didn't answer.

"Oz!" Pete yelled at her.

Still no answer.

"If you don't stop this, I will blow him off the ship!"

Oz answered, *Keanu Barbarino Nikpoo.*

The robot lowered the visor back over the red light and remained at his post, a metallic sentry as still as a statue.

What in the world was that?

It's a fitting conclusion.

Oz, stop with the movie references already. I did not see this movie. If I did, I don't remember. So I have no idea why you're doing these things.

Oz flinched. *Pete, he's there to protect us. These morons are firing at you. The robot sees that as a threat.*

I don't care, Oz. I told you, no shooting.

Okay, he's shut down now.

The president yelled at everyone to get off him. "Get the hell away from me!" he shouted.

He stood up and brushed the grass off his clothes. Several agents started to help wipe the grass away.

The president looked at them. "Stop it, please. Just back off!"

The agents moved away. The president walked up to Pete. "Sorry about that. They're all just scared."

Pete looked at the president and then scanned the area. "Am I going to be able to get to the White House without any problems?"

The president nodded. "Of course. I'll make sure they all know not to shoot at you."

"Thanks, I appreciate that."

Pete handed the rock to the president. The president stood beside Pete, took his wrist, and raised their hands together in victory. The crowd grew excited and cheered louder than they had been screaming before. Then, the president and Pete walked across the National Lawn to the president's limousine. The crowd applauded the president's efforts as he escorted the alien from his flying saucer. The president waved at the crowd as they walked from the ship to his limousine.

The president snickered to himself, "Guess who's getting re-elected?"

Pete couldn't hear the president over the crowd noise, "Did you say something?"

The president shook his head at Pete and continued waving to the voters. Pete copied the president's movements and started waving as well. When Pete began waving, the applause grew even louder.

The agents opened the doors when they finally made it through the mass of cheering people to the limo. The president stopped and stood up, using the inside of the car door to step up. He was a little higher than the crowd and could see the growing mass of people. The president waved to them, sending an uproar through the gathering. Then, he got into the limo, and Pete followed suit.

As the limousine started to move, the crowds gave way to let the vehicle slowly pass. The president had ordered the Secret Service to allow people close access to the car. He wanted them to be able to see the president riding alongside the alien. After all, it was an election year. The ride worked through the street slowly, waiting for the onlookers to part like the Red Sea. The president was thrilled with the development of their plan.

The president turned away from the window and looked at Pete.

"This is going to work, my man. I think you've got the world's attention now!"

Pete smiled and turned back to the window, waving at the crowds. Even with all the excitement surrounding him, all Pete could think about was scratching his butt.

31 ON THE CLOCK

Day one of the three-day deadline proceeded as planned. When Pete and the president entered the Oval Office, the phones began ringing off the hook. Leaders from every country, whether American allies or not, wanted to be involved in this event. They all wanted to meet the alien and see the spaceship for themselves. So, the president ordered a robust communications system in the East Room of the White House. The leaders who could not make it to DC in time could participate via secured visual communication.

The president's aides tracked which leaders would commit to an immediate visit. By the president's order, the Federal Aviation Administration canceled all commercial air traffic into Reagan National Airport to allow for emergency flights worldwide. All flights still en route to Reagan were redirected to Dulles and Baltimore-Washington International airports. The president ordered his military commanders to beef up security and escort all leaders from the airport directly to the White House. The military created an uninterrupted route between Ronald Reagan Washington National Airport and the White House. All public access to the restricted road was blocked. Route 395 looked desolate except for the escorted limousines of arriving world leaders occupying the route.

The chaos around DC was building as more people assembled around the spaceship. More troops were needed to reinforce the barricades and keep people from getting too close to the flying saucer. People began pushing each other to get a closer view and take selfies with the spaceship. The military was joined by local law enforcement to try to keep the crowd from getting violent. People who insisted on being rude, arguing, and fighting with others were escorted off the National Lawn by local officials. Some went willingly, while others had to be dragged off by several officers.

All the primary news channels and networks ran constant coverage—their media trucks were parked on the National Lawn. Camera operators were on top of the media trucks to get a good shot of the spacecraft over the crowds.

Pete was in the Oval Office with the president. Only one Secret Service agent and the same two advisers as before were in the room with them. The advisers talked to each other, discussing papers in front of them while the president was on the phone. He was taking calls from other nations' leaders, explaining the plan.

He hung up the phone and looked at Pete. "Why don't you sit and relax?" he asked.

Pete looked around the room and then at the president. "I prefer to stand, thanks."

"Okay, suit yourself. It looks like we should have the majority of the leaders here by tomorrow. Those who cannot get here will have it available via secure online transmissions."

"Sounds good," Pete said.

The president seemed concerned about Pete. "You don't sound too thrilled about how this is going."

Pete raised his hand and waved it as he began to speak. "No, no. I'm impressed with how well all this came together so quickly, that's all."

"You don't see a problem with this, do you?"

"No, sir. I think it's great. I believe the Wen will accept this gesture."

"I hope so." The president looked at Pete, then picked up the phone and started another conversation.

Pete looked out the window behind the president. He could see the sun setting; this day would soon be over. They had done their part. Everything was going well.

Pete spoke to Oz. *Hey, what do you say we get out of here?*

Oz perked up. *I thought you'd never ask.*

The president didn't notice Pete vanish from the room. He looked up while he was listening on the phone. He looked at his advisers sitting on the couch and gestured to them, asking where Pete had gone. The advisers shrugged their shoulders to indicate they did not know. The president looked at the Secret Service agent. He, too, shrugged his shoulders. The president swung his free hand out, swatting at the air before him. The agent showed no emotional response.

Pete remembered an alley he had passed while in the president's limo. So that's where he teleported.

Why here?

I didn't want anyone to see me, and this alley was deserted. Please get me my coat. I can't walk around the city like this.

Are we walking around?

Don't get so excited. I just needed to get some air, that's all. But I can't do it without my coat. I need to blend in.

You have it on.

Pete looked at his arms. He was wearing his trench coat.

You could tell me before you do that.

Sorry. It's easier this way.

Pete started walking out of the alley across the street from the National Lawn. He noticed that the crowds still gathered around the spaceship. The groups seemed to double in size in the few short hours. To avoid the masses, Pete walked opposite the city towards the Potomac River.

Let's keep away from this madness, he said to Oz.

Pete utilized different alleys whenever possible. As Pete viewed the river from one alley, he began to feel a warm breeze blowing off the water. It felt good on his face. Pete lifted his head and closed his eyes as he slowed his pace. Finally, Pete opened his eyes and saw an overpass four to five blocks away that stretched over the river. He spotted an area below the bridge where he could sit and pretend to enjoy the beautiful summer evening.

How are the repairs to your tech going?

The repairs are proceeding as they should. I should be 100% in a few hours.

And that's the last thing Pete remembered until Oz began to wake him up.

Pete. Pete, wake up. You need to get up now.

Pete was dizzy, and he tried to sit up. When he did, the back of his head throbbed. Pete reached around and touched the sensitive area. He pulled his hand back and saw blood on his fingers. Pete looked at the blood, shocked that he was bleeding.

"That's right, mutha. We knocked your ass out!"

"What?" Pete was still a little dizzy. His surroundings were hazy, and he squinted his eyes to clear up his sight.

"Get up slowly and empty your pockets, or I'll shoot you right where you're sitting."

Pete tried to stand up. It took him a few tries, but he eventually made it up. His vision cleared, and he knew three Black men were standing around him. The biggest of the three men stood directly in front of him while the other two stood off to his right.

Oz was angry. *Let me make them disappear!*

"No!" Pete yelled out loud.

The man with the gun said, "What you mean, no? Empty your pockets now!"

Pete's mind was finally clear. He looked around to assess the situation. He could feel the summer breeze on his face, so he knew he was close to the water. They were in an alley lit poorly by one street light on the corner. Turning in the opposite direction, he could make out the overpass he was initially heading to. Pete rubbed the back of his neck and turned again. He noticed a young kid sitting a few yards away on a pile of discarded wooden pallets. Pete raised an eyebrow.

"Is that little boy with you?"

"What is wrong with you, man? Do you see this gun? This gun means I ask the freakin' questions."

Pete looked at the man. "What gun?"

"This gun, mutha–" But the gun was gone from his hand. He looked at the other two young men, who were as confused as he was.

Pete looked at the three of them and approached the individual who no longer held the gun.

"I cannot believe you knocked me out. I didn't think that was possible. Oz? How was that possible?" Pete never took his eyes off the man standing in front of him.

"You are freakin' crazy, man," the big man screamed. "Who's Oz?"

Oz answered Pete's question. *You are still human, Pete. You are vulnerable if you aren't wearing any armor or don't have the forcefield up. And I was busy making repairs. So, my system shut down the forcefield to direct more energy to the repairs. Sorry.*

Pete shook his head and smacked the man on the shoulder. "Thank you, sir!"

The big man's eyes opened wide. "What for?" The man was confused, and his two friends stood with pipes in hand, still frozen in place. Both fixed their gaze on Pete.

Pete grinned, "You, sir, just taught me a life lesson. You have awakened me to a new insight about myself. I can bleed! And the blood is red! I am human!"

Pete's comments made the assailant angrier. He picked up a pipe that was on the ground next to him. The other two men readied themselves.

"Okay, man, you realize we gonna beat your ass, right? You some dumb white boy to stand there and argue with us."

The man lunged forward toward Pete. He swung the iron cylinder hard at the top of Pete's head. The iron tube stopped with a loud clang just before touching Pete. The man's hand stung from the force of the pipe, hitting the forcefield. He immediately screamed and dropped the iron pipe in front of Pete.

"What the ..?"

Pete smiled, pointing to the pipe. "See, that is what was supposed to happen when you hit me in the back of my head. But, unfortunately, Oz let the energy field down, and you took advantage of a vulnerable moment. I have to say, sir, your timing is impeccable."

The other two men just stood and stared at Pete. They immediately dropped their pipes. Pete looked at them and nodded his head, agreeing with their choice. They looked at each other, not knowing what to do next.

Pete looked at the angry man standing before him and assumed he was the leader. He was a lot older and more hostile than the other two. The man was taller and broader than Pete. He was wearing a tight white t-shirt that clung to his bulging muscles. The streetlight didn't provide enough light for Pete to read the tattoos on the man's arms.

Pete had a slightly closed, tight-lipped smile. "I'm sorry."

The man stared with wide eyes. "What you sorry for?"

Pete sighed, "For this."

Pete moved his right hand in a backhand motion, and the man came off the ground and flew into the nearby brick wall. He slid down the wall and landed on the ground, unconscious. Pete sighed slowly and turned to the other two young men. The other two looked scared, as if they wanted to run, but it was apparent to Pete that they couldn't leave without the little boy.

Pete spoke up. "My name is Pete. What're your names?"

They looked at each other, and then one spoke up. "LaQuan, ass wipe. And this is Reggie."

"Okay, LaQuan Asswipe. Let's just say this was a misunderstanding, and we just go home."

The two men were younger than their leader, who was still unconscious against the alley wall. Pete guessed they were in their early 20s. Both dressed similarly, wearing white T-shirts and jeans. Their jeans hung down below their waists, almost to their knees, exposing their underwear. They had toned bodies but weren't as muscular as their much bigger friend.

Pete looked over at the little boy, still sitting on the pallets. "Is this little man with you?"

LaQuan clenched his fists. "Yeah, so what?"

"I'm just wondering why he's hanging out with you at this time of night. That's all," Pete said.

"I gotta watch him for his mamma. She's workin' tonight."

"You're telling me you're babysitting?"

Reggie started to laugh. LaQuan got angrier. "Shut up, man," LaQuan yelled at Reggie.

Pete walked over to the young boy on the pallets. He was sitting there, not saying a word. The little boy had a blue ball cap on his head with the letter W sewn onto it. He was wearing jeans, a black sweatshirt, and red high-top sneakers.

Pete introduced himself. "Hey, I'm Pete. What's your name?"

"Andre," the boy answered.

"How old are you, Andre?"

"I'm five."

Pete looked over at LaQuan. "Five? You brought a five-year-old kid out into this?"

"What does your white ass care, anyways?" LaQuan yelled at Pete.

"You're using him to see white people, aren't you?"

LaQuan shifted nervously and didn't answer.

Pete turned back to Andre. "Your mother is at work?"

"Uh-huh," the boy affirmed.

"Do you have any brothers or sisters?"

"I had a brother, but he was kilt."

Pete froze. It was like his mind shut his body down. Pete didn't understand what was happening inside his head, and he wanted to continue the conversation, but couldn't. He felt enclosed in a small space and couldn't move. It was as though his mind had flipped a switch and turned him off. The claustrophobic feeling felt familiar, and he called Oz for an explanation.

Oz, what's happening to me?

I think the tech is trying to suppress an emotion. I've heard about this program but have never seen it in action.

That doesn't help. I don't understand what set it off.

The blow to your head may have activated some of the unknown techs. Andre caused you to have an emotional reaction. As a result of the strike to your head, the program kicked in before you could experience the emotion.

Pete regained control, walking away from the boy and pacing around the alley. LaQuan and Reggie moved over to Andre. LaQuan took Andre's hand, and they began to walk away.

Pete turned around. "Hold on a minute, please."

"What, man?" LaQuan asked angrily.

Oz, I need to explore this reaction more deeply. This incident could lead us to answers about regaining my human emotions.

I don't know how to proceed, Pete. We cannot hold them against their will. They will most likely get angrier and refuse to cooperate if we do.

Pete looked at Andre. "Want to see a spaceship?"

LaQuan looked at Andre and then at Pete. "Why are you asking him that? We can't get close to that ship right now."

Okay, Pete, I am confused. What are you doing?

I don't know, Oz. Bringing them to the ship may be the only way to keep them around longer. But, on the other hand, I think if I let them walk away, I may lose an opportunity to unlock some of my emotions.

I don't know, Pete. I am not familiar with the program that kicked in. There could be dangerous consequences if you continue. We can't afford to screw up our mission.

I won't screw it up, I promise. Oz, this is important to me. I have to look into it further.

Pete looked at Andre. "So? You want to go see the spaceship?"

Andre nodded excitedly.

LaQuan walked up and got into Pete's face. "Look, I don't know what you want. Maybe you're one of those perverted white men that likes little kids or somethin'."

"No," Pete said. "Look, you're watching him for his mother, so I'll take you too. I'll take all of you."

"How are you going to do that? You just a crazy white boy, that's all. You ain't got no money or pull in this town."

Pete looked at Andre. "You want to see an alien?"

"You mean from outer space?" Andre asked.

"Watch this." Pete took a few steps back from the group and started levitating.

LaQuan and Reggie started screaming. Andre's eyes grew wider as he watched Pete rise in the air. Andre began grinning from ear to ear. Then, he began laughing at LaQuan and Reggie while they were freaking out.

Pete looked down at them. He saw Andre jump up and down, laughing. Reggie and LaQuan were trying to figure out how Pete was levitating right before them. Pete drifted down and looked at Andre.

"Well, what do you think?"

Andre laughed. "That was cool."

LaQuan was still angry. "You some magician? How did you do that?"

"Do you all want to see the spaceship now?"

Andre was screaming Yes and hopping around. LaQuan still needed some convincing.

"So you do magic. How's that supposed to get us to the spaceship?"

Pete looked at Laquan. "You're already here."

LaQuan glanced around, and his eyes looked like they would pop out of his head. He stumbled backward and fell on the floor. Andre started laughing at LaQuan, and Reggie joined in. Reggie pulled LaQuan up, and they slapped each other's hands.

Andre was continuing his hopping. "This is it? Am I in the spaceship?" he asked Pete.

"Yes, you're inside the spaceship." Pete looked at the joy on Andre's face. Then, something started happening inside his head again. It was a sensation that Pete had yet to experience. Pete couldn't figure it out.

Oz, what's going on?

I think you are trying to experience emotion again. I believe the program will kick in…right… about…now.

Pete felt frozen again, like in the alley. But this time, Pete was able to snap out of it more quickly.

Oz was surprised. *How did you do that so quickly?*

I don't know. I guess I'm adapting to the program.

How did you bypass the program?

Oz, I don't know, but something is different now.

What do you mean?

My body is lighter; I don't feel as heavy as before.

I don't know what that means.

Neither do I. But I'm not going to resist it. I'm going to see where it takes me.

What about the mission?

Nothing has changed; I'm still focused.

Andre ran up to Pete. "Tag, you're it." Andre ran in the opposite direction, laughing. Pete ran after Andre. He wanted to be around him as much as possible to see if interacting with him would cause another emotional reaction.

While Pete and Andre were running around the ship, LaQuan and Reggie stood in the middle of the room, puzzled. There wasn't much to see. Solid metal walls and a metal ceiling. For all they knew, they could be in a warehouse somewhere.

LaQuan blurted out, "What the heck is this man? It looks like an old sci-fi movie set in the 1950s. 'Member that crappy old black and white movie we saw at yo mamma's? It looks like that."

Reggie agreed. They were disappointed and confused about what they were seeing.

Oz spoke up through the control system.

"We have to hide our tech from human eyes, so we put this out here in its place."

LaQuan and Reggie started to laugh at Oz's voice. Reggie looked at the control panel and said, "That's a load. My computer looks more futuristic than this piece of crap. Look at all these flashing, ridiculous lights. What a joke."

The two of them started laughing harder.

A blue beam of light radiated down from the ceiling. A white circle of light on the floor surrounded the blue ray. Reggie jumped back and looked over at LaQuan. LaQuan was frozen, staring at the beam.

Reggie screamed at LaQuan, "You ticked it off, man!"

LaQuan snapped out of his stupor, "Me? What you mean me?! You talked about it, too!"

The blue beam began rotating in a circular motion within the white light. The two young men stood there, staring. Then, the blue light slowly turned into a female body. Oz looked out at them as she emerged. She walked up to LaQuan and flipped the bottom of his chin up. His mouth closed with a snap as his top and bottom teeth clicked together.

"Your grandma's TV do that?" Oz smiled.

They didn't answer. Reggie and LaQuan just stood there, shaking their heads. Both were afraid to respond or move.

Pete came around the corner with Andre. "I see you guys have met Oz."

LaQuan looked at Pete. "This is Oz? She's the voice you were talking to before?"

"Yup, that's her."

"This is some crazy stuff, man." LaQuan walked over to Pete. "I can't believe you actually brought us here. I can't believe you did this for us."

Reggie nodded his head in agreement.

Pete tilted his head, "Why wouldn't I?"

LaQuan looked at Pete and shook his head. "Come on, man. If you're an alien, you gotta be smarter than that."

Pete looked at Oz and then back to LaQuan. Oz was confused, but Pete knew what he was saying. "Sorry, I didn't mean any disrespect. I guess it's easier to ignore the truth than to deal with it sometimes."

Reggie nodded his head in agreement. "That's right," he said.

"I know you meant well, man," said LaQuan. "I get you, I really do, but life on this planet is pretty messed up for people of color. We can't cut a break with all the racist bullcrap going on in this country. And it ain't no better anywhere else. They still be sellin' off Black people in other countries. And the messed up part is they're bein' sold by other Black people.

People of color can't even agree on what's important. It's like everyone forgets about us in the inner cities. No human being should have to live like us. It's depressing and frustrating. It makes us angrier every day. We don't know who to trust anymore."

Pete lowered his head. "Yeah, I know. Unfortunately, humans can't live with each other with mutual respect."

"Too bad you guys can't come here and fix this."

"The beings I represent are called the Wen from the planet Wen'q'rixsh. What if I told you these aliens are doing something right now?"

"Like what?"

"The affliction."

LaQuan stepped back. "Y'all are responsible for this?"

"Yes, the affliction is how they are trying to help."

LaQuan looked between Pete and Oz in shock. "You know not everyone likes what's going on with this, right?"

Pete nodded. "I know. But this is what the Wen decided to offer as help. They are a highly advanced intelligent race, and they spent a lot of time and research on this protocol because they believe it's the only way."

"Well, it may work out in the long run, but it's going to be a tough sell right now."

"No doubt," said Pete. "But they had to do something. This planet is on a course to self-destruction, and drastic measures are needed to save our planet."

LaQuan agreed. "No, I get it. Believe me, I got you on this. But it's hard for people to come to grips that they been racist all along, you know?"

Pete nodded. "Yeah, that's a hell of a wake-up call, isn't it?"

Everyone laughed.

Pete decided to explain how the affliction works.

LaQuan shook his head. "You know a lot of people can't tell the difference between judging someone and being racist, right? So, if you judge people by how they look, you must feel like you're better than them. And that's some racist bull."

Reggie walked up to LaQuan, slapped his hand, and they chest bumped. "Tell it, brother."

"Yeah, I know," said Pete, "but this is what the affliction does. It doesn't allow anyone to pass judgment on how a person looks in the moment they see them. It isn't saying the person is racist or not. Well, the person could very well be racist, but it doesn't mean only that. I know it is going to take getting used to. Still, the only other solution is to round up every racist and take them out of society."

LaQuan laughed. "I am definitely okay with that. Shoot all the white racist muthas!"

Pete looked at Laquan. "I don't believe they would all be white."

LaQuan looked at Pete and then at Reggie. "But that's a good place to start."

Reggie nodded. "True dat."

"I know it sounds like the right thing to do, but if you can't change how a society treats the people within it, removing some of them is not the answer."

LaQuan and Reggie nodded their heads in agreement. LaQuan pressed his lips together, "Yeah, maybe."

Pete looked at Andre, who was playing at the console. He saw Oz walk over to him and turn the screen on so he could see all the people outside the spaceship.

A big grin filled Andre's face, "Wow!"

Pete turned to LaQuan. "So what can I do to help you guys and Andre? I know you aren't asking for my help, nor am I saying you need it."

LaQuan laughed. "Chill, man, you're cool. We appreciate you. I don't know what you can do for us, man. We still got to go on with our lives, you know?"

Pete looked at LaQuan. "Well, I need to do something."

"Why?"

"I feel responsible for bringing Andre out with you to that alley tonight."

LaQuan looked confused. "Why?"

"You brought him because of the affliction."

"Bringing him wasn't my idea. That was B-Boy's."

"B-Boy?"

"Yeah, B-Boy, the mutha you flung against the building."

Pete nodded. "That makes sense. I'm glad it wasn't your idea."

LaQuan shook his head. "I kinda agreed with it because I didn't want us to beat on no brother in the streets."

Pete shared a warm smile with LaQuan. "Look, I am not judging you. I just wanted you to know I got you, too."

LaQuan and Reggie nodded.

Pete had an epiphany, "You know if you walk out of this spaceship, you'll be pretty famous, right?"

LaQuan nodded, "I suppose so, yeah."

Pete took off his coat, revealing his uniform.

"Nice threads," LaQuan smiled. "Who's your tailor?"

Oz started bouncing. "See?! I told you it was a good uniform!"

"Thanks," Pete said, "you just inflated her already huge ego."

Oz smiled, "Since you like the outfits so much…."

LaQuan and Reggie looked at each other. "No way!" they shouted together. They were now wearing uniforms like Pete's.

LaQuan started laughing when he looked at Andre. "Look at you, little spaceman."

Andre giggled. "I'm a spaceman!" he shouted.

Pete looked them up and down. "Damn, you guys look much better in this uniform than I do."

"Yeah, they really do," Oz agreed, "really."

Pete smiled, "Thanks, Oz."

"So, what's the game plan?" LaQuan asked.

Pete said, "Nothing major. All you do is walk out the door with me. My guess is you'll be doing the talk show circuits right away."

"I know that's right." Reggie smiled in agreement.

Pete looked at Oz. "You ready?"

"Yeah," said Oz. She glanced over the three new aliens. "You guys look great, and it was nice meeting you."

They all returned Oz's salutation and watched her disappear.

"I'm so glad I didn't disintegrate those guys," she chirped.

"What?" LaQuan and Reggie's eyes opened wide.

Pete spoke up. "Oz, you were speaking out loud."

"Oops! Sorry."

Pete looked at everyone. "You guys will do well. It was nice meeting you. Thanks for the souvenir." Pete said, rubbing the back of his head.

LaQuan shook Pete's hand, and they chest bumped. "I'm sorry about that, man. You know, you're alright. I hope we see each other again."

Pete nodded. "Hey, little man, you going to be okay?"

Andre ran up to Pete and hugged him. "Thank you for taking me on your spaceship!"

Pete felt his eyes water a little. "Thank you for being my friend. You do good, okay? And listen to LaQuan. He's a good guy."

Andre nodded in agreement.

Pete turned away from Andre and wiped his eyes with his sleeve. Pete stood there for a moment, taking it all in.

The water in my eyes is a good sign, he thought. He looked back at everyone and had Oz open the door.

The crowds of people became deathly quiet as the door to the saucer started to open. The light poles the military had erected around the dish lit up the walkway like daylight. Cameras flashed, and reporters began calling out a play-by-play of what was happening. Pete started walking down the ramp, holding Andre by the hand. LaQuan and Reggie followed behind, their faces hurting from frozen smiles. People started pointing at them, cheering loudly. Finally, Pete paused on the ramp so LaQuan, Reggie, and Andre could take it all in.

A guard sitting at his desk in an office building was watching the television, observing the events unfolding at the flying saucer site. He recognized the little boy walking down the ramp of the saucer with the alien visitor. He shouted to the custodian cleaning the floors to hurry to the TV, "Kendra, come quick. You got to see this."

She dropped her mop and ran to the guard's desk. When Andre's mother saw him on the TV along with LaQuan and Reggie, she began to cry and laugh at his spacesuit. Kendra's tears were joyous as her baby boy held hands with the alien. And though she knew she should have been frightened for Andre's safety, the look on the alien's face calmed her fears. When the camera zoomed in closer to the alien, she saw a warmth radiate from his eyes. She wiped her tears and sighed. She knew she would remember this day for the rest of her life.

The camera flashes increased as the four aliens reached the end of the ramp. They stopped and stood close together in a group. Pete looked down at Andre, and Andre jumped up and hugged Pete. Pete nodded to LaQuan, and LaQuan nodded back. Then Pete shook LaQuan and Reggie's hands before returning to the ship. The ramp slowly closed behind them.

LaQuan, Reggie, and Andre stood alone on the grass. The crowd cheered as the three young men started waving at everyone. LaQuan lifted Andre so everyone could see him waving as well. The three continued waving and soaking up the moment. Finally, a soldier approached and escorted them across the National Lawn to the military base tent. LaQuan's smile was as big as Andre's.

32 THE CLOCK IS TICKING

Day two was as hectic as the one before. All the White House staff allocated to help were running around putting the finishing touches on their respective assignments. All political issues were set aside to enable 100% focus on putting this meeting together. The president ordered all House and Senate sessions to be put on hold until further notice. This meeting with the aliens would be the only item on every D.C. politician's to-do list.

The president called for a meeting with his advisers. "Okay, we need to keep everyone busy until the Wen contacts us again," he said. "Please work with the staff and contact any senator who has volunteered their time. We need to create a plan to meet every leader's needs. I want to ensure we verify with everyone participating what and how we will communicate before the Wen arrives. Understood?"

The advisers nodded their heads in agreement.

"Now isn't the time to second-guess these aliens," the president told them. "If the world leaders do not comply, we are all doomed. We must all speak with one voice. It is important to have these discussions before the contact happens. Get the word out to all attending."

The advisers jumped up and hurried out of the office. The president rolled his eyes as he watched them rush out the door. "Idiots." The president shook his head as they hurried away.

He stood up and walked to the window. He stared out and lost himself in the moment. Nothing he had faced in his political career was as important as this meeting. The president was concentrating so hard on the scene outside the window that he didn't notice Pete walk up next to him. Eventually, the president saw Pete's reflection in the glass.

The president acknowledged Pete and returned to staring. "This is a great country. There are a lot of good people in it. It's just sad that groups of blockheads get all the publicity, and their hateful messages are communicated to an unknowing public."

The president sighed and continued, "It seems the American public is more concerned with how many hits and views their posts receive than caring about each other. But I still believe Americans will come together and do the right thing when the time comes."

Pete also looked out the window as he spoke. "Maybe there will be more good people and good deeds to publicize now."

"We can hope."

"Yes. A very human trait."

The president looked over at Pete. "You should know, right? Because you are human."

Pete nodded, not moving his gaze. "Yes, I am. The Wen stripped me of my emotions so I would be more logical during this mission. But I still know what hope is. Hope keeps humans going when the odds are against them. It is something that the logical, super-intelligent Wen will never understand."

"Well, if a super-intelligent life form can't figure us out, how the hell will we be able to do it?"

"By working together. That's how we will prevail."

The president laughed. "I may use this conversation to address all the world leaders later today. Or you could do it for me?"

Pete smiled, "You don't need my help. You've got this."

The president turned toward Pete, and Pete turned toward the president. They shook hands. "I'm glad you're on our side."

Pete just nodded. The president went back to his desk and his phone calls.

Pete walked around to the front of the desk. "So, what time do you think everything will be ready?"

The president looked up from his desk. "I believe everyone will be set up by six p.m. tomorrow. I'd like you to be in the East Room to talk to everyone and prepare them for the Wen contact."

"I can do that," Pete agreed.

"Oh, and by the way, nice touch with the kids coming out of the saucer last night."

Pete tilted his head, "Touch?"

The president laughed. "You really should be a PR man. You missed your calling. It's all over the news today."

Pete tilted his head, "What is?"

The president laughed, "The headlines are about how friendly the aliens are."

Pete shrugged. "It wasn't my intention to publicize our position."

"Even better. It made it more authentic," the president laughed and picked up the phone.

33 BACK HOME

"Tell me what the president is like in person." Jessica was sitting on her couch next to Pete.

"I don't know," Pete answered nonchalantly. "I think politics may have turned him into a person he doesn't like."

"What do you mean?"

"It seems the president is overly concerned with public opinions of himself."

"How do you know he wasn't like that to begin with? Maybe politics just brought it out of him."

Pete sighed, "He has moments when he would rather be somewhere else. He speaks within those moments as if he misses a time when things were different."

Maggie and Bill sat in the two chairs across from the sofa, where Pete and Jessica were. They shared a bowl of popcorn. Pete and Jessica had their bowl sitting on the couch between them.

Bill and Maggie were listening attentively. They wanted to hear the details of Pete's DC visit as well. Bill spoke up. "Seriously? Come on. You have to share the details, man."

"I don't know what you want me to say."

Maggie chimed in. "Start from the beginning; how did you get in to see the president?"

"I just teleported into his office."

The three of them were frustrated. Jessica looked at Bill and Maggie. "He's not good with explanations."

They all laughed. Bill, Maggie, and Jessica stopped when they noticed Pete was smiling. He looked at them. They fell silent and stared at him like he was a stranger.

Pete sat up straighter. "What?"

Bill smiled. "Dude, you're smiling."

Pete grabbed a handful of popcorn and sighed, "So?"

"So? So you never smile," Bill insisted.

Pete leaned forward, "Oh, yeah. I think I had an epiphany while I was in DC. I think that's the right word for it."

Jessica screamed, forcing Pete to jump back a little in his seat. "Why didn't you tell us?" she shouted again and lunged across the couch to hug Pete, knocking the bowl of popcorn onto the floor.

Pete struggled to speak between Jessica hanging all over him and the popcorn in his mouth. "Well, I guess I didn't think of it."

Maggie laughed. "Typical male. Yeah, you are definitely human." Everyone started laughing again.

Jessica had an idea. "Pete, can Oz play the recording of your visit?"

Pete shrugged, "If you want to see it. It wasn't that exciting."

Jessica got up and picked up the bowl from the floor. She put all the popcorn back in it and headed into the kitchen. "Okay, great," she said from the kitchen. "I'll get more popcorn."

She walked back into the living room with a new bowl. "Oz, come out, come out, wherever you are!" Jessica called out.

Oz popped up on the coffee table. "I didn't think I was going to be invited to this shindig. I felt so left out."

Jessica smiled at her. "Oz, you are always welcome here."

Oz looked at Pete. "What the freak, man?"

Pete narrowed his eyes. "What did I do?"

"You didn't invite me out. And Maggie's right. You are becoming more human."

Pete took another handful of popcorn. "Sorry."

Oz turned the lights off and played Pete's visit to DC. When it ended, they started with their questions again.

Bill was the first. "So, is the president as much of a dick in person as he is in public?"

"As you saw, he was okay."

Maggie was next. "So you just appeared in the president's office? And you were sitting in his chair?"

"Yes."

"You were like Dirty Harry. Such a badass!"

"Dirty who?"

Maggie smiled. "Never mind."

Bill parted his lips, "The agent outside the door didn't feel anything when you took the whole room into space. Was that an illusion or something?"

"Yes."

Pete's three friends looked at each other, then over at Pete, who kept eating his popcorn.

Jessica spoke. "Pete, it would help if you elaborated a little when you answered our questions."

"Okay."

Bill went on. "Was that the first time you saw a Xan? He looked pretty scary."

"Yes." Pete looked at Jessica; she leaned her head forward as if to ask, '…and?'.

Pete went on quickly. "Oh, okay, yeah. He was scary. The Xan wore protective armor, and I didn't get to see what he looked like underneath. I wish I could have had time to check him out more."

Jessica smiled at Pete. "See, that wasn't so hard, was it?"

"No."

Bill kept going. "Do you know how they take on the body and persona of a human being?"

"No. But it appears that the Xan kills the host and then assumes their identity. I am not sure if they have to kill the host or if it is something they choose to do."

"By the looks of them, I am sure they take pleasure in killing."

Oz chimed in. "It's not a pleasure they seek. They kill out of a sense of necessity. The Xan are highly intelligent beings, like the Wen. The only difference is that their logic comes from a common belief, or, as you would say, religion."

"Killing is killing," Bill answered.

"To the Xan, killing another being serves a purpose. They cannot arbitrarily kill another lifeform; it is against their logic belief. Killing that agent and assuming his identity was part of the greater plan to annihilate Earth. Therefore, it was justified."

Pete nodded, "You have done your homework, Oz."

"We must know everything about the Xan to predict their next move. So it is only logical."

Bill had yet another question. "Krix'x wasn't shocked about you killing the Xanoclax warrior, Pete. I thought Oz said no one kills a Xan? Krix'x took the whole thing pretty much in stride."

Pete nodded. "You picked up on that; it must be the cop in you. I was thinking the same thing. I waited for him to ream me out, but he wasn't concerned. Oz and I have spoken about this and couldn't develop a logical explanation."

Oz said, "There are many peculiarities about this mission that trouble me."

Bill raised his eyebrows, "Like what?"

"I have been on other missions similar to this one. I have guided different lifeforms the way I am guiding Pete. Across all my missions, the lifeforms I guided acted and responded as expected.

Pete is different. Pete is showing signs of evolving into something else."

Pete shifted in his seat, "Evolving how?"

"You do things you should not be able to do, Pete. My tech makes some of your actions possible by integrating with your mind and body."

"And others?"

"You shouldn't be able to control and redirect energy as you do."

Pete tilted his head, "Well, how do you explain it then?"

Oz shook her head and bit her lip, "I can't explain it logically. My only theory is that the Council enhanced you somehow to enable these abilities."

Pete frowned, "Enhanced me?"

"I am not sure what they did, Pete. It is unclear if the Council considered your new capabilities even a possibility. I can only assume that the enhancements, combined with your biology, created a new set of abilities for you to utilize. I have never been exposed to this protocol before."

The atmosphere of the room became quiet and gloomy. No one knew what to say. Pete just stared down at his popcorn.

"Well, look at the bright side, Pete," Bill offered.

"What bright side?" Pete spoke into his bowl.

Bill smiled. "You're unique. Out of all the lifeforms in the universe, the Council chose you."

"Why settle for the rest when you can have the best?" Oz

exclaimed.

Bill, Maggie, and Jessica laughed. Pete looked up, smiled, and nodded. After that, everyone seemed to liven up a little.

"Pete," Maggie made eye contact with Pete, "what you did for those kids was awesome."

Pete smiled. "Thanks."

"Virgil watched the whole thing at the shelter and started crying. Then, he stood before everyone like a proud daddy and yelled, That's my boy' several times."

Pete looked at Maggie. "I have been thinking of Virgil." Then Pete noticed Jessica wasn't saying anything. "You okay?" he asked her.

Jessica's eyes began to water. "I'm just so happy for you. You got a taste of your feelings back. No matter how small it was. It's wonderful."

Pete raised an eyebrow, "Yeah, about that. I must work on repressing whatever I have gained before tomorrow night's Council visit."

Bill looked at Pete and groaned. "Man, that sucks."

"Yeah, but I can't let the Council know. It may jeopardize the mission."

Oz spoke up. "If they know Pete has some of his feelings back, they could try to take them away again."

***

When Maggie and Bill left, Jessica asked Pete if he planned on staying the night.

"I didn't give it much thought," he answered her.

"Oh," Jessica said in a soft voice. Pete could tell she was bothered by his comment.

"I'm sorry. I didn't mean to sound like I didn't care. I was so focused on wanting to visit you that I didn't think about where I would be sleeping."

Oz jumped onto Pete's shoulders and smacked him on the head. "He's evolving into a human male. Or should I say devolving?"

Jessica laughed, and Pete rubbed the back of his head. "Okay, I get it."

Oz said she was leaving. Pete told her to shut down. "No problem. Goodnight!"

Jessica smiled at Oz. "Goodnight, girlfriend."

Pete looked at Jessica, "I need to keep taking everything as slow as possible. Maybe we can lie together like we did that first night in the motel?"

Jessica grabbed Pete's hand and led him to the bedroom. "No problem," she smiled. "Promise you won't blow up my new place, okay?"

"No problem," he echoed.

When they got to the bedroom, Jessica threw Pete's coat onto a chair. They lay on the bed together, fully clothed. Jessica stared into Pete's eyes and smiled. She slowly caressed his hair as their gaze remained locked. Jessica found it difficult to take her eyes off Pete. The innocent look he was projecting was so honest that it melted her heart. Finally, she pulled away slowly and reached over to her nightstand to turn off the light. She cuddled up to Pete and put her head on his chest, and they both fell asleep.

34 ONE LAST MEETING

The following day, Pete arrived in the Oval Office around five-thirty pm, and the president was pacing in front of the window. He was practicing his speech. Pete just stayed in the shadows and did not interrupt him. When the president finished rehearsing, Pete spoke in an encouraging tone,

"I think that will do fine."

"Jesus, I hate it when you do that!" The president jumped back, surprised. Then, he laughed and shook Pete's hand.

Pete smiled. "I think you're ready."

The president smiled and nodded. "As ready as I am ever going to be."

A Secret Service agent opened the door, and the president walked out. Pete followed behind him. Pete stepped out of the Oval Office and surveyed his surroundings. Three agents were before the president, and two were directly behind Pete. They began walking toward the East Room. The president had his head down, staring at the papers in his hand, occasionally looking up to see where he was walking. Pete asked Oz to scan all the personnel. Oz began the scan and immediately noticed something was wrong.

Oh no! No, no, no! Oz sounded worried.

Pete yelled out to her telepathically. *What is it?*

Oz was breathing rapidly. *Everyone is blocked, Pete. The Xans know we are here, and they blocked us out, so we can't pick up their trace!*

Pete looked at the president and the agents. *Oz, what are our options?*

I'm thinking. Hold on!

We don't have time to think, Oz. We have to act. If they blocked their signal, they are here and will try to mess up this meeting.

Oz screamed back at Pete. *I know that!*

The president kept walking, unaware of what was going on. Pete concentrated on the agents. He had to stop them before they got to the East Room. Pete approached the president and spoke under his breath so only he could hear. "Sir, I need you to stop for a moment, please."

"What for?" The president turned around to Pete.

Pete grabbed the president by the arm and gently pulled him to the side. He whispered into the president's ear. "I need you to dismiss your agents right now."

The president looked at Pete. "Oh, crap," he said under his breath, startled. He looked at Pete and nodded his head slightly in agreement.

The president spoke up and addressed the agents. "I want all of you to stay here while I proceed to the East Room with the herald."

The agents left the hallway and let Pete and the president pass. They stood in the passage, not saying a word. The president and Pete continued to walk away from the agents toward the East Room. Pete looked back at the agents. They were all doing as ordered. Not one of the five agents insisted on escorting the president.

Pete slowed down. *Oz, this doesn't seem right.*

Yeah, Oz agreed. *They didn't put up a fight to escort the president. So maybe we're okay then.*

Pete wasn't convinced. *No, we're not okay. What are we missing?*

Maybe they're not here.

Why would they jam the signal if they weren't here?

Yeah, I realized that after I spoke. So who is it, then?

How strong is the jamming signal? Is it traceable?

Oz perked up. *Maybe. Let me try something.*

Pete was getting anxious. He and the president were about to approach the East Room door.

Oz yelled out, *Holy crap!*

What is it?

The signal is powerful right here. Pete, I think it's the president!

Pete was already grabbing the president's arm before Oz finished her sentence. Pete turned the president around and came face-to-face with him. The president looked at Pete, and they locked eyes. They stood there staring at each other, neither saying a word. It was as if one was waiting for the other to say something.

Oz would later say that the next moment reminded her of a scene in a movie she saw. It was as though time slowed to almost a stop as the president's serious look changed. His cheeks began to wrinkle as he formed an enormous, menacing grin. Then, the president tilted his head toward Pete and froze in that position.

"Damn!" the president said, keeping his terrifying smile expanded, "I thought we would have been able to get into the East Room before you figured it out. What gave me away?"

Pete looked into the president's eyes and clenched his fists. "You called me the herald."

The president lunged at Pete, and Pete quickly moved to the side, avoiding any contact. The president had his back to Pete and turned his head around, still grinning from ear to ear. His smile appeared frozen in place, making the president look horrendous. He swiftly shifted his body to face Pete. The president paused momentarily, and his face changed to a stern expression. He decided to kill the herald slowly and savor the victory. His right hand came up straight before him, and he pointed his palm toward Pete.

Pete! Oz yelled.

I see it!

The president discharged a ball of energy, and Pete's forcefield took it head-on. The blast lifted Pete off the floor and blew him backward through the East Room door. As the fire burned around the newly expanded doorway, Pete rolled off his back onto his hands and knees. The president casually walked through the burning doorway and cautiously stepped over the debris on the floor. The president brushed ash and dust off his suit as he addressed the dignitaries sitting in the room. He perused the room with his terrifying grin. Finally, the president bowed to all the present dignitaries and acknowledged the many LCD screens displaying those who couldn't attend in person.

"Ladies and gentlemen, how are we doing this evening?" He kept the same chilling grin on his face while he was speaking.

He pointed down at Pete and raised his hand over his mouth as if surprised by what he saw. The president removed his hand from his mouth and tilted his head sideways. He held his index finger in front of his face and nodded rapidly toward the attendees, gesturing to give him a minute, "I need to take the alien trash out before I get to you, so please make yourselves comfortable. And by all means, enjoy the show!"

The president pointed to Pete and levitated him quickly, banging him into the concrete ceiling. Pete broke the cement in the ceiling, where he made contact, and immediately plummeted to the marble floor. Pieces of concrete from the ceiling fell onto him.

Pete immediately spoke to Oz after hitting the floor. *Oz, what's happening?*

He's trying to weaken our forcefield. He knows that your body will only be able to sustain a few more of these powerful blows.

As Oz finished, Pete was hurled backward, flying across the room and crashing against the opposite wall. The forcefield made an awful thudding sound when Pete hit the wall.

Pete shook his head. *I am feeling the impact. How is this possible?*

He has tremendous power, Pete. The energy he is using exceeds measurements I have never seen before.

Pete slowly stood up and brushed the dust off his coat. He clenched his fists and took a step toward the president. "Okay, it's my turn now."

Wait, Pete! Stop! Oz interrupted him.

Why?

342

He wants you to engage. Everyone in the room dies if you participate in an energy blast fight with him!

Pete sighed. *Then what do we do?*

Before Oz could answer, the Xan fired another blast. Pete braced himself once more as the explosion slammed him onto the floor. The president laughed out loud. "Come on, herald, fight back. Or are you too afraid to confront me?"

Pete got up and walked in a semi-circle around the room. The president circled in the opposite direction. The dignitaries were still sitting in their seats, afraid. Pete had succeeded in turning the Xan away from where the dignitaries were seated. The president had his back to the window, and Pete had his back to the burning door. Before the president could speak, Pete leaped at him with all his power. He was so fast that the president had no time to react. Pete held onto him, and they crashed through the window. Pete held onto him as they fell rapidly. Pete levitated them both before they could hit the ground. The president's grin was gone, and his jaw dropped.

"How is this possible, herald? No Wen has this ability or power." The Xan spoke in a deep, rough voice, not that of the president.

The Xanoclax warrior raised his arm to release his weapon.

Before the weapon materialized, Pete looked the Xan in the face and stopped a few hundred feet above the ground. Pete held him as they floated above the clouds. The warrior was so shocked at Pete's ability to hold them both up that he forgot about his weapon.

"Impossible," the Xan screamed in his low, raspy voice. "How?"

"I am no ordinary herald, you Xan bastard!"

Pete's right hand caught fire with energy. The president looked terrified as he saw it energize. His eyes turned blood red as he met

343

Pete's stare. He appeared frozen in shock, and the president's mouth fell agape. He could only repeat himself: "How?"

Pete smiled and punched the president. Pete's entire arm continued through the president's chest and out his back, and Pete quickly intensified the energy. The president's terrifying expression froze on his lifeless body as Pete held the slumped, dead body by the collar. He hesitated a few moments, hovering in the air. Pete gazed at the dead president and bowed his head. He felt a weight in his chest like he said goodbye to his friends in Bends Creek. *Sadness is a complicated emotion*, he thought. Pete nodded and took a few deep breaths.

Pete drifted back down through the broken window and tossed the president's corpse onto the floor for everyone to see. Smoke slowly drifted up from the president's chest wound as his skin started to disintegrate, revealing the armored Xan warrior beneath. The dignitaries looked on in horror as the president's skin melted away. The cameras focused on the transition, which enabled the rest of the world to watch. The clamor of voices grew louder. No one could sit still as they watched the president's skin dissolve.

Once the president's skin had fully melted, Pete continued his observations, which started with the first Xan. The hole that Pete's energy blast made in the Xan's chest was oozing a green liquid. Pete looked inside the hole and tried to see the skin of the Xan underneath the armor. He couldn't see anything but green fluid. Pete refocused on his body armor. Bending over the Xan, Pete began tapping on the Xan's chest with his fingernails. The tapping made a clinking sound. The light was brighter than the Oval Office. Pete could clearly see the blackish-green metal armor.

The Xan's legs and arms were covered in armor as well. His metal hands had four digits shaped like long, thin spikes with sharp points on the ends. There was no way for Pete to tell if the fingers were a part of the armor or the Xan's physiology. Pete turned the Xan over, and there was a quick mechanical swishing sound from his leg armor. The back of the Xan's leg armor exposed the sharp points of four individual blades shaped like shark fins. Pete pushed on one of the edges with his foot; the blade retracted and immediately snapped back when he removed his foot.

Pete wanted to continue observing the Xan, but the chatter in the room from the dignitaries turned into a roar and distracted him. Pete told Oz to record as much of the Xan as possible for further investigation. Pete was still breathing heavily as he stood over the Xan. He held his hand up, and the dignitaries fell silent. When the last murmurs had subsided, Pete spoke to everyone in the room.

"Ladies and gentlemen, this was not the President of the United States."

"Where is the president?" one leader asked.

Pete sighed, "He is dead. I am not sure where his real body is."

The world leaders were shuffling in their seats and talking to their interpreters. Pete raised his arm again. "Please, listen to me for a few minutes. It would be best if you prepared for your encounter with my leader. The president wished you all a quick meeting to discuss what to expect and ensure everyone is on the same page. We need to honor his wishes."

Another leader spoke. "Why should we stay here? It's dangerous for all of us to be in one room together like this." The chatter picked up, and they seemed to all agree.

Pete continued, "Please listen. Give me five minutes. Then you can decide if you want to stay or not."

The leaders all calmed down and became silent.

Pete looked out at them. "Thank you. My leader will appear before you in a few short moments with a plan to help you save the human race. What you see at my feet is a Xanoclax warrior. This species looks for planets that are destroying themselves."

"Why?" a voice called out.

"They suck the energy from the planet for themselves. This alien race is technologically advanced, like the Wen'q'rixshi I represent. They intend to invade our planet and enslave us. When they get what they want, they will terminate everyone on this planet. The Xanoclax will succeed unless we change immediately and attain peaceful coexistence among ourselves."

Pete could feel the fear and chaos exuding from the dignitaries increasing. It was suffocating. The dignitaries all began asking questions at the same time. The volume of the chatter was rising, and no one in the room was paying attention to Pete. Finally, Pete paused and looked down at the body of the dead warrior who was lying at his feet. He stared for a few seconds, waiting for the room to settle down.

He realized that the chaos in the room would not dwindle and sighed. *Oz, can you please do something to get their attention?*

Suddenly, a loud bang went off and shook the room. It felt like a bomb had gone off and forced everyone to shut up and look directly at Pete.

Thanks, Oz.

My pleasure.

Pete continued. "We are continually scanning this room for Xan presence. You are safe. We will enclose you all in a forcefield that will protect you."

I'm scanning, but how will you do the force field? Oz asked Pete.

They need to believe it's there to remain calm for Krix'x's presentation.

Wow, Oz said.

What?

You should go into Earth politics; you'd fit right in.

Pete raised his voice, "Okay, ladies and gentlemen, the Wen will be here shortly. Please pay attention. And please, this is a big one, *do not* interrupt. I promise you that the Wen'q'rixshi get no benefit from helping our planet. So if you show no interest or disrespect, they will leave us all to our fate. Do you understand?"

All the dignitaries nodded. Pete signaled for a staff member to lower the screen from the ceiling.

The lights went out, and the screen went black. A few people were whispering, but the majority sat in silence. The dignitaries on the LCD screens were silent and attentive.

"I am addressing the leaders of Planet Earth," Krix'x spoke through the black screen. His voice resonated through the East Room. No one said a word or made a sound.

Pete began, "J9-1-7 reporting in. All the leaders are either present in this room or attending via secured visuals."

"Well done, J9-1-7." Krix'x's tone did not change. Pete couldn't tell if he was pleased or not. "I am Krix'x. I am here to help save your planet from an impending invasion from the Xanoclax. You must heed my warning and take action to avoid the Xan invasion."

Like his first broadcast, he showed his face when Krix'x finished his sentence. Again, the blue light radiated from the screen and filled the room. The dignitaries were startled when his face appeared.

Krix'x's face bulged out of the screen slightly. The back of his head remained inside the screen, hidden from the dignitaries. "We are here to help your planet. The Xanoclax will come to Earth and take it for themselves, leaving no one alive, and your world will cease to exist." Krix'x looked around the room and observed that everyone was paying close attention. No one spoke or interrupted him. Most were too scared to respond.

"We are a race called Wen'q'rixshi. Our mission is logical: to try and save different civilizations from total annihilation at the hands of the Xanoclax. The Xanoclax are an alien race whose sole purpose is to exterminate weaker species to become more powerful. The Xans have been doing this for thousands of Earth years. They can only prey on civilizations that are self-destructing. When I finish, my herald will be available to go into greater detail and answer your questions. For now, listen to what we have to offer."

Pete recognized this speech. It was almost word-for-word what Krix'x had first told him. Krix'x explained his offer to the dignitaries as he had to Pete. When he finished, there was silence throughout the room. No one wanted to say anything. They were either too afraid or in shock.

"Chush seboya," a voice bellowed through the room. "How do we know it is not you who wants to invade us?"

Pete put his head in his hand and sighed in disbelief. *What the hell is this guy doing?*

Uh oh, Oz said quietly.

Krix'x looked around the room and, in a commanding voice, asked, "Who speaks?"

"I do! The president of Russia." The response came from one of the digital displays on the wall.

Krix'x's face came off the screen as it had from the wall of the Oval Office. As the headless face moved away from the screen, it left the same blue trail of liquid light. The blue light path stretched out from the screen as if it were attached to it. Krix'x's headless face moved slowly toward the display of the Russian president. Everyone in the room was sitting with mouths wide open, staring at Krix'x hovering above their heads. His face slowly entered the LCD and became absorbed by the glass. Someone in the room pointed to another LCD and screamed, "Look!"

Krix'x was face-to-face with the Russian president. As he had in his Oval Office meeting with the American president, Krix'x stopped just before touching the Russian president's nose. The Russian president looked like he was going to have a heart attack. He was completely motionless. The beads of sweat running down his face had turned into small rivers of flowing water.

This guy is soiling himself right now, Pete said to Oz.

No doubt.

Krix'x's eyes turned blood red, which caused the flowing rivers of sweat to flood the Russian president's face.

"Listen closely," he began to speak in a low voice, almost a whisper. "If I can do this right now, why bother trying to help you? I could eliminate you at my whim, as the Xan will. Do you understand what I am saying to you?"

The Russian president nodded his head rapidly.

Krix'x continued in a deep, calm voice, "I am not logically invested in your planet; therefore, I don't care if you believe me. I don't care if your planet falls to the Xan. I have offered you my help. Your fate is sealed if you are foolish enough to ignore my warning."

Krix'x slowly backed through the camera, never taking his eyes off the Russian president, who was still shivering in his seat. Krix'x exited the same display he had entered, appearing again in the East Room. As Krix'x's blue trail crossed the room and retracted back into the main screen, nobody in the room made a sound. The chamber was deadly quiet. You could hear a pin drop. Krix'x surveyed the room and saw the Xan warrior on the floor.

"Another one?" he cried out.

Pete walked over to the Xan and looked up at Krix'x. "Yes. We stopped him from blowing up this room."

"Very well. I will see to the Xan." Another blue light from the screen came out and engulfed the Xan. The blue light glowed brightly around the body. Like the Xan in the Oval Office, the warrior floated to the screen and disappeared behind Krix'x.

Krix'x continued moving backward toward the screen. Silence remained as he moved effortlessly across the air to the screen. When he entered it, he stopped and spoke one last time.

"Humans, you must not ignore the help we offer. Make the affliction work and become more civilized toward one another. Through constant effort, you will not always need our help. Your minds will advance and develop. With more advanced minds, you will realize that your petty treatment of one another was always unnecessary."

The screen went black.

When the lights came on, the interpreters immediately bombarded Pete with questions. Pete stayed in the East Room for three more hours, answering questions and explaining alien species and their differences. When Pete decided to end the Q&A session, he felt most leaders understood the situation well. Pete left the embattled room and headed to the ship.

***

Pete walked to the chair in front of the control panel.

Oz approached and placed a hand on his shoulder. "You okay, Pete?"

"Yes. I must sit for a minute to digest what we just went through."

Pete was holding the manila envelope that Bill had given him. He realized he had never opened it. Pete shook the envelope and tapped it on his other hand several times. Pete couldn't take his eyes off the envelope as his mind wandered about what he would discover.

It can't be too bad, Pete thought, *because if Bill had found something peculiar or damaging, he would have discussed it with me first.*

He decided to open it, and before he ripped the envelope, the screen above the control panel turned on. Pete could see everyone watching the ship from the outside.

Pete squinted his eyes, "Did you turn this on?"

"I thought you did."

"I don't know how. Maybe—"

Pete stopped and stared at the screen as the visual distorted and became snowy. The screen then shifted to a bright blue-white tone. Krix'x's face appeared on the screen.

Pete was stunned. Krix'x had chosen to talk directly to him. Finally, Pete would be able to confront the alien responsible for turning him into what he is now. Pete wanted to be angry. He wanted to lash out at the screen.

He wanted to yell at the top of his lungs, "What gave you the right to do this to me?"

Pete couldn't, of course, because he desperately needed answers from this face. He was confident that Krix'x was responsible for erasing his emotions and memories, making Pete feel like he needed to scream even more. But all those thoughts disappeared as quickly as they came when Krix'x's face became more explicit.

On the screen was the leader of the Wen'q'rixshi High Council. This Wen was respected above all others for his high intellect, and he was about to speak to Pete directly.

I would feel nervous if I knew how he thought to himself.

"You have done well, J9-1-7."

"Thank you." Pete decided to be patient and see where the conversation would lead.

"I know you have questions. So I decided that you deserved answers in honor of your success."

So here it was: Pete's opportunity to get answers to the questions that encumbered him daily. But, unfortunately, he didn't know where to start.

"I will begin to allow your mind to settle."

"Thank you."

"You understand that our race has chosen you to protect those who cannot protect themselves from the Xanoclax?"

"Yes."

"The Xanoclax is not the universe's only violent, warring species. We chose the Xan because of their direct relationship to the Wen'q'rixshi."

"What relationship is that?" Pete was surprised when he asked. He wanted to talk about what the Council did to him. Pete wanted to cry out Why me, but he remained patient.

Krix'x continued in his deep, calm voice, "We have learned that the Xanoclax have set their interests on Wen'Q'Rixsh."

"I thought they only attack civilizations that are destroying themselves?"

"That is true. But the Xan have decided through the Xanoclax logic belief that enslaving our species and receiving our life force will help them increase their ability to accomplish their goals. They would reach a higher level of intelligence and become unstoppable. With our collective intelligence, the Xanoclax would become the most superior life form in the universe."

"Is this why you enhanced me?"

"It was the logical next step to enhance lifeforms to enable self-preservation from the Xanoclax."

"Sounds like you're creating an army to deal with the Xan."

"It is logical to expect our successfully enhanced heralds to protect us when needed."

"So there it is. You are not unselfish in your so-called logic, are you? You're only looking out for yourselves."

Oz stood off to the side of the room, watching from around the corner. Oz gasped. No one had ever spoken to a High Council member this way, especially not Krix'x. She wanted to get back inside Pete to help him keep calm and show respect. But, she decided a sudden interruption may cause more problems, so she remained quiet.

Krix'x revealed no emotion when answering Pete, "We have to ensure the survival of our species. Who will be available to stop the Xan if we become extinct?"

"Logic is difficult for humans because of this very premise. No emotional decisions made; no looking out for the few, only the many. I get it."

"Yes. Emotions are not logical." Krix'x blinked for the first time. Pete wondered if that was a gesture of agreement. There was another flash of familiarity. He wasn't sure if it was Krix'x's proximity to him, but something felt strange. It was as if Pete and

Krix'x had previously shared the same space. They would have had to since Krix'x experimented on him…but this felt like a moment that only the two of them had experienced, not as a scientist and a guinea pig but as a teaching moment between master and student.

Pete continued, "That's why you took my emotions away."

"Yes."

"And my memories as well."

"Yes."

"What about memories moving forward? I can still create those and keep them, correct?"

"Yes. Our technology cannot prevent new memories from being created."

"And emotions? Will I be able to develop emotions again?"

"That is an area for which we have not reached a logical conclusion."

"So you are saying there's a possibility that I can relearn feelings? Like a child does?"

"Logically, it is possible."

Pete felt a glimmer of hope rise through his body. Krix'x was telling him now, face to face, that there was a possibility he could relearn his emotions. *I am definitely human*, Pete thought. *Hope is a good thing.*

"What about the affliction?" Pete went on, not wanting to waste his time with Krix'x. "Is it permanent, or can a human with good intentions become unafflicted?"

"The technology we created and exposed humans to allows this to be a possible logical conclusion."

Pete didn't want to dwell on any one subject. He didn't know when he would have the opportunity for a one-on-one with Krix'x again. He changed the subject.

"How many heralds have you successfully enhanced?"

Krix'x looked at Pete and paused. "You are the only one."

"Out of how many attempts?"

"Hundreds."

Pete squeezed his eyebrows, "Why am I the only one?"

"We have not reached a logical conclusion as to why only you could adjust to our enhancement programs."

Then, a thought quickly filled Pete's head. A terrifying thought, "You're not planning to dissect me for future science projects, are you?"

"No. But we will continue to observe you." Krix'x did not say goodbye when he disappeared suddenly into the blue screen. When he was gone, the visual outside the saucer returned.

Oz walked up to Pete and sighed. "Man, that was a lot to ingest."

Pete stared at the visual of the crowd outside. "Yes. Krix'x answered a lot of questions."

"A lot? Which one did he not answer?"

Pete looked down at the manila envelope. "What happens now?"

To be continued…

ABOUT THE AUTHOR

MJ Petrin was born in Biddeford, Maine, and spent his early years in the coastal town of Camp Ellis, where small-town life set the stage for big imagination. At ten, he traded quiet shores for the buzzing streets of Miami, Florida, where wandering downtown became its own kind of education—one filled with colorful characters and life lessons you won't find in any classroom.

Music was his first love, and in his twenties, MJ hit the road with his brother in a rock band, playing clubs across the country and collecting stories along the way. The amps are turned down these days, but that energy shows up in his writing.

Now living just outside Baltimore, Maryland, MJ prefers a quieter pace, steering clear of social media drama and political shouting matches. Instead, he channels his creativity into writing science fiction and adventure stories, often weaving in threads from his own experiences and today's world to keep his stories relevant, meaningful, and unpredictable.